"The tight plot is enriched with Amos's wry observations ("Free is what you are when you don't want to retire yet but nobody's beating a path to your doorbell. It's a terrible thing to be free like that"). Descriptions of Amos's tender yet increasingly fragile feelings for his dementia-stricken wife add poignancy. Hopefully, Amos still has a long career ahead of him." —*Publishers Weekly*

AN OLD MAN'S GAME (BOOK 1)

"Delightful . . . Mr. Weinberger writes as his hero detects, at a measured and thoughtful pace. Most of the book's violence takes place offstage, leaving the detective to ponder and ruminate in contemplative fashion. And Amos himself proves pleasant company: a gruff mensch whose avowed atheism is balanced by a humanism that sees him tenderly caring at home for his dementia-prone wife. 'Everybody matters,' he says at one point, and as we follow his quest to find out what happened to Rabbi Ezra, we know he means it.

—Tom Nolan, *Wall Street Journal*

"While the mystery is intriguing, the thoughtful, retired Jewish PI is the draw for this debut mystery. As he and his wife age, he deals with her onset of dementia with love and patience, that patience being a part of his nature as an inquisitive PI." —*Library Journal*

"Andy Weinberger has created an absolutely charming private investigator that readers will follow from book to book. L.A.'s Fairfax District—get ready for your close-up!"

—Naomi Hirahara, author of the
Edgar Award–winning Mas Arai mystery series

DIE
LAUGHING

More Amos Parisman Mysteries
by Andy Weinberger

The Kindness of Strangers
Reason to Kill
An Old Man's Game

DIE LAUGHING

An Amos Parisman Mystery

ANDY WEINBERGER

PROSPECT
·PARK·
BOOKS

Prospect Park Books
an imprint of Turner Publishing Company
Nashville, Tennessee
www.turnerpublishing.com

Die Laughing

Cover art by Ben Perini
Book and cover design by William Ruoto

Library of Congress Cataloging-in-Publication Data
Names: Weinberger, Andy, author.
Title: Die laughing / Andy Weinberger.
Description: First. | Nashville, Tennessee : Turner Publishing Company/
  Prospect Park Books, [2024] | Series: An Amos Parisman Mystery
    Identifiers: LCCN 2022037185 (print) | LCCN 2022037186 (ebook) |
  ISBN 9781684429615 (hardcover) | ISBN 9781684429608 (paperback) |
ISBN 9781684429622 (epub)
Classification: LCC PS3623.E4324234 D54 2021 (print) |
  LCC PS3623.E4324234 (ebook) | DDC 813/.6—dc23
LC record available at https://lccn.loc.gov/2022037185
LC ebook record available at https://lccn.loc.gov/2022037186

Printed in the United States of America

For my Dad, who loved a good joke.
Or any joke, really.

DIE
LAUGHING

CHAPTER 1

I must have seen them a thousand times. Wolf and Pupik—they were the kings of late-night television for so many years when I was growing up. They were the interlopers, right? No, more than that: the disrupters, the rascals, *paskunyaks*, as my grandmother used to say, the wisenheimers you wanted to send to bed without supper, the family that put yours to shame, the family you only wished to hell you had. They were also the brothers from Mars. Over the top. Always waiting for Godot, you know. Running in place to catch the train. Crazy, but logical to a fault. TV couldn't book them fast enough. Once, I turned the knob, switching from channel two to four to seven, and damn if they weren't still there, everywhere, in the flickering living rooms of America all at once, throwing spitballs across the plate. I thought I had lost my mind. I didn't get it. But even when you didn't get it, even when it was meaningless what they said, it didn't matter; they were so goddamn smart, so slick, those two.

And another thing: they were always such a dapper duo. Dressed to the nines. Wolf was, anyway. Not Pupik. God, no. He was the philosopher, the maniac, the pineapple. He'd do anything; he'd wear a dirty dish towel on the set if he thought he could squeeze a laugh out. Light his hair on fire, smack himself with a cream pie. Anything, anything for a laugh.

Of course, in the end his appearance couldn't save him. Al Pupik didn't look so good, sprawled out half-naked on his living-room floor. That's where the house cleaner found him when she opened the front door, the morning light streaming into his hilltop hideaway at the end of Beachwood Drive. Lieutenant Malloy was kind enough to show me the photos.

"I adored that man," I tell him. "Even now I'll wake up at night sometimes—I swear, Bill, he makes me laugh in my sleep."

"Yeah, well. I shouldn't be sharing any of this stuff with you, Amos. Strictly speaking, that is. Since it's you, though, and since your client was his friend and former partner—"

"'Former partner' doesn't begin to describe it. Hell, he was his alter ego. His brother. They were Siamese twins."

"Alter ego, brothers, sure, whatever. Anyway, I guess it's fine. But let's just keep it between the two of us, okay?"

Malloy has a deep affinity for the law. The law is his savior. He knows what he's supposed to do. He rarely steps over the line. But he also values friendship, our friendship especially, which has lasted as long as the Wolf and Pupik act ever was.

We're sitting around his office at the Parker Center. Malloy's inbox is piled high with alerts and memos and legal documents. His ashtray is clean and empty. He hasn't smoked in a month and a half, and he swears this time it's for real—this time he's going to quit. He's chewing this special gum he says helps with the urges. The air-conditioning is going full tilt. It's a hot afternoon in the middle of June, one of those blistering days in LA where old men sit around in their underwear and talk about frying an egg on the sidewalk and they mean it—only it's too damn hot to step outside, let alone go looking for a piece of sidewalk.

"So, what can you tell me, Bill?" I set the photos down on his desk. "Are we calling this a break-in? A burglary interrupted? I can't imagine he had many enemies, sweet old guy like that."

Malloy wags his head. "Doesn't look like anything was stolen," he says. "The housekeeper didn't think so, anyway."

"She's been with him a long time?"

"Nine years. Her name's Inez. Inez Beltran. You want her address, I'll give it to you. Remo talked with her, said he doesn't think she's documented, but who cares, right? We don't. She seems like a decent sort, just doing her job, and she sure as hell didn't need to walk in on that." He taps his finger on the top photo, which is a close-up of a bare-chested Albert Pupik lying in a pool of blood.

"And we know for sure how he died? What'd forensics say?"

"Combination of things," he says. "Blunt-force trauma to the head. Two bullets. One in the neck. Another in the shoulder. Heart attack, maybe. Coroner's still working on it. Not clear which came first."

"Any weapons recovered?"

Malloy shakes his head. "No, not yet. But whoever did it was friends with him, I figure. Known to him, at least. He had to be, to get into his living room. And to get that close."

I pick up the top photo again, glance at it, then lay it down. "There's also the little matter of his nudity," I say. "What do we make of that?"

"This is California, Amos. Where nudity was invented." He gives me a disparaging look. "We don't make anything of it, you want to know. Albert Pupik was a nut."

I'm the last person on earth to argue differently. If not a cer-tifiable lunatic, Albert Pupik, at a minimum, occupied his own private, pulsating universe. I'm guessing they rehearsed their lines, that it was all written down beforehand; but so much of what he said in front of the camera seemed like pure, unredacted pap. And Benny Wolf—Benny, the straightest of straight men, the soul of propriety—would stand there in silence. His rubber face said it all. Sometimes he was embarrassed or humiliated. But mostly he was confused, appalled, shocked, as if Pupik had just handed him a live grenade or a pile of warm dog poop. That was the joke. You felt for Wolf, the long-suffering friend. You wondered why he put up with this insanity. In the back of your mind, you were always asking why a nice guy like that didn't have any normal acquaintances in his life, people who didn't cause him to turn away, to roll his eyes in despair, or to look for the nearest exit.

*   *   *

Benny Wolf lives clear on the other side of town, in Granada Hills, where the Tehachapis loom in the distance, where Los Angeles starts to fade away, where my Uncle Max moved to before he got sick with diabetes and died. It's a placid neighborhood, well-heeled. Big boring houses on even bigger boring lots. Swimming pools. Spanish tile on the roofs. Endless sunshine and endless views of other big boring houses. Uncle Max thought it would be a good place to raise kids, but he was a bachelor until he turned fifty; when the one woman, Riva, took pity and finally consented to marry him, well, that ship had already sailed.

I was surprised when Benny called me a few days before meeting with Malloy to see if I was interested in a job because, you know, he's famous—a rich, well-connected man—and who am I, I ask you? Really? I'm nobody. Okay, not nobody—but a guy like that, you'd think he'd pick one of those four-star agencies out of the phone book, give them a try first, let them sell him a bill of goods. I know, I know; they don't have phone books anymore, but you get the drift. The internet has my name listed under private investigators, but I'm way down in the P's, just a phone number, no ad, no spiel about my accomplishments or the people I've sent to prison, nothing. It's not that I'm suspicious. Not at all; I'm grateful. I mean, a job's a job, right? So I went.

Benny's street is broad, smooth, manicured, and tree-lined, far better than most of the streets I lived on as a kid, a step up from ordinary, but not fabulous. Something called Montague Court. I pull up to the curb, kill the engine. This is the address he gave me over the phone. It sits on a slight rise. If he'd planted a lawn, it would be a challenge to mow, but he didn't bother. I study the lot, which feels barren and unloved, and at the whole structure, trying to grasp what it's all about. The metal railing, the plain concrete steps leading to the oak front door. The solarized roof overhead. The mullioned windows. Confusing. My feral detective's brain kicks into gear. You wouldn't think a TV star, a big *macher* like him, would deliberately choose to spend his sunset years here. I sure wouldn't, not if I had his dough. Makes no sense to the naked eye, but maybe that just proves how little we know about people.

I hike up the steps and, as soon as I catch my breath, poke the buzzer. There's a mezuzah tacked up at an angle on the door jamb— nothing ostentatious, just a nice tin memento with Hebrew letter- ing on it. That's another curveball. In all the years I watched them prancing around on Jack Parr and Johnny Carson and Jay Leno, it never dawned on me that Wolf and Pupik were Jews. Not once. I mean, yeah, maybe I might have known somewhere in the third-class steerage of my mind they were Jews. Had to be. Guys called Wolf and Pupik aren't exactly your standard Episcopalians, right? And you'd never mistake them for British royalty. But in the flesh, in per- son, they were so beyond Jewish. Their words, their delivery, their facial expressions—to me, none of it automatically registered—not like the old borscht-belt comics did. They were postmodern. They spouted nonsense. They were always stuffing ideas into centrifuges and spitting them out; it was the absurdity of everything we cherish and hold dear. The whole universe baked like a pizza. I never even pigeonholed them as comedians. How could you? They were ban- dits, anarchists.

Knock, knock.
Who's there?
Oh, wait. There's been a nuclear war. You say knock, knock.
Okay, knock, knock.
Who's there?

It takes a minute for Benny Wolf to let me in.
"My name's—"
"Yes, I know," he says. "I've been waiting. Come in, come in." He shoos me quickly and unceremoniously into the den. It's not an enormous room, but it's functional: no art on the white plaster walls, no tchotchkes, no distractions at all, in fact just three black fake-leather couches that form a U around a gigantic glass coffee

table. "Here," he says, pointing vaguely toward the couches. "Sit where you like; sit and we'll talk."

I plop down on a couch. This is where he likes to do business, I guess. It's cool and inviting, which I attribute to the furniture, but then I realize he has the ceiling fan cranked all the way up to ten. He takes a seat opposite, crosses his legs, smiles.

Benny Wolf is a rakish little fellow, unlike his former partner. If he weighs a hundred and twenty, I'd be surprised. He's wearing a gray silk suit and what looks like a white linen shirt without a tie. He's undone the top button to show off his neck. Still has a fine head of white hair. The other thing he's without is shoes. He's barefoot, which is weird, okay, but his feet aren't bad looking, and, besides, it's his house. I figure he can do what he wants.

We exchange pleasantries. I admire his suit. He says it's Italian. Not only that, he picked it up last time he was in Milan. I tell him I've never been. He says don't go; it's noisy and overrated. Except for the minestrone, he says. Go for the soup. Then he asks me point-blank, do I want something to drink, like, you know, it's a hot day, and I tell him no, thanks, I'm cool. And he says, no, you're not, you're hot. Which is maybe the beginning of another one of their comedy routines, I dunno.

"Let's get down to brass tacks, Mr. Wolf. You wanted to hire me?"

"To look into Al's murder, yeah. Check it out."

I wag my head. "I can do that. I'm happy to do that, Mr. Wolf. But before I take a job, there's one or two questions. Preliminary things, that's all. I like to know who I'm dealing with."

"Please," he says, "please, call me Benny. Mr. Wolf sounds so high-and-mighty. I'm not high-and-mighty. Not these days. Of course, you have questions. Anything you want, feel free."

"I guess what I mean is there's a difference sometimes between a movie star in front of a camera, and that same person, someone like you, in his living room. Sometimes they're one and the same, but, you know, not always."

"Sure, you bet." He's very confident, or at least he's good at projecting confidence, which I've seen a lot of in Hollywood. He fingers the buttons on his suit. His hands never seem to stop moving.

"Okay, great," I say. I pull out my notepad and pen. "So, let's touch on the basics. You live here in Granada Hills? You're retired? And you and Al Pupik? You haven't been an item for what—ten years? Fifteen years?"

"Al and I haven't worked together for ages," he says. "I'm not good with dates. We did a week in Vegas, at the Sands. A Christmas show. That was the last time. It didn't go so well, as I remember. And after that, I went back to his dressing room. I said *dayenu*, enough."

"You had a fight? Can you tell me why you broke up?"

"No, no," he says, "nothing like that. But it was an odd chemistry we had. We got under each other's skin sometimes. You can understand. And we were getting older. Both of us were feeling it. The gigs weren't coming like they used to. What can I say?" He waves his hand in the air derisively. "It was time."

"All right," I say. "I'll accept that. Next question—and don't take this wrong, Mr. Wolf—"

"Benny, please."

"Okay, Benny. What I want to know is—and this is more than idle curiosity—why'd you choose me?"

"You?"

"To look into Pupik's death. I mean, me, specifically. You looked me up, right?"

"Something like that."

"And your next-door neighbor didn't call you and tell you what a handsome, talented detective Amos Parisman was, did they?"

"You weren't recommended, it's true," he says. "I just—I just went on my computer and your name popped up. I liked your name. Parisman. There's a lilt. I was drawn to it."

"Okay," I say. "Okay, let that slide for now. It's a little off-base, but you know what? Never mind."

"I disagree," he says. I see I've touched a nerve. He shakes his head, points at me with his finger. "That's who I am." His voice grows more strident, like he's about to make a speech. "In the moment. My whole career has been like that. The big decisions in my life—every one—I've made them all on a whim. Where to live.

Who to marry. Who I worked with. You should ask my ex-wife, Alma; she understood. You know what she used to say?" He looks at me intently. "That I was a seat-of-the-pants guy." He winks, grins. "Those were her words. I think that's what she liked about me, my spontaneity."

"And is that how you did your act with Pupik? You didn't rehearse? Just improvised? It was all—seat of the pants?"

"Oh, no, no," he says, "we rehearsed constantly. Sometimes we wore each other out. Day and night. In the beginning, anyway. Nothing was left to chance. We had a script, you know, step by step by step. But after a few years"—he's talking with his hands now—"we started to trust each other. To loosen up. We always brought in jokes, but really, we'd stopped writing. We had this—I can't explain it—it was magic, like we suddenly saw where the other person was going. That's when the act took off."

I nod, make a mark in my notepad. Drilling down to the bottom of Benny Wolf's creative well is going to be difficult. Also, time-consuming. But then that's not why I'm here. *No, Parisman, it's a job, remember that. You should be grateful. Just stick to the facts.* "Fine," I say. "So you turned on your computer and found me. I'm much obliged. And now the question I have is, why? Pupik was murdered. What do you expect me to do? Find his killer?"

"It couldn't hurt," he says.

"Or, let me be even more blunt: What do you think I can learn that the cops can't?"

Wolf uncrosses his legs and leans in over the glass tabletop. His voice drops. "The police . . ." he says, with some hesitation, ". . . the police haven't been huge fans of mine. Not lately, not for a while."

"So? What does that have to do with it?"

"I'm worried, Mr. Parisman. I'm not all that well anymore. I'm not well at all, in fact. And I don't know how much time I have left. I'm wasting away here. Look around you. I'd like to live out the rest of my days in peace. Am I making myself clear?"

"No, you're not," I say. "Are the cops hassling you? Is that it? They think you're involved with this? Really?" I was willing to believe Al

Pupik was a nut—Malloy didn't need to convince me. But Benny Wolf? Benny Wolf had always been the soul of propriety. At least on television.

He sighs. "It was a courtesy call. Two officers came to the door. Young men. I don't remember what time. Late. Or maybe it wasn't late, but I was in my pajamas, about to turn in for the night. They said they had some bad news. They wanted to let me know he was dead. Your friend, they said. Mr. Albert Pupik of Beachwood Drive in Hollywood. They said they were sorry. Then right away they got accusatory. Where was I the day before, they wanted to know—when did I last see Al, what did we talk about. Could I remember? No, not really. I was confused, shocked. Violated. Well, for a minute I got emotional and lost my mind. Anyone would, right? 'Please,' I asked them—I might have been angry by then—I pleaded with them, 'Will you please just tell me what the fuck is going on?' Maybe I shouldn't have used that language—maybe that was a mistake."

"And?"

"Oh, you know. They clammed up. But I'm not stupid, Parisman. I could tell by the officer's voice, by the way he stared at me: something was very wrong."

"Yes, but didn't you just say the police weren't fans of yours? You're losing me, Benny."

He turns aside and coughs into his open hand. His face goes red, then he looks at me again. "I was in an accident a few years back. T-boned by a guy on Melrose. He'd been drinking, but he wasn't over the limit. I was shaken up, I had a couple of cracked ribs. I knew I wasn't in serious danger. I would survive. The problem was, my date was killed. Died instantly. And they found a bag, a rather large bag of cocaine in my glove compartment. I didn't put it there, of course. Just so you know. I don't do cocaine. I told them that."

"So, who did?"

"Ah, now that's a mystery, isn't it? I still don't know for sure. But there was only one other person in the car, right? The lady. So who else could it be?"

My mind immediately goes over to the dark side. I don't want to muddy things up by telling him that the LAPD have been known to plant bags of cocaine now and then—that for a small minority of cops, it's another way of doing business, supplementing their income. No, in this case, I think Wolf is right. He should just blame his dearly departed date.

"We were driving to a party in Silver Lake," he says. "I had just begun to circulate again after my divorce. What a splendid creature too. Her name was Connie Shields. I don't suppose you've heard of her? She was in a batch of daytime soaps. *Days of Our Lives. General Hospital.* Credits long as your arm."

"Sorry," I say, "I don't watch much."

"Yes, well, it was terrible. Like I say, she died instantly. And they found these drugs. They didn't end up charging me, but it was awkward; I had a devil of a time explaining them away. My publicist had to work overtime."

"That was years ago, you said."

"Yes; and now it's like I'm always on their radar. I feel cursed. Every time I'm pulled over for running a stop sign or changing lanes without signaling, something stupid, they want to throw the book at me. That's why I moved here, in fact. You think I like this house? I don't. It's horrid, to be honest. Once upon a time, I had a perfectly lovely place in Brentwood. Now I hardly ever go into Hollywood anymore. Hollywood scares the bejesus out of me."

"And now that your partner's suddenly turned up dead, you want me to do what? Prove that you didn't do it?"

"I *know* I didn't do it, Mr. Parisman. It's the police I'm worried about. I don't need their skepticism."

"And you have a good alibi? What did you tell them?"

"The truth. That I was here at home the entire day."

"You have witnesses? Friends? Neighbors? People you spoke to on the phone? Emails or text messages they can pull up to corroborate this? Anything?"

He gazes at me. He starts to finger his coat buttons once again. His eyes are watery, like he's on the verge of tears. "I might be able to come up with an alibi," he says. "Not a perfect one, though. I wouldn't bet the bank on it. You see, my—my gears have been slipping lately. There are days when I get up in the morning, I brush my teeth, and the sun is shining, and then, the next thing I remember, it's time to go to bed."

CHAPTER 2

In less than half an hour, we settle things up. He agrees to my fee, which has risen a bit over time in line with the cost of living but still isn't astronomical like some of those detective agencies; in fact, he agrees so quickly and he's so elated that I wonder whether maybe I'm the one getting taken to the cleaners. Oh, well. He writes me a check on the spot. In my business, you can't ask for more than that.

At some point, I'm going to sit down and have a long heart-to-heart conversation with the police, I know that much already. I have friends there. That could be the end of it. Maybe it's a personal vendetta; maybe that's all it'll take to nip this problem in the bud. If it really is a problem—I'm not convinced of that yet. There's a whole bunch I don't know about Benny Wolf, but I count myself a pretty good judge of character. I'll admit, I could always be wrong, but he's still a handsome man, an elegant man, a *shayna punim* as my mom would say. Even if he's pushing ninety, he doesn't *look* guilty. Let's just stipulate: he wouldn't be the first guy I'd choose, you know; I wouldn't pick him out of the lineup of likely killers. And yet he was worried enough to write me this fat check that's tucked in my wallet that I'm sitting on, so go figure.

I drive down to the end of the block and park my Honda Civic in a nice shady spot beneath an enormous pepper tree, reach for my cell phone, and call Omar Villasenor. Omar's my pal. We aren't at all alike, but we've worked together for years. I admire his energy. I also like bouncing ideas off him. He keeps me young.

I fill him in on the details. He owns a television, but of course he's never heard of Wolf and Pupik. That's not surprising. Omar is young enough to be my son, possibly even my grandson, if I had been a more active twelve-year-old. He lives in Boyle Heights with his new wife, Lourdes. It's been a roller coaster of a year for him. He claimed he wanted to be a cop, but he was a street kid. Brilliant, but emotional. A proud Mexican. He had a hard time taking orders from the white instructors at the Police Academy, and one afternoon something just snapped in his brain. He quit—just walked off the field. Then two weeks after that, he met Lourdes in his cousin's kitchen and fell desperately in love. She changed his life, he said, by which he meant she inspired him to go into business for himself. It was like he'd found his muse. She had opinions, but maybe because she was fresh off the bus from Guadalajara and even more old-fashioned than he was, she didn't tell him what to do; all she wanted was for him to succeed. What man doesn't respond to that?

To make ends meet, he drifted into security work—surveillance, guard duty, patrolling air-conditioned shopping malls. That paid okay, but it took too much precious time away from Lourdes. Then, a year and a half later, he cobbled together enough to start a small detective agency of his own, catering to fellow Latinos in the barrio, offering them help on a sliding scale. Great idea, I told him then; God knows they could use it. I cheered him on like that, even loaned him some extra cash I inherited from my aunt on the theory that it wasn't mine to begin with. How could I not? He wanted to be like me; but, see, I know a little something about business, how easy it is for things to go sideways, and even if they don't, that it always takes time, that it's bound to be a struggle. I kept my mouth shut, but in the back of my mind I never thought it would fly. Recently, he let his two part-timers go and gave up the lease on his office. Now he's freelancing again, doing odd jobs here and there—construction work—and helping me out whenever I call. He's not bitter anymore: that's the saving grace. Guys like Omar are built to last.

"So I figure we should go talk with the house cleaner," I say, "this Inez Beltran. I could use a translator. The cops talked with her; but, you know, they're not always so thorough, and besides, she might be shy around them. What do you say? You interested?"

"Por supuesto, man. You bet. You just tell me where and when. I'll be there."

"There's no rush," I say. "On second thought, forget about her. Right now, I'm still trying to figure out just who our client is."

"You said it was this Benny Wolf dude."

"True. But there's something doesn't smell right about his story."

"Such as?"

"Such as location, for one. He lives way the hell out in Granada Hills. Albert Pupik was killed in Hollywood."

"So?"

"So that's what you call a long drive in a Buick, especially for an old man. Hell, it's a long drive for me, Omar, and he's got me by twenty years."

"That what worries you?"

"That's just the tip of the iceberg. The distance and his age. Then there's the murder itself."

"What about it?"

"Well, Lieutenant Malloy said—and I agree—Pupik must have known his assailant. There was no forced entry. Also, he was found with his pants down on the floor, which suggests either a major comfort level with his killer, or, less likely, that he was caught off guard. Or maybe he'd just stepped out of the shower when the doorbell rang."

"Was his hair damp?" Omar asks.

"Good question. I should ask. Anyway, Pupik got hit hard with something on the head, then shot a few times afterwards. So what happened to him wasn't just violent—it was a huge emotional experience."

"For Pupik, sure. You better believe it."

"It was wrenching for both of them, Omar. Think about it. He was hit. He was shot. This wasn't a casual murder. Somebody was angry. Somebody had it in for him."

"And that somehow points to Wolf's innocence?"

"No. It points to the difference in their body types. Wolf is scrawny. Pupik's six-one, six-two. Pupik might allow his old partner to come into the living room, which, granted, puts him in striking range."

"There you go," says Omar, "case closed."

"But any good defense lawyer would point at Benny Wolf and say 'That's nonsense, your honor. As you can plainly see, my client is a frail old man. A wuss. A noodle. One of those hundred-pound weaklings on the beach. Common sense says he wouldn't have the strength to kill him.'"

"I don't know if I'd buy that," Omar says. "He had a gun, the killer. That kinda levels the playing field. Doesn't matter what you weigh."

"You're right. I'm just saying that to me—to my mind—it looks weird. And I'm guessing it would to most people as well. A jury would be chewing on that for half a day if it ever got that far."

"But they haven't even charged him yet. So what the hell are we talking about?"

"That's another thing, yeah. He hasn't been charged with anything. Now, I can't crawl inside Wolf's head. I'm not his psychiatrist. But he and Pupik weren't a couple anymore. It's been a long, long time."

"Maybe he's leaving things out."

"He probably is. Maybe they'd had a fight, maybe Al was blackmailing him, maybe Benny still had some kind of grudge going, but I didn't hear that from him."

"He's not going to tell you. Not if he wants your protection."

"He wants me to prove his innocence. Which I could probably do. Hell, he's already an improbable suspect."

"He's loco, is what he is, man. You know what I'd do? I'd just talk it over with Malloy, then cash his check and tell him it's all taken care of."

"I can't do that, Omar. It wouldn't be fair. Crazy or not."

*   *   *

I figured his ex-wife might be much easier to talk to, and Wolf gave me her address without hesitation.

"You *should* ask Alma about me," he said. "That's a terrific idea. We were together nearly twenty years. She knows me better than I know myself. Friends with Al too. You'll get a lot out of Alma."

Alma Wolf owns a hip hair salon on Doheny near Beverly— A Cut Above. She also has a small, upscale apartment on San Vicente. Benny has written down both numbers. I call the hair place first, but they tell me she's not in today. From Krystal, I get the distinct impression that Alma doesn't come in so often, also that the staff at A Cut Above has pretty much everything under control and they'd be just as thrilled if she stayed home and worked on her nails. She doesn't say that, naturally, not in so many words, but there are hints of hostility in her voice. I thank her, turn right onto San Vicente, and go hunting for a parking space.

Alma is a short-haired, trim, fashionable woman. Age? Unknow-able. Large, blue-green rimmed glasses. Lots of makeup and hair color going on—that's the first thing I notice as she ushers me in. I don't fault her for this. Women are always experimenting on them-selves, especially as they get older. Why should she be any different? She's got on a simple reddish top, black pants, and ballet slippers that give her a Chinese vibe. Her apartment also has a very spare Asian sensibility—recessed lighting and tan walls set off with a few abstract paintings. *She has taste,* I think. *Or if she doesn't have taste, at least she knows where to buy it.*

"Benny called ahead to say you'd be coming," she says as we sit down across her kitchen table. "He said you had questions only I could answer. Is that true, Mr. Parisman?"

"I'm not sure you're the only one, Mrs. Wolf. But your husband—"

"Ex-husband," she corrects me gently. "I kept his name—it's an improvement on who I used to be—but after the property settle-ment, that's about all we have in common anymore. I've moved on."

"Sorry," I say, "your ex-husband. My mistake. He still has a very high regard for you, by the way. I hope you know."

"Oh, I know. I wish I could return the favor."

"Well, maybe you can. You heard the news about Albert Pupik?"

"It was in this morning's paper," she says. "Poor old Al." She shakes her head in sympathy. Or, I dunno, maybe it's not sympathy, maybe she just doesn't want to speak ill of the dead. Then she looks down and rubs her hands together, and I see the several silver rings on her fingers. Nothing that resembles a wedding band, though. That finger is bare. "Would you care for some coffee, Mr. Parisman?"

I wave her off. "Thanks, but after three o'clock I have to call a halt. Otherwise, I'll be up all night, know what I mean?"

"Benny has the same problem," she says. "Not me. I must have a cast-iron stomach. I drink espresso at midnight and still sleep like a baby."

"Mazel tov," I say. "Anyway, Benny has a lot more tsuris than that. Maybe he told you how worried he is about the police? He thinks they're out to get him."

She rolls her eyes. "When it comes to Benny Wolf, Mr. Parisman, let's get one thing straight: the sky's always falling. It took me forever to learn this. That's why I finally threw in the towel. I couldn't handle it. I'll give you an example. He used to tell me regularly—at least once a week—that inanimate objects hated him."

"I beg your pardon?"

"Things," she says. "Ladders, garden hoses, stone walls, the whole dead universe. Benny believes it's a malicious force out there. He really does. That's why we trip on the sidewalk. That's why we cut ourselves slicing tomatoes."

"That didn't come up in our discussion."

"Count yourself lucky, then. So, what did he think I could help you with? Are you supposed to find out who killed Albert? Is that it? Lord knows, he doesn't trust the cops."

"We talked about his run-ins with the police, yes. I might be able to clear that up. I have some good friends there, people I've worked with on other cases, people I trust. I could sit down with them on his behalf."

"He'd pay you well for that."

"Actually," I say, "he's already paid me plenty. And not necessarily to find Al's killer, but to prove to the police—to the world—that he didn't do it. That's why I'm here."

"That's just like Benny," she says. "That's who he is. Can't stand surprises. He's always peeking around corners, looking for trouble ahead of time. I get it now. He thinks the cops are going to charge him with murder, right?"

"Something like that, yeah."

"And I'm supposed to do what? Give him an alibi? Write him a note?"

I take out my pen and notepad. "His memory seems shaky," I say. "At least when it comes to the immediate past. He can talk about his childhood like it was yesterday. He told me about playing marbles when he was nine years old, but he can't account for his whereabouts in the lead-up to the murder. Also, since he's all alone, there are no witnesses—nobody he can think of who'd place him somewhere else."

"Sure," she says, "and now he lives in that dump in Granada Hills, and Al is over on Beachwood. How many miles is that? Did he mention that he never comes to Hollywood anymore?"

"All of those things, yes. I think he's hoping maybe you can tell me something about his character."

"Oh, he's a character, I'll give you that," she says. "He played the straight man when he and Albert worked together, but the truth is, they're both lunatics."

"Benny said he never planned anything out, nothing was scripted, that his whole life really was a seat-of-the-pants operation. That so?"

"He liked to improvise," she agrees. "He was funny when he did that. Beyond funny. Made me laugh so much, once I wet my pants."

We move on to other topics. She tells me she grew up in Minot, North Dakota, of all places. Her maiden name was Morgenstern; her father was a butcher. She was the only Jewish kid in her high school.

"I can't imagine," I say.

"No," she says, "you can't. It was cold and bleak and lonely there, like Siberia, only without the culture."

Her parents were devout, but they kept to themselves. As a girl growing up in Minot, she struggled with her identity, braced herself against the freezing wind and the snow and the stony faces of her teachers and classmates. Everywhere she turned, she thought she was always locked down, and she felt like she must have done something terribly wrong to have landed here. Why else would God choose this particular spot for her exile? Her parents had no good answers. We're living on the moon, they told her, get used to it.

I find myself nodding a lot. I've never been to Minot, or the moon for that matter, but it sounds perfectly awful. Anyway, she was ecstatic that bright September morning when she boarded the Greyhound that took her away to college in Los Angeles, far from Minot. I ask her how she got involved in the hair-styling business, and she says Benny bought it for her as part of the settlement. It was something for her to occupy her time, he thought, until she could find her footing in the art world again. She's really an artist at heart, she says. "At least I was when we first got together. Now I'm not sure. Every once in a while I go back into my studio and try my hand at painting again. I still make the effort. Twenty years ago I had promise. Now, I dunno. It's just not there anymore."

She looks at me hard, then turns away. I see her fidgeting with her fingers again. "I guess I ought to be grateful for what Benny gave me," she mumbles. "He's really not a bad man. A nut job, yeah, and I'd never live with him again. But for what it's worth, in his ex-wife's humble opinion, he's not your killer. You can tell that to the police."

*　　*　　*

I thank her for her time and head back to my car. The shadows are lengthening. It's quitting time. Young men are pouring out of their offices, loosening their ties. Young women are letting their hair down. But before I head for home, there's one more stop I need to make. I turn east on Wilshire and hang a right on La Cienega.

The night shift is just coming on at Olympic Terrace—nurses and aides in their lavender uniforms. I take the faux marble steps two at a time, past the large potted plants, past the pleasant if primitive collection of oil paintings, the sunsets and waterfalls. I walk quickly down the hall to Loretta's wing. She's in Room 212. Usually she has a roommate, another white-haired woman named Patricia who has yet to say a word, but this afternoon she's all alone and Patricia's bed is freshly made up.

"Hey, sweets," I say, and lean in and kiss her cheek.

She's been staring up at the ceiling, it seems, although the television, which is suspended from the opposite wall, is on and murmuring contentedly. The television is always on. I think it's part of the overall therapy, a subtle (or maybe not-so-subtle) reminder that there's life beyond these walls—real, purposeful human beings going about their daily tasks. Today the staff has tuned it to Channel 4, the local news-and-weather folks. Everyone is sitting around a boomerang-shaped table. They're a cheerful group of young men and women, well-dressed, smiling, and joking the way you do when you've got the world on a string.

She turns slightly in my direction. "Oh, hello," she says.

"Hello. Have you been waiting for me? You knew I'd be here. Am I late?"

"What time is it? No, you're never late." She grins.

I take her hand, squeeze it. These are the conversations we have these days, when we talk at all. Some days, she is so lost inside her head I can't reach her. I try, but often I end up just stroking her head. Sometimes the drugs they give her make her unresponsive. Sometimes she just nods off.

Today I decide to tell her about the new case I have. "You remember Wolf and Pupik, don't you? The comics on TV?"

"Wolf and Pupik," she says, "Wolf and Pupik." Maybe she remembers them, maybe not. It was a long time ago, but who cares? All I know is something makes her eyes light up a little. "They tell jokes. Are they funny? They make me laugh."

"That's right," I say. "Well, you'll be happy to know I just got hired by Benny Wolf. The one and only. So what do you think about your boy now? Am I famous, or what?"

She nods. Her lips move as though she's slowly forming words, but no sound comes out. I bend over, try to hear. Whatever was on her mind is gone.

Loretta is well into her second season at Olympic Terrace. The nurses love her here, they treat her like family, but it wasn't my idea; I had to be talked into it. I'm not good at delegating. I would have soldiered on with her at Park La Brea until they carried us both out on a board. Sooner or later, though, you have to listen to the pros. Dr. Ali laid it on the line. She needs more than you can give her, Amos. It's time.

*　　*　　*

Wolf and Pupik are doing the Johnny Carson show. Pupik's wearing a black long-sleeve T-shirt, dark pants, black sneakers, and a beret. He looks like a mime, and velcroed onto the front of his shirt is a crudely printed sign that says PLEASE. He's carrying a red ceramic salad bowl. They stand there together, and Wolf announces he has big news. His dear friend and partner, Albert Pupik, has had a vision. He's joined a religious sect. He has sworn off the trappings of fame—no more wine, women, and song for him. His days as a craven comedian are over. No, all he wants from this moment on is to live simply, to honor God, to serve the poor. He will now walk out among you and humbly beg for alms in the ancient tradition of his order.

Pupik bows from the waist and walks with great solemnity down among the audience. People applaud him, they pat him on the shoulder, they shower him with dollar bills. The red bowl quickly fills up. He nods and silently shows his gratitude to each and every donor. He even kisses one old woman on the forehead before returning to the stage. He hands the bowl to Wolf, then he grabs all the cash and stuffs it into his pockets. He pulls the PLEASE sign off his shirt. Beneath it is another crude sign that reads THANK YOU. Wolf looks at Pupik, astonished. Pupik smiles, bows to the crowd, and exits.

*   *   *

It's only a few short miles from Olympic Terrace on Pico to where I hang my hat now on Creston Drive in the Hollywood Hills. But I learned a long time ago that you don't measure distance in LA by how the crow flies.

It takes about forty minutes to get through the late-afternoon traffic. Once you get onto Argyle and start to climb, the streets narrow. Young people are out, exercising, walking their dogs. There are many twists and turns, and you need to watch out for oncoming traffic.

I could have stayed on at Park La Brea, I suppose, but I would have been rattling around all alone; and now, looking back on it, I'm glad I didn't. I pull into our driveway. I say *our driveway*, but of course it's not. Everything here—the house, the driveway, the amazing view—belongs to Mara. I couldn't afford a square of sidewalk in this neighborhood. I'm just a squatter. She bought it a couple of years ago, to be closer to Gus.

That's how we met: I was tending Loretta, she was visiting Gus at Olympic Terrace. Gus died in March. And now, more and more, Loretta's in her own permanent dream world. Neither one of our spouses ever knew what we were up to, but it wasn't like we were cheating, not in the old-fashioned sense. We never skulked around. I mean, how can you cheat on someone who's forgotten what planet she's on?

Mara has her feet sprawled across her favorite chair; she's sipping white wine and reading the latest *New Yorker*. She gets up, and we kiss. "Where've you been?" she wants to know. "I thought you were just going to Granada Hills."

I peel off my sport coat and hang it in the closet. "I did. But I ended up talking to Benny's ex-wife in West Hollywood. She took forever to tell me how crazy he is. And then, after that, I dropped by to check in on Loretta, see how she's doing. Just for a while."

"And?" she asks. "How is she doing?"

"Oh, about the same," I say. "I dunno, maybe a little worse. I told her a bit about the murder case and—"

"You did? Really? Why on earth would you do that?"

Mara has only known Loretta as an invalid, which may explain why she thinks my wife is a delicate flower. It's true, Loretta wasn't crazy about how I made my living. Hell, Mara isn't either, for that matter; but so what? The only difference, I guess, is Loretta and I both had day jobs. She managed the LA office for the Garment Workers Union, I covered for a couple of law firms before I went off on my own and started freelancing. Thing is, we always depended on a paycheck to make ends meet. It was work, that's all we ever cared about.

Mara comes, more or less, from the same stock we did; but in her case, she got lucky. She won the lottery the day she married Gus. All of a sudden there was money. Trouble was, it came with Gus. That was the tradeoff. In the early years, she played the good wife, I guess. She tried to do what was expected of her: learned to cook, managed the help, and, even though it was a difficult birth, produced a fat, pink, gorgeous baby. Meghan was a handful; it was all on Mara's shoulders to raise her. Gus, she said, was always too busy for kids; he never said so, but she always knew he thought they were an impediment to his career. He ignored the little girl, came home at all hours, and complained bitterly whenever she cried at night and interrupted his eight hours of sleep.

Gus had gone to all the right schools, but he wasn't what you'd call a perfect gentleman. I would have punched him; Mara was more tolerant. She put up with his shady shenanigans, his right-wing politics, the occasional mistress. Now, if she lives to be two hundred years old, she'll never spend all the dough he left her. Me, I don't care about that. I didn't move in just so I could sit around and count her money. It's a problem for her, is what I'm trying to say.

She's of two minds whenever we talk about my career. She's supportive. She's gracious. She likes it when I solve a case; she'll give me a congratulatory kiss and maybe we'll go out to dinner to celebrate. But underneath it all, I can't help but feel like there's another agenda going on. It's like she's sort of adopted her late husband's attitude: work—the kind normal folks do—is a foreign commodity.

Now and then I watch her when she talks to workmen who come to the house to install new lighting or repair the deck. She's always friendly, but she doesn't get them; it's like she's talking to a race of extraterrestrials. She'd never bother to pick up a hammer or a screwdriver, never consider learning to do it herself.

"You don't need to worry," I say. "Loretta doesn't remember what I tell her from one minute to the next. She used to, but not anymore. And besides, I censor myself. I leave out all the juicy parts. By the time she hears about it, it's suitable for families."

"I doubt that," she says. She goes to the kitchen and returns with a refilled glass of wine for herself and a fresh one for me as well. "I'm just recalling my own time with Gus. There were days when it seemed like he was unreachable, you know? Nobody home. But then he'd open his eyes and suddenly he'd mention something I'd told him earlier in the week. You've got to be careful. You just don't know what she takes in, what stays in her brain."

"I *am* careful," I say.

Then she asks me what Benny Wolf is really like in person, and I say his ex-wife is right, he's meshuggah, and she says that covers a lot of behavior, and I say okay, he's paranoid. He thinks when he cuts himself slicing bread that the knife is his mortal enemy. He also thinks the cops are going to try to pin Al Pupik's murder on him.

"Were they enemies?" she asks.

"Enemies might be overstating it," I say. "They broke up a long time ago. They hadn't worked together for years. Maybe there was some animosity still going on, but I kinda doubt it."

"And you're never wrong," she says, rolling her eyes.

"I'm usually wrong, honey. I just don't have any evidence in this case."

"So why would he be worried about the police?"

"Dunno. He's had a few run-ins with them over the years; but to hear him tell it, there's an organized cabal down at the LAPD. He's on their hit list."

"Is that possible?" Mara appreciates the police, probably even more than I do. They've always been Johnny-on-the-spot whenever she's had trouble. There were a couple of daylight burglaries up the street the year she moved in, and they ramped up patrols to the point where every other stranger you saw in the neighborhood turned out to be carrying a badge.

"I'm going to talk it over with Lieutenant Malloy this week, see if he knows something I don't," I tell her. "Benny's an odd duck. He might have acted out, which, yeah, probably ticked the cops off. But there's no conspiracy at that end. For now, I'm sticking with his ex-wife. She slept with him. She did his laundry. She knows who he is."

CHAPTER 3

Three Jews walk into a room.
That's not how it goes.
What do you mean? This is my joke. Let me tell it, okay?
All right, but you're screwing it up.
Oh, really? I'm screwing it up?
Yeah, it should be: a Catholic, a Protestant, and a Jew walk into a bar.
That's your joke.
No, that's the joke.
It's not funny. Three Jews walk into a room, that's funny.
What kind of room? A living room? A bathroom?
I dunno, a room. Just a room. Doesn't matter.
For what? You don't just walk into a room. And why three Jews? What's the point?
There is no point. It's a joke. What do I look like? A punchline?

L ucky for me, Lieutenant Malloy agrees to meet me at the last minute for breakfast at the Beachwood Cafe. I was going there anyway; it's not all that far from where I live, and it's also a stone's throw or so from Albert Pupik's house up the hill. It's a pleasant, artsy hodgepodge—from the venerable Spanish exterior to the white anti-nuclear peace sign painted in the window. The food is good, I've found; that's all that matters. Even Mara enjoys coming here—that is, if she can ever force herself out of bed.

I order their hash and eggs and black coffee, Malloy gets the pancakes and a tall orange juice with ice. It's early. People are out, trying to get their chores done before the heat takes over, which the weatherman on Channel 4 is cheerfully predicting.

"Any news on the late, great Mr. Pupik?" I wanna know.

Malloy adjusts the knot on his silver-and-blue-striped tie before he opens his mouth. He's kind of a throwback to an earlier time; most cops I know don't bother with a tie anymore, not if they can help it. But Bill is stubborn; he pays attention to form. With him, the way he dresses every morning is an expression of honor. "I'm on my way over there after breakfast," he says now. "Remo and Jason have been canvassing the neighborhood. They have two potential witnesses they say I should follow up with. Elderly couple that lives across the street."

"Wonderful. You mind if I tag along?"

"You're a civilian, Amos. C'mon, you know I can't bring you with." He sips his orange juice, carefully daubs his mouth on a napkin. "Besides, what I'm doing is just a little bit out of your lane, isn't it?"

"I don't follow you," I say.

"I mean," he says, "what do you really care who killed Al Pupik? As long as it's not your client, right?"

"That's not the way I see it." I frown. "To me, it's all one question. Wolf and Pupik were joined at the hip for years. You want the murderer, I want to make sure he's not named Benny Wolf. We work together, I figure in the end we'll both be happy campers."

"You figure, huh? Well, that's very nice, but the Los Angeles Police Department figures differently."

I take a few tentative bites of my hash and eggs, lay down the fork. "Well, then, maybe you can at least help me out with my piece of the puzzle."

"If I can, sure."

"The reason Benny Wolf hired me is because he's worried—panicked, in fact—that you're going to accuse him of killing Al."

"Is that so? And why on God's green earth would we do that?"

"My thought exactly. At first glance, it seems like a stretch, you know. He's old, he must be pushing ninety, doesn't live anywhere near Beachwood Drive. Hasn't had much to do with Pupik in years. Still, he called me up. And he cared enough to give me this." I yank out my wallet then, unfold the check, and hold it up for Malloy to admire.

"Okay," he says. "I'm impressed."

"You should be. He talked my ear off, kept trying to justify what he was doing by telling me all the times the police harassed him. Said he was in a car wreck a while back, that they found a bag of cocaine in his glove compartment."

"And they didn't prosecute?"

"I don't know what happened. He denied it was his. He thought it might have belonged to his date. I didn't tell him this, but just looking at him, who he was, a celebrity and all, it crossed my mind that the officers on the scene could have planted it. It wouldn't have been hard."

"Based on what?"

"Based on what I read in the papers. God knows they've done it before. You know that. Not often, maybe, but there are a few bad apples, crooked cops, whatever you want to call them."

Malloy frowns, shakes his head in disbelief. He knows what I'm getting at. He works side by side with imperfect human beings every day; he's seen his share of racists and knuckle-draggers, but it's the institution he cherishes above all, the institution he trusts will endure.

"Somebody told me once," I say, "that among Blacks and Jewish people, the word 'paranoia' has no meaning. You know why, Bill?"

"Why?"

"Because people really *are* out to get us."

He stops in the middle of lifting a forkful of pancake to his mouth, puts it down, stares at me. "I'm not going to argue with you, Amos."

"And I don't want you to, Bill. All I'm looking for is a little help." I fold Benny's check and slip it back into my wallet. "I'm just trying to give him his money's worth."

"What do you want me to do? Tell you he's not a suspect? I can't do that. Not yet."

"Why not?"

"Because we have no suspects. Zero. Which means, for the time being, everyone is a suspect."

"How about this, then? He says driving into Hollywood these days terrifies him because he's always getting hassled by LA's finest. Can you at least look into that? Tell me what that's all about?"

Malloy finishes his orange juice, smacks his lips. "Oh, sure," he says, "no problem. I can pull his file, find out who the officers were on the scene, what they wrote in their reports. All that stuff. It'll take time, you realize, some leg work, but I can do it." He pauses. "Now, do I think that's going to change anything? No, I don't. Not one iota." He taps his index finger on the table. "Here's the truth: there is no conspiracy, no organized group of policemen out to nail your client. He's had a few run-ins, apparently. He's been in an accident. Maybe he's a careless driver. Maybe it was his fault. He may have been arrested, I don't know. But you want my honest opinion? He's full of soup."

"His ex-wife would agree with you. When I talked to her, she called him crazy, okay; but the way she put it, it was almost a compliment. Like, you have to be a little bit nuts, you want your own gold star on Hollywood Boulevard."

"I can't comment on that. I don't follow these people's cockamamie careers."

*   *   *

Malloy's right. Benny Wolf probably *is* full of soup. Or beans. Or blarney. Which could mean no one wants to see him in jail; and if that's so, then he's just given me more money than I'm likely to see for the rest of the year. After the lieutenant gets up and leaves, I sit there fiddling with the last of my breakfast. Part of me wants to return Benny's check and say thanks but no thanks, you don't need my services. Better he should put it toward a good psychiatrist. But then I think, what if I'm wrong? What if Alma Wolf doesn't really understand her husband as well as she claims?

I get in my car and start to drive down the hill. Alma knew how Benny behaved in the bedroom. She knew how he liked his eggs in the morning. His shirt size. Fine, but she didn't tell me much about what he did on stage. The stage was where he came alive. Maybe she didn't understand how he made his living. Maybe that wasn't part of their marriage.

There is one person I could talk to, though, someone who knows the ways of the rich and famous. A professional. Joey Marcus.

We haven't spoken in a long time and I haven't called ahead, but that's never stopped me. Joey still has an upstairs office on Sunset near the Bank of America. His office hasn't changed much. There's still a small barren reception area, with a desk, a phone, a computer, and a young girl in a short skirt sitting there thumbing through a movie magazine. He's added a few classic film posters to the walls, reproductions you could pick up anywhere—*Casablanca, Dial M for Murder, High Noon, Airplane, Throw Mama from the Train*. I know they're meant to add color and ambiance to the place, but they actually make it look empty, desolate. Beyond the desk and the girl, there's an opaque glass door marked PRIVATE. The girl has a side swirl of pinkish hair. The rest of it is dyed dark black. She's wearing aquamarine plastic earrings shaped like stars. She's probably nineteen. I somehow doubt that she's planning on staying here forever.

"Is Mr. Marcus available?" I ask.

She glances up from her reading material. "You have an appointment?"

"No, no. I was just in the neighborhood. We're old friends. Well, acquaintances." I hand her my blue business card.

She takes it, nods, rises from the desk, tugs at her skirt so it comes slightly closer to her knees. I don't think she particularly cares whether we're friends or acquaintances. If anything, she's annoyed that I interrupted her fantasy time, but she's trying not to show it. "Gimme a minute. I'll check, see what I can do."

She knocks once on the door behind her, then enters and closes it behind her. A minute or two later, she's back. "You can go in," she says, returning to her magazine. "It's okay."

Joey hasn't aged a bit. He's still a scrawny, unshaven, energetic guy in designer jeans, the one I recall from a few years back. Hasn't gained a pound. Once, in another lifetime maybe, he was a boxer, I heard, a featherweight. Now he's leaning forward in his leather chair, scribbling something. On his desk, he's still got the same brass statuette of Charlie Chaplin, the little tramp with the cane, and behind him on the walls are the same glossy black-and-white celebrity photos thanking him for his help and brilliance. Joey Marcus is indispensable. That's what he'd like you to believe.

"Hey you, Parisman." He looks up, grins. "It's been a while, huh?"

"A couple, three years, Joey. I'm surprised you remembered me."

"I didn't, except when I saw your business card. Then it all came back. Made me think about that rabbi I had lunch with down at Canter's. What's his name—Diamond?"

"Diamont," I correct him.

"Yeah, that's it. The one who dropped dead in a bowl of soup. He coulda been somebody."

"Yeah, well, that case is closed, Joey. But you're always on top of things, right? I'm hoping you might be able to tell me something I don't know about Wolf and Pupik."

He gets a startled look on his face, lays his pen down, drums the desk. He's an emotional guy, Joey Marcus. A smart guy, sure, but someone who probably feels about as much as he thinks. Maybe more. "I read about Al Pupik in the paper," he says. "Sad, what happened to him. Kinda broke my heart."

"You knew him? I mean, personally?"

Joey cocks his head, gives me a goofy face like how could I even make such an idiotic suggestion. "Of course," he says. "This is one big happy fucking family, Parisman. Music. Movies. Television. All the talented people mushed together. And we like to party, don't we?"

I shrug my shoulders. "I've only heard tell, Joey. I've never been invited."

"Trust me," he says. "You want to make it in this town, it's all about the parties."

"I'd like to hear about the parties. But first, what do you have on Wolf and Pupik? You know why they split up?"

"Sure," he says. "They had a fight. It was supposed to be a private affair, but I heard about it. Everybody did." He leans forward. "You need to understand how teams work. Take your classic ones, your Abbott and Costello, your Dean Martin and Jerry Lewis. There's a straight man and a comic. They may both write the material, and maybe you feel a little bit sorry for the straight man, you're supposed to, but it's always the comic who gets the laughs. Word is, Wolf got fed up being the straight man. That's what it came down to in the end."

"And how did Pupik take the news?"

"Not well, I guess. I mean, would you? When you work with someone for twenty years? He probably felt resentful, betrayed. I wasn't in the room when it happened, naturally. But there was a lot of noise. The tabloids picked up on that. How they make the rent. You could have read about it at the supermarket checkout stand."

"That's not how you learned about it, though, was it?"

He clicks and clicks the ballpoint pen in front of him. "Like I say," he insists, "I go to parties. It's the horse's mouth, know what I mean?"

"I think I do, yes."

Then he scratches the back of his neck and gives me a puzzled look. "Now let me ask you something," he says. "What difference does all this make to you? You're not a cop, Parisman. Somebody hire you to track down the killer?"

"You could say that," I say guardedly. "In a manner of speaking."

"But . . . isn't that why we pay the police?"

He's fast on his feet, Joey. I could tell him about my meeting with Benny Wolf, I suppose, or show him the fat check in my wallet, but what good would that do? He'd have something juicy to pass on at the next party he went to, and two days later it'd be all over the front page of the tabloids. "My client wishes to remain anonymous,"

I say. "For the time being, anyhow. But I was hoping for more about Wolf and Pupik. How they worked together. How people saw them in the business. I already had a long chat with Benny. And another one with his ex-wife, Alma."

"Oh, yeah?" he says. "And what'd they tell you?"

I make a small dismissive gesture with my open hand. "Oh, they're both sad, you know. Like you, shocked. They said nice things about Al. But who doesn't say nice things about the dead, right? It was chummy. But I need something extra."

"Extra?" He has suddenly become animated. "All right. Maybe you'd be interested to hear what I learned at Charlie Teitelbaum's last week. That Wolf was making noises about taking Pupik to court. That he was ready to talk to a lawyer. Claimed that Al had been nickel-and-diming him for years, that he'd been getting the short end of the stick on royalties and residuals."

"Teitelbaum told you that?"

Joey nods. "Charlie said he was furious, too. That as of a few days before he died, you couldn't even say Al Pupik to Benny Wolf. You want an exact quote from Benny? He called Pupik a four-letter word."

"So, what about my meeting with Wolf? What was that?"

"Search me," he says. He looks skeptical.

"You don't believe he was shocked when he heard? You think that was all an act?"

"Here's what I'm sure of," he says. "First off, Charlie Teitelbaum would never lie to me, not in a million years. We're brothers, you understand? Second, Benny and Al had come to the end of their run, regardless. Maybe it was because, like Benny says, Al was acting like a *gonif,* stealing him blind. Or maybe Benny was tired of living all cramped up inside Al's head. Tired of being ignored, being the straight man, the nobody. Any way you look at it, it was *fercockt.* Fucked. Finished."

I tell him then that Alma Wolf said I ought to realize that Benny Wolf was a crazed individual. Maybe not certifiably insane—he had a lot of good qualities, and you couldn't bring yourself to get him locked up—but you know, off the rails, different.

"Every comic I've ever met has been insane," Joey replies. "That doesn't mean squat. Think about it. The public—those people that go to clubs and bars—who are they? Take it from me, they're rowdy. They can be mean. And you gotta be nuts to stand up in front of a crowd of drunks and make a damn fool of yourself night after night. But that's the requirement. If you're not nuts and brave, if you're not willing to die, to walk straight into the lion's den, well, then, forget about it. When I was in my twenties, I tried doing stand-up. I lasted one week. Scared the shit out of me, Parisman."

*   *   *

Before I let any charitable second thoughts get the better of me, I drive over to the Wells Fargo on Vine and deposit Benny's check. Then I turn around and head for Boyle Heights. Omar said he'd be home around now; the construction site he's on has more crew than they need at the moment; besides, it's too damn hot, so he offered to take the afternoon off, and they graciously accepted.

"You want a beer?" he asks as I step past the screen door into the living room. He and Lourdes have a small fenced-in bungalow with a porch and a yard that's mostly baked dirt. They're planning to move once the baby is born; Omar has his eye on a tract home in Hacienda Heights off the Pasadena Freeway. His brother-in-law thinks it's underpriced and he's going to help with the down payment, but this is real estate—everything is still up in the air.

"One beer, amigo, but por favor, no more, okay? I don't want to get slowed down in the heat."

"Hey, man, that's what you do in the goddamn heat. Slow down." He disappears into the kitchen and returns with two glistening bottles of Modelo Negra.

We settle in on his second-hand couch. We have to talk quietly because Lourdes is taking a nap in the bedroom, where there's a rotating fan.

"So, what do you have for me?" he asks. He's barefoot, he's wearing Levis and a clean white T-shirt. His bald head is shiny, and he looks fresh from the shower he just got out of.

"This is a first for me," I say. "I need to chew on this again, Omar, just to see if maybe I'm missing something. You tell me where I go wrong."

"Okay," he says, "shoot."

I take a long swig of beer, clear my throat. "My client—our client, that is—has it in his mind that he's about to be charged with murder. He's had a few negative experiences with cops. So what else is new, huh? He also has some kooky ideas about conspiracies. I get that, but that doesn't make him a murderer. In fact, I don't think he is."

"You talked with Malloy?"

"You bet. And according to him, they have nothing. No weapon, no motive, no prints or DNA, certainly no suspects."

"They're just getting started," Omar cautions. "Give them time."

"Yeah," I say, "but on Benny's side of the scale it still doesn't add up. Wolf and Pupik lived miles apart. Wolf said he hardly drives anymore, and almost never into Hollywood. Why? Because he's sure the cops there are gunning for him."

"That all you got?"

"Did I mention that he's old and frail?"

"I think you did."

"In other words," I say, "not your typical Jack the Ripper."

"Okay, so maybe he didn't personally do it," Omar says. "But he's still scared enough to bring you in, right?"

"Yeah, so what's that mean?"

"I dunno. You said he was crazy."

"His ex-wife did. Also, Joey Marcus. Remember him? The promoter?"

Omar nods, sips his beer, sets it gently down on the coffee table. "You know what stands out for me? It's the money. I keep coming back to that. You walk through the door, and Benny Wolf writes you a fat check. You, a total stranger. For no reason. You only do that if the cops are breathing down your neck. Or if you think they are."

"Or if you're wacko."

We sit together in silence for a minute. Except it's never silent around these parts. I hear a clock ticking in the kitchen. A muscle car goes by with a muffler that needs to be tamped down, then another car, pumping loud, indecipherable music. Outside his open screen door, I see a couple of stout dark-eyed women trudging back from the local corner market. They're chattering away in Spanish, and they're both lugging several white plastic bags hanging from their arms.

"So here's something else to think about," Omar says. "We're talking crazy, but it might be simpler than that. He's an old guy, you said, *un viejo*. I have relatives like that. People around his age have memory lapses."

"Hey, people *my* age have memory lapses, amigo."

"Just try this on," he says, ignoring my lame attempt at humor. "Everyone you've talked to so far says Benny Wolf is slipping. Crazy. Not crazy. Who the hell knows. He forgets stuff. He doesn't *think* he killed his old partner, but he remembers they had a fight once upon a time, and maybe in his heart there's still some leftover anger. When he hears Pupik's been murdered, what's the first thing he does? He panics. He hires you. Not to find the killer, but to show the world that he's innocent."

I let what he says sink in. "You make a lot of sense, Omar. A whole lot of sense. It fits. I like it."

"Me too." He takes a long, satisfying pull on his beer.

"But that leaves us with another tough question. He doesn't think he did it. But what if he did?"

Omar looks confused. "Hey, man, didn't you just make a great big long speech telling me he couldn't have? That he was too weak?"

"Not him personally. But what if he paid someone to do it for him? He's not too weak to write another check, now, is he?"

Omar shrugs, gets up and goes to the kitchen, comes back with two more beers.

"Hey, I already told you, one's my limit."

"They're both for me," he says. "I think better on three beers."

Shortly after that, we arrive at a plan. On the theory that Benny Wolf is not quite who he says he is, Omar's going to start tailing him around beautiful downtown Granada Hills, see who he talks to, how he spends his time and money, chat up the gardeners in the neighborhood. And me? I'm going to finagle a way to meet with Charlie Teitelbaum somehow. Maybe ask Joey if I can be his date at the next soiree in the Hollywood Hills. Or if that's not in the cards, maybe I'll just waltz into CBS one afternoon and hope I get lucky.

CHAPTER 4

I've got good news and bad news.
What's the good news?
I can't tell you.
Why not?
First of all, it's a secret. Second, just between you and me, it's not that
good.
Okay, then, what's the bad news?
You don't want to know. It's bad. Really bad.
How bad can it be? You just said the good news wasn't so good.
I didn't say that.
Yes, you did.
I didn't mean it. What I meant was, the good news wasn't that bad,
really. It could be worse.
The good news is worse?
Could be better.

Joey Marcus calls the next morning. He's got the phone number of someone who used to be their manager back in the day, a guy named Darius Shapiro. Darius quit before the famous breakup in Las Vegas, Joey says, but he worked with them for a dozen years. That takes stamina. According to Darius, they gave him an ulcer. "You should go see him. He knows the inside dope."

I call him up. Darius Shapiro's retired. It sounds like he spends
his day sitting around watching baseball on TV—that, and waiting
for his kids to produce grandchildren, which is not a good bet. He
and his wife are in Pasadena, a town I still have fond memories of.
I learned to drive at the Rose Bowl parking lot, and I used to date a
girl from Pasadena when I was in high school. In fact, I still think
about her every once in a blue moon. As in, whatever happened to
Pamela Singer? I figure I must not want to know the answer to this.
I'm a detective, after all. I could track her down if I had to.

Anyway, I tell Darius my spiel. I don't tell him Benny is my
client. Just, you know, I have a client who wants me to look into
things. He's heard about Al Pupik's demise. It was on the nightly
news. Sure, come on over, he says now. My Molly'll fix us lunch.
We'll talk.

He has an upscale tract house on the lower end of Brigden Road—
lots of tall trees and dappled sunlight. It dates from the sixties, but
it's well built and cared for. You can look out his living-room window and behold the San Gabriel Mountains, which are enormous
and impressive, mainly because they're right there in your face. He
greets me at the door and waves me into the kitchen without cere-
mony, where Molly is whipping up an elaborate niçoise salad and a
pitcher of iced tea.

"Sit," he says. "Go on, sit, make yourself at home." He's in
his seventies—bald, pudgy, heavy black plastic glasses, and, now
that he's stopped punching the clock, not all that fastidious about
what he wears—khaki shorts and flip-flops and a wrinkled gray
T-shirt with a picture of a red playing card face down that reads
Jokers for Obama. He also walks with a limp, which may be neu-
ropathy or gout, I don't know. Given all his other attributes, it's
not a football injury, that's for sure. His wife, Molly, is a shy,
cheerful sort in a long white apron—she sets the food down in
front of us and leans back to take it all in.

"You're trying to find out who did it?" he asks, shaking his head.
"And you're coming to me? Really? I'm supposed to know about
that?"

"Not at all," I say. "But you knew Wolf and Pupik. Who wrote their material. How they worked together. Their style."

"Sure, but what does that have to do with who killed him? Who wrote the punch lines?" He grabs the salt shaker and jiggles it vigorously over his salad.

"Taste it first," Molly says. "Go on, taste it. It has salt."

"It needs salt," he says. "You never put enough salt."

Molly heaves a sigh, looks at me. What can you do?

"Why don't you ask Benny?" he says to me now. "I booked them, but I wasn't in the room when they put that stuff together."

"I tried. Benny and I had a long chat. He looked old, tell you the truth. Older than I remember him on television."

"Television takes ten years off everyone," he says. "That's just a given. Plus, he had a makeup man. Amazing what they can do."

"Still," I say, "I had this feeling in the back of my mind. Like maybe he lost a few marbles over the years."

"You know something?" Darius says. "They were lost when I knew him too."

"What about Al?"

"What about Al?" he replies, defensively.

"Well," I say, "was he just as crazy?"

"Oh no, no, no. Albert Pupik—he was the funny man, you understand, the one they laughed at—but if you went backstage, what you got was always the sober adult." He takes two quick forkfuls of salad and begins to speak again, chewing at the same time. "About their style, how they worked and all that, they both wrote their own jokes and then tried them out on each other. It was like a melting pot. Not like the Lower East Side, but still."

"Are you sure?"

"Sure I'm sure," he says. "Al had an office on Fountain. It was near a Romanian bakery, if I remember. And Benny had a place on Melrose. Every Friday afternoon they'd pick an office—one or the other—and they'd meet, just the two of them." He slaps his hands together. "And that's where the jokes came from."

At Molly's urging, I keep pounding away at the niçoise salad. It's good, although it's pretty hard to muck up a niçoise salad; you'd have to work at it. "How did they get along?" I ask, between bites. "Would you say it was an equal partnership?"

"They were equally famous," he says. "They had their own separate stars on Hollywood Boulevard. But you couldn't say Wolf without Pupik, and vice versa. A good comedy team has that kind of power. Laurel and Hardy, right? In the public's mind, they were never separate units."

"Still, something was going downhill. That's what Joey Marcus heard through the grapevine."

"That was after my time. But yeah, I heard it, too. Not much is secret in this town."

"What'd you hear, Darius?"

He unfolds his palm for the greasing. "In my time, mostly what they fought about was money. I got them gigs, but they had an accountant in Century City back then who handled the receipts. His name was Barton—Jack Barton, Jeff Barton, something like that. I never had much to do with him. He turned out to be a gonif, and they ended up letting him go. After that, it was Albert who managed things. But I was gone by then."

I put down my iced tea. "And even without the accountant, they still fought over that? Over money?"

His shoulders go up and down inconclusively. "That I couldn't tell you. But let's be honest, okay? When you get to that level, there's a lot of money sloshing around. They signed contracts, and contracts are full of fine print. And money tends to disappear in the fine print. But what I always felt in here"—he taps his fist on his heart—"what I felt most of all was a diminishment. Albert didn't seem to mind—he kept quiet—but not Benny. Drip, drip, drip, you get me? More and more, day by day, Benny felt like he was less and less. In all kinds of ways. Does that make sense?"

"You want seconds on the salad?" Molly jumps in. "I made extra."

"For God's sake, leave the young man alone, Molly. He ate already. Be grateful."

I rub my stomach appreciatively, shake my head, thank them and tell them I wish I could, but I have to be shoving off. Darius Shapiro nods. He's said everything he intends to say, made his pronouncements. Now he walks me to the door. I'm fond of this couple. I've only been here for an hour, but I feel like I've known them forever. That he has the chutzpah to call me a young man takes me back to my childhood. My dad, Irving Parisman, may he rest in peace, was always making little sideways digs like that. In fact, it's frightening how much these two remind me of my parents.

"You timed it perfectly," he confides, with a twinkle in his eye. "I was just about to throw you out. There's a Dodger game starting in ten minutes."

"Hey," I say, "timing's everything, right?"

*   *   *

Darius didn't give me the accountant's phone number or anything. Maybe he would have if I'd asked, but I decided I really didn't need to talk to someone who was stealing them blind. A gonif is a gonif is a gonif, as Gertrude Stein probably wrote once upon a time. You won't learn anything going down that rabbit hole.

I head for home. Traffic is light, the palm trees are waving, the sun is shining, and I'm cruising along on the Pasadena Freeway at Orange Grove when my cell phone goes off. It's Malloy.

"Hey," I say. "I didn't think you'd want to talk to me anymore."

"What gave you that idea?"

"Well, for one, you've got a real live murder on your hands. You're lucky, Bill. All I've got is a rich lunatic who can't remember what he ate for lunch."

"Actually," Malloy says, "that's the reason I called. Your client may be slightly demented, I dunno, but he's now a person of interest."

"No kidding. What changed?"

"Evidence," he says. "They found a wine bottle on Al Pupik's kitchen counter."

"So? You'll find those in every kitchen in LA."

"I'm sure," he says. "Only this one's a little different. It's a private label. Pinot noir. Came from a limited production winery up in Sonoma. Place called Travesty Vineyards."

"Okay, but so what? He had a wine bottle in his house."

"Here's what," Malloy says. "Albert Pupik was a recovering alcoholic. We think he hadn't had a drop of anything stronger than apple juice in twenty years. He had the Big Book on his shelf. He had a heap of sobriety chips in the bedroom. We don't know for sure, but we believe he still went to meetings."

"And? I can think of a dozen ways a bottle of wine might have ended up there. His wife, a new acquaintance—"

"Al lived alone. Never married. He had a boyfriend once, a kid named Chip Alexander. Died of AIDS, but that was years ago."

"So all right, it's an anomaly. Maybe you can't explain it," I say, "but still, by itself, what are we talking about? *Bupkis*. Nothing."

"Not quite nothing. Sergeant Remo was the one who first noticed it. You may not be aware, but Remo's turned into a wine geek in the last year or so. Anyway, he'd never seen that label before. He's the one who looked into it."

"And?"

"And the winery—Travesty Vineyards—is owned by your man, Benny Wolf."

"I see."

"Actually, Amos, there's more. Forensics thinks someone might have used that bottle to smack Al Pupik on the head. Or to be more precise: they found bits of his DNA on the label. Along with some of his blood."

"The bottle's not broken?"

"No."

"Okay, fine. But that still doesn't place Wolf in Pupik's living room. If you ask me, it's a stretch, Bill."

"We're not accusing him. We're a long way from that," he says. "Forensics is still seeing what they can find. Like I say, we're just interested."

At this point, I'm past the Southwest Museum. I'm past the Lummis Home and Avenue 52. I'm starting up the long, dismal grade that goes past Chavez Ravine and Dodger Stadium. This is where my old Honda usually coughs and loses steam, just as the traffic bunches up and another slew of cars veer off the Golden State. I look around. I need to merge into the right lane, but people in better, flashier, more expensive vehicles than mine are already jockeying around, their turn signals are blinking, and they're inching into position before we hit the top to begin our descent into the city.

"I'll tell you what," I say. "How about I go and have another chat with him before you send your boys over and scare the bejesus out of him?"

"We need to talk to him, Amos. That's how it works."

"Oh, I know, I know. But eventually, is what I'm saying. It's not like he's on the run, right? Hell, he barely leaves the house."

There's silence on the other end. Or maybe he mumbles something and I don't catch it. I see a small gap in the traffic then. I signal, and in the same motion, swerve deftly into the right lane so I can catch the ramp for the Hollywood Freeway.

"I'm not telling you how to run your business, Lieutenant, but if all I had was a suspicious wine bottle, well, I'd hold off, you know? Give it some time. Let it age."

"You would, huh?" He's not laughing at my teeny tiny joke.

"Yeah," I say. "Why don't you wait at least until you have a decent motive. Maybe a witness or two. Something. If you bring him in for questioning now, all he's gonna do is wet his pants. Embarrass himself. Is that what you want? Confirm what he already believes? That you really are out to get him?"

"We're not out to get him. Unless he's the killer, that is."

When you've spoken with the same man for years, like I have with Bill Malloy, familiarity takes over; it can't be helped. You hear things in a person's voice you wouldn't ordinarily hear. It's his choice of words, for sure, but also it's the hiccup in his voice, the defensive tone, the way he pauses between certain key phrases. Maybe he can't say it out loud. Maybe he has private doubts. He's thoroughly committed to the rule of law; but in the end, none of that matters because you're his friend. That's what seeps through. You're the one he counts on.

I'm on the Hollywood Freeway now, which is slow at first, but then it opens up once you get past the eternal clot around Alvarado. I tell him again that his news about the wine bottle is interesting, and he should also know that, as it happens, I've got Omar scoping out Benny Wolf too. "Not because I think he's the culprit, mind you—quite the opposite, in fact."

"What are you looking for?"

"I dunno; he claims he's innocent, and he's paying me to prove it. I'm trying to figure out what makes him tick, I guess. Wolf and Pupik were partners for decades. Johnny Carson. Jay Leno. As long as Loretta and I were together. And I'm thinking you don't stay in a relationship like that for years and years if it's all wrong. It was a marriage. Something had to be worthwhile about it; you don't stay if it's not working."

"Is that your way of saying he couldn't have done it?"

"It argues against it," I say, "but what do I know? I just spoke with his ex-manager, who told me he always seemed to have a screw loose. Darius Shapiro in Pasadena. Nice old guy. A *landsman*."

"You told me what that was once. Tell me again."

"A fellow countryman. A Jew, in other words. You should give him a call."

"Sounds like you already did."

"Yeah, but I might have missed something important. I don't have a legal mind. I don't ask the same questions you do."

While I'm on the subject, then, I add that Wolf's ex-wife thought he was bananas, too: she couldn't bear to live with him, but she also said he was very generous, that he set her up in the hair-styling business after they split. That doesn't sound like someone who carries around a grudge, does it? Malloy agrees, it does not.

"And when I first met him," I say, "I didn't know what to think. You'll see, he doesn't own a mansion out there in Granada Hills. Far from it. I mean, it's okay, but it doesn't compare with Al Pupik's house."

"We haven't taken a gander at his finances yet," Malloy says. "Who knows where that will lead us."

"Which is all the more reason why you shouldn't talk to him directly. How about this—give me some space to poke around. Whatever I find out, I'll pass on to you, promise, scout's honor. If I can't get to the bottom of this in a week or two, he's all yours." I pause a moment before I put in the clincher. "He trusts me, Bill. I can't tell you why, but he does."

"And you know what, Amos? I trust you, too."

"So we have a deal, then?"

There's a short, stilted silence on the line. I see the exit sign for Gower Street. "Yeah," he says slowly. "Yeah, okay, it's a deal."

CHAPTER 5

Albert Pupik's obituary in the *LA Times* is shorter than I expect, especially when you consider that he's famous and he's just been murdered. There's a handsome photo of him taken maybe thirty years ago surrounded by two bikini-clad starlets. He's smiling, mugging straight at the camera while the lovely ladies caress his shoulders. Below that are the bones of his biography, how he was the third of seven children born to Shmuel and Esther Pupik, a mention of his rough-and-tumble upbringing on the Lower East Side, his service in the navy, and some drivel a publicist probably threw in at the last minute about his illustrious career in showbiz, how he and Benny were a regular feature on late night. Nothing insightful, beyond the fact that the funeral itself was small and private. And yesterday. They deposited him at Hillside Memorial Park in Culver City, where the other big *machers* in his line of work are housed. Milton Berle, Jack Benny, Eddie Cantor. All the good people. Okay, a few bad apples as well. The last time I was there, I spotted the crypt where they'd laid Mickey Cohen, the mobster, to rest. He's in the Alcove of Love. Go figure.

Omar, meanwhile, has been making the rounds in Granada Hills. In three days, he's become pals with Manuel Morales, the jovial gardener at the house next door. He knows the park Benny goes to every morning on his daily walks with Greta, his white Pekinese, and the bench he sits on while he catches his breath, the trashcan where Benny drops off the tiny plastic bags of Greta's poop. He knows who Benny talks to on these excursions (no one). Most importantly, Omar has started what he calls a "serious flirtation" with Yelena, the shy young Guatemalan woman who cleans his house every Tuesday and Saturday.

"I followed her to her bus stop and we got to talking," he says. "She calls him El Señor."

"Isn't that the name for Jesus?"

"Yeah. But you have to be in her shoes. He pays her in cash, and it's more money than she's ever seen in her life. It's a miracle. He might as well be Jesus, as far as she's concerned."

"I only hope you're not getting yourself into hot water with Lourdes over this," I say.

"Oh, Lourdes knows this is all an act," he says. "I told her sometimes detectives have to fudge things a little, tell *una mentira*, a lie, here and there. She grew up watching lots of soap operas on Mexican television. She understands."

We're sitting in Art's Deli on Ventura Boulevard in Studio City. I've been filling him in on my adventure in Pasadena with Darius Shapiro. Also the "person of interest" stuff Malloy told me on the phone. Art's is a standard-fare place—nice muted atmosphere, linoleum on the floor, large portraits of food on the wall, ceiling fans. Valley Jews seem comfortable here; it lacks the frenzy of Canter's on Fairfax and isn't as uptown as Nate 'n Al's in Beverly Hills. But the food works, that's all they care about. Omar has a glass of cold beer and a hot pastrami plate in front of him. He's eaten about half, it's a free lunch, and he's happy.

"Yelena thinks I'm a contractor," he says. "She says Benny's house is fine, she could live there, but it needs all kinds of improvements. He wants a new bathroom, a new kitchen, new windows in the bedrooms. El Señor has lots of ideas."

"Question is, does El Señor have the cash to do these things?" I ask.

"That, we don't know," Omar says. "He has enough for her, that's for sure."

I'm drinking iced coffee. They bent the rules and made me a grilled-cheese sandwich, which I didn't see on the menu, maybe it's only available for kids. I don't mind buying Omar the pastrami; he's got a cast-iron stomach; but me, I get heartburn these days just looking at that kind of *chozzerai*. "Have you asked what Benny does with his day? Does Yelena know? I mean, besides cleaning up after the dog? Does he have visitors? Write letters? Make phone calls?"

"He has an office upstairs, she told me. That's where he is most of the time. But we haven't gotten that far along yet. She only works two days a week. I'm going to drop by next Saturday while he's out, let her give me a quick tour. Maybe I can learn more then."

"You have a good excuse for showing up out of the blue? I hope so."

"I'll make something up if she asks. But she won't. Maybe I'll bring her a box of candy. That's all the excuse she'll need."

"I don't see what that's going to do for you, Omar."

Omar puts down the sandwich. "You told me you wanted me to check him out, right? That something's weird about him?"

"Right."

"So I'm doing what you want. I'm checking him out. Or planning to, anyway. Give me a little credit, okay?"

"I don't mind how you weasel your way inside," I tell him. "But it's more complicated than that. You're not going to find a bloody knife or a gun lying around in his bathroom. And he probably doesn't have a diary saying how he plans to murder Albert Pupik."

"So what am I looking for?"

"I dunno. If you find stuff like that, then we do have a problem."

"If I find a knife or a gun or a diary, *he* has a problem."

"No, we do, because he's paying us to prove he's innocent. Personally, I think he is. But he's not well, Omar. His mind is on the fritz. So maybe what we really need is his doctor's name."

"Okay, fine, I'll look for that."

"The alternative route is to try to find the killer ourselves."

"That's what they pay cops for," he says.

"Yeah," I say, "and at the moment they think Benny Wolf is their man."

Omar shakes his head. He's caught in the push-and-pull, the same as me. "They're just clutching at straws. Or wine bottles. Or whatever."

He downs the rest of his hot pastrami and leaves. As I watch him go, I decide I'm wasting my time running around trying to prove a negative. There's just no way in hell Benny Wolf could be the killer. I know that in my bones. He's a goofball, no question. But if Malloy wants to haul him downtown and grill him for a few hours, in the end what difference does it make? What'll he get for his efforts? And honestly, do I care?

I climb back in my car and drive back to Laurel Canyon. Halfway up the hill, I realize there is somebody I've overlooked, someone who knows the business and can help me out, somebody I haven't thought of in years. Besides, he owes me a favor.

*   *   *

For decades, Marvin Rich tried his hand at stand-up comedy. I saw him first at the Ice House in Pasadena when I was a high school senior and still pursuing the beautiful and elusive Pamela Singer. I saw him again at the Comedy Store on Sunset when I'd just got back from Vietnam. He always wore a ratty old sweater, and he had a self-effacing sweetness about him, a kind of "aw, shucks" humility that made you feel like you were being given life lessons from your dad—that is, if your dad was all thumbs around the house, a lackluster employee, and a total washout when it came to the opposite sex. Marv's jokes were predictable, cozy and moth-eaten, like his favorite sweater. He didn't try to unnerve people the way Wolf and Pupik did on television. He was always a brand-new puppy, a sweet loser, your best friend. You might want to set him down gently on a newspaper to keep the floor dry, but he didn't catch fire with the audience, and he never made it out of the local clubs in LA.

Our paths had crossed a few years ago. He'd hired me to find out who was stalking his teenage daughter; that's how we became close. By then, he had quit racking his brains day and night for fresh material; he'd landed a decent job teaching drama at Fairfax High nearby, and even though he could retire now with a pension, he was resisting it.

The two-bedroom cottage on Sweetzer where he and his wife, Karen, still live has been repainted an avocado green in the intervening years since I worked for him. I remember it being yellow or tan. Other than that, it looks the same.

"I enjoy the kids," he says as we sit down in his living room. I haven't said a word, but it's as though he's already trying to read my mind, trying to explain why a brilliant man, a genius like him, would be consigned to a place like this. "What can I tell you?"

The house is a shambles: it's filled with books jammed in every which way. Karen still has a job as a pharmacist; she gave up keeping house long ago. And he's put on a little weight, his hair looks thinner, and he hasn't bothered to shave in a few days.

"You look good, Marv," I say. "You're happy. You don't have to tell me anything."

"Great," he says. "The less public speaking I do, the better."

"How's your daughter? What's she up to?"

His face brightens. "Teresa got married last year. She's six months pregnant. I'm about to be a grandfather."

"So no one's stalking her anymore."

"Just her husband. And he's allowed." He asks me if I want some coffee, but I wave him off—it's too late in the afternoon.

"Actually, the reason I'm here is because of Albert Pupik," I say. "You heard the news?"

"It was in the papers." He wags his head. "He was a talent, that guy. Off the charts."

"You knew him, didn't you? Back in the day?"

"Oh, yeah," he says. "He'd come around to the clubs and watch us work. I don't think he was interested in my jokes, of course. I wasn't in his league. But he would sit there and watch. Sometimes afterwards he'd tell me little things he noticed—not mistakes, but things he'd maybe do different. A word or a look. You know, change the routine to tighten it up. He sort of mentored us. We all did that for one another. It was a mutual admiration society."

"And after the show," I ask, "you'd go out for drinks?"

"Usually, yeah. We spent time. Al liked to drink. I just tagged along to socialize. I had this idea—it never happened, but still—I thought that maybe being in his company, something magical could happen. I might get lucky, meet an agent who would point me to a TV spot. Like I say, it never happened."

"So what did happen?"

"Not much. We'd all go to a bar and drink. I never had more than I could handle. Not like Al. Sometimes he'd drink himself into the third circle of hell."

"Really?"

Marvin rubs his hands contemplatively together; it reminds me of the way Boy Scouts are taught to rub two sticks to start a fire. "You knew, right?" he says, as if to clear the air. "That Al was gay?"

"I did. His partner died of AIDS."

"Yeah, well, when that happened, it was like a gypsy or someone like that came along and put a hex on him."

"You wanna explain, Marv?"

"You could see it written on his face," he says. "One minute he was smiling, then suddenly he'd be bitter—he'd lose it. All the more so after he'd had a few. You never knew what to expect. His whole personality could change on a dime. It was a Jekyll-and-Hyde kind of thing."

"Sounds hard to be around. Why'd you put up with it?"

Marvin pauses. "Because he was famous. We all just shrugged it off. You know, it was the price of admission."

"Yeah. I get that. But still."

"He was a mean drunk," he continues. "He acted impulsively, from his gut. I'll never forget this one night. There was a bunch of us sitting at a table, and Sammy Abrams—you remember him?—he was doing his signature bit about the Nazis, his alternative history. How Hitler and the Nazis were really misunderstood; that when they started out, they weren't thugs, not at all. If anything, they were more like health nuts."

"Oh, I remember that guy, sure. Sammy Abrams was the only comic with the chutzpah to go out on a limb like that."

"Yeah, well. It helped a great deal that he was Jewish. Anyway, Sammy was playing the academic, and he was holding forth. He said, I would not think of the Nazis as evil. No, further research now suggests that they were driven, they were obsessed, hell-bent on a mission, kinda like . . . Jack LaLanne. They were against indolence, he said. *Indolence ist verboten!* When he was on stage he'd do his Hitler impression, prance around and sieg heil in all directions. Everyone must work! Everyone must exercise! Everyone must eat their Wheaties! Only he pronounced it Veaties! Nothing inherently bad with that idea, right? All Germans agreed. Push-ups. Sit-ups. Everyone agreed. Everyone, that is, except the Jews. The Jews, they didn't care for the push-ups. Or the Veaties. Nein, not so much. That was the whole problem, according to Herr Professor Abrams. Vel, vat can you do? They were indolent. Always writing books and reading books and scribbling little mathematical nonsense on blackboards and composing symphonies and sitting around cooped up in their doctors' offices. They were trapped inside their heads, poor things, suffering. They needed to take deep breaths. They needed to get outside in the fresh air and run around."

Marv pauses then. "He was setting it up," he says, "and we were smiling, listening, waiting for the punchline. That's when Albert turned and flung his drink at him. We were all stunned. Sammy, Sammy just sat there, not moving, his face was wet. Nobody said a word. Then Albert stood up. 'Go fuck yourself,' he said, and left."

"Guess he didn't like the joke. I mean, it's a touchy subject, you gotta admit."

"Yeah," Marv says, "but that's what comedians do. Push the envelope. Benny and Al did that all the time. All the time. And even if you don't like somebody's stuff, that's not what you do. Not when you're out with a group of comics. You talk to him in private, maybe. Later on, when it's just the two of you. You take it apart word by word."

"I get it."

"I don't know if you do, Amos. It's a brotherhood, what we have."

"Some folks would say it's more like a disease."

"That, too." He grins, then he asks if I'd like to explore his garden in the back. This is how he spends his summer vacation, he explains.

I've never been much of a botanist, couldn't really tell you the difference between a rose and a pansy; but it's his house and I want to pump him some more. He's got a nice bunch of plants in various pots and various stages. They're mostly ornamental, but he also has a few rows of tomatoes and peas and lettuce going near the fence. They're like his children, he says; some are doing better than others.

He points to the agapanthus and the salvia and the succulents. "What's important," he tells me, "what's critical is to notice how each one has a distinct personality."

"So, was that the end of the incident?" I ask. It seems to come out of the blue, this question, especially since we're standing here in this scented paradise.

He gives me a nervous look.

"Did Pupik and Abrams ever see each other again?" I ask. "You said it's a brotherhood, didn't you? Did anyone say they're sorry?"

Marvin stuffs his hands into his pockets. "No. No, they never spoke again. Sammy was devastated by what happened. Ruined. His friends tried to console him, but no one really knew what to say. A couple of guys tried to laugh it off. They said, oh, that's so Al, that's just who he is. A drunk, a *shicker*, what can you do? He probably won't even remember it in the morning."

"Sammy did, I bet."

Marvin nods. "Sammy remembered it, oh, you bet. He signed up for another gig or two at the Comedy Store, but something was different. You could feel it when he walked out there and the spotlight hit him, his heart wasn't in it. And he wouldn't touch the Nazi monologue anymore. Wouldn't go near it. I can't tell you whether or not he was ever meant to break out and be a star, but I know this much: Al Pupik destroyed his career."

"So d'you think Sammy might still be angry with him?"

"For sure."

"Angry enough to kill him?"

He shrugs. "Long as I've known him, Sammy's been a decent guy. He wasn't religious, but he had aunts and uncles, cousins he never met. Most of his people never made it out of Poland. That Nazi material was his way of wondering what happened."

"That doesn't answer my question, Marv. How angry was he?"

He squats down around a potted plant labeled *datura* to feel how damp the soil is. "I can't answer that. You'll have to talk to him."

Marvin gives me Sammy's phone number, also those of two other younger comedians who Al Pupik had wronged. "Jay Wilder and Bud Cornelius," he says as I head out the door. "They weren't as dedicated to doing stand-up, but I always thought they had promise. Al hated them. He heckled them off the stage. Can you believe? I never saw anything like that in my life, where the heckler wins."

As I get into my car, I think gosh, this is not a brotherhood I want to belong to.

*   *   *

Sammy Abrams lives with his sister in Midtown, in an old beige builder's tract house on Gramercy Place that their parents used to inhabit before they passed away. There's a Japanese maple in the yard. It's all part of a lovely, well-kept, leafy neighborhood, and now, in the midst of a real estate boom, it's worth a whole lot more than his parents paid for it back in the forties. Well, that's not true. It's the same house. What's true is he could sell it tomorrow and make a bundle, but then what? Where would he go? Anyone who owns a square of sidewalk in LA has the same problem, I tell him.

He and I sit on a padded bench that occupies half the porch and watch the cars go by. "Bessie's napping on the couch," he says quietly, pointing with his thumb. "She's up half the night sometimes when her pain meds wear off. I hope you don't mind."

He slides from one topic to another, trying without success to gain traction. It seems to be the story of his life. The clowning around in high school, his failed marriage, how his circumstances have changed. After he quit trying to break into show biz, he went out and got a job reading meters for Southern California Edison. He liked the work, he found; sure, it was mindless, but he enjoyed being outdoors and hiking around in the sun. The money was good enough, and the pressure to constantly achieve fell away as he trudged from house to house. "For me, you know, it was pleasant," he says. "Not to think. Not to have to think."

Sammy Abrams is short and dark and muscular. He has rimless eye-glasses and a serious, scholarly demeanor. It's a hot day, so he's wearing tan shorts and a rumpled blue long-sleeve shirt, rolled up to the elbows. As we talk, I try my best to quietly figure him out. That's what I do with everybody—read between the lines. He might be fifty years old, but his work keeps him in shape. When I told him on the phone who I was and that I needed to chat with him about Al Pupik, he didn't act surprised. He also didn't resist. I took that as a good sign. A person who has something to hide, he'd just blow me off ordinarily. Sammy didn't. All right, he's not happy to see me exactly, and he doesn't much want to talk about Al Pupik. But you know something? If Al Pupik had destroyed my career, hell, I wouldn't want to talk about him, either.

"Marvin Rich is a former client," I say. "I did a job for him once, and he told me about the run-in you had with Al Pupik—the beer in the face?"

"I think it was a cosmopolitan he threw," he corrects me, "but it was a while ago."

"Marv said it was humiliating. Shocking, even."

"I felt something snap inside, yeah." He frowns, gives me a rolling-eye look that suggests it was more like an earthquake.

"So you've heard about what happened to Al?"

"Is the Pope Jewish?"

"Not last time I checked," I say.

"It's an old joke," he says. "Of course I heard about Al. I'm out of that game, but he was an icon, a notable. I even considered going to his funeral—that is, if I hadn't had a root canal scheduled that day."

"You're funny," I say.

"There are some leftover feelings," he mutters. "You can appreciate that, I'm sure."

"But when you heard the news, what was your reaction?" I try to keep a sober expression. "I'm guessing you didn't shed a tear."

"The truth? That what you want? When I saw them announce it on television, I smiled. A weird, warm gushy feeling flooded over me. I know you shouldn't do that—smile, take pleasure in someone else's death. It's wrong."

"But you couldn't help yourself."

"I smiled, Mr. Parisman. I admit it. I was happy. Is that a crime?"

"No, not a crime. I'd call it rude, maybe, but then no one's ever tossed a drink in my face before. What can I say?"

Sammy gazes at me. "He didn't just throw a drink in my face. He ended my career. Ended it! I don't know if I could have graduated from the clubs—I don't know if I had what it takes to make it. But thanks to Al, I'll never get a chance to find out, will I?"

There's something familiar about Sammy Abrams. I stare at him, and in that moment I realize what it is: I've met his type before. They were the whiners and goldbricks in the Marines; they were also the smug, self-satisfied students at Berkeley, the demonstrators who stopped opposing the war in Vietnam the minute they learned they'd never be drafted. They were the cowards—the critics who just talked, who never wore a uniform, never took a principled stand one way or the other. "Shit happens all the time, Sammy. You know that. You don't let it get you down. You pick yourself up and go on."

"Meaning?"

My hands make a small shrugging gesture. "Sounds like you used that incident to call it quits, that's all. Maybe you knew you didn't have what it takes, that your career was already heading for the exit. Maybe you were already standing on a ledge, and Al—Al came along and pushed you."

"That's not so," he says. "Al shamed me in front of everyone. Everybody in Hollywood heard what happened. You don't get second chances in this business, Parisman. There are no fairytale endings. Now I'm a meter reader. That's what I do. Now I look out for my sister, Bess. That's okay. She's in pain day and night, but it's good work. Honest work. I'm not ashamed of it. But let me tell you, I'm a long fucking way from the spotlight."

We're sitting in the shade; I notice his cheeks have turned red and he has started to sweat. I have a small internal debate with myself. Should I put this next question to him? Will that be stepping over the line? Will it end our discussion? I don't know. But then, before I can think it through, it just comes hurtling out of my mouth. "So, how much would you say you hated him, Sammy?"

"Huh?"

"You hated him, right? He fucked you over, stunted your life. Turned you into a meter reader. So my question is, how much? Enough to kill him?"

He tenses and his hands mold into fists, but he doesn't stand up and throw a punch, which I thought was a vague possibility. "I hated him, you bet your life I did," he says. "But if you're asking did I kill him? Did I kill him? The answer is no."

"That's good to hear. And I believe you, Sammy, I do."

"Thanks."

"Unfortunately, the police won't much care what I think. You know cops. They have their own peculiar way of doing things. You have to walk a mile in their shoes."

"I don't follow you."

"No," I say, "I don't expect you do. See, the problem is, you had a decent motive. He did you wrong. That means a lot to the LAPD. That's nine tenths of the law in their book. Right now they're fanning out all over LA, hunting for people with motive. You're not alone, though. Apparently, Al managed to put the kibosh on several budding careers before he died, not just yours."

He pulls his glasses away from his face and tucks them carefully into his shirt pocket. "The thing with Al Pupik happened years ago," he says. "It's ancient history. I don't know when I stopped losing sleep over it, but it's not an issue anymore. Not as far as I'm concerned. I like to think I've moved on."

I stand up then, brush the schmutz from the padded bench off my legs. "It's great you feel that way, Sammy. And I'm sure—if and when the time comes—you'll have a solid alibi all prepared. Nothing you can do about a motive, so maybe you can think real hard about where you were the night Al died. I'd work on that if I were you."

I make a mental note in my head that, in the interest of thoroughness, Sammy Abrams is deserving of further research. But if I were a betting man—and I am—I think he's a pretty unlikely suspect. He's a meter reader, not a murderer. I feel for the car keys in my pocket, turn to leave.

"Hey, Parisman, can I ask you something?" Sammy asks.

"Sure."

"Why are you doing this? Huh? Coming around here and hassling me?" His voice starts involuntarily to rise. "I told you, I have a sick sister inside—" Suddenly he grows quiet, fearful that she might awaken.

"It's not about you, Sam. Don't take it personally. It's a process. I'm just looking for the truth."

"Yeah, well, go look somewhere else, will you? I've got my own goddamn problems."

*　　*　　*

Omar calls to let me in on the progress of his romance with Yelena. They met for coffee, and afterwards he insisted on giving her a ride home to her apartment in North Hollywood where she lives with her three sisters. Yelena was excited because a reporter and a photographer from the *New York Times* had spent an hour with Benny Wolf, talking about Albert and their career together.

Yelena didn't understand most of the things they talked about; the reporter was a very brisk woman in a black pantsuit. She had long blond hair, and Yelena thought she was named Arlene something. She asked a lot of questions very fast, one after another, and used a notepad and a tape recorder as backup. When she wasn't jotting stuff down, she played with the split ends of her hair. She smiled every so often, but Yelena could tell just by the rigid way she sat on the couch with her feet pressed together that many of life's pleasures had eluded her; she wasn't a very happy soul.

The photographer was a young fellow with twinkling eyes named Hank Rothchild. He was much more relaxed. He had nothing in common with the reporter. He wore an old Angels cap and kept it on, even inside the house. He reminded her of a rowdy boy she'd once had a crush on in Guatemala. His name was Guillermo. Hank Rothchild had two large cameras slung over his vest. He walked around and squatted in the corner. He snapped dozens of pictures of El Señor, but he never said anything, never told him to make a funny face or to turn one way or another.

"So what are you telling me, Omar?"

"I'm saying Yelena is not all that useful, I guess. She's sweet, she's smart, but I'm saying you wanna know what they talked about, you better read the story when it comes out in the *Times*."

"Lourdes told you to stop."

"She did, but the truth is, unless we bug his phone or put a tail on him 24/7, we're not going to learn much."

"Did you manage to get in on Saturday and case the second floor? Wasn't that the plan?"

"I looked around while Yelena was finishing vacuuming downstairs. I had to be quick, though; I couldn't spend a lot of time. He's got an office and a bedroom up there. Also a huge bathroom. I think whoever owned it before had a thing about bathing."

"What's in the office?"

"Papers, files, unpaid bills. There's two big white metal cabinets with everything. In the first one he's got a file on his winery in Sonoma. There was a manila folder with his stock portfolio from Morgan Stanley. Didn't look like he had much. A couple of medical folders. One about his divorce. I think there was a will there, too."

"Did you look in the medical file? Get his doctor's name?"

"I told you, man, I had to be fast. So no, I didn't."

"And the second cabinet?"

"The second one is full of jokes and ideas, that kind of thing. Little scribblings. A couple of full-length movie scripts. Once I saw what it was, I stopped poking around."

"Anything interesting in the bedroom?"

"There's no porn under the bed, if that's what you mean. He keeps his drawers nice and neat, everything folded up just so. There's some art on the walls, but I couldn't tell you what it was."

"And no posters of Wolf and Pupik? Nothing like that? No trophies? Plaques? Memorabilia?"

"Not that I could see, man. Unless he stores that stuff somewhere else. What about a museum? Isn't there something like that in Hollywood?"

"I'm sure. Or maybe Benny doesn't choose to remember those days. Which—if you believe the stories I've been hearing—is more likely."

"It was his whole life, Amos. How long were they together?"

"Has to be twenty, thirty years, at least."

"That doesn't smell right, you ask me. It's not against the law, or anything, but the cops are going to wonder."

"Maybe we ought to hold off, then. Let the wheels of justice grind it out. Lieutenant Malloy is building a modest case against Wolf as we speak. It's all circumstantial. Personally, I think he's barking up the wrong tree, but hey, it's a free country."

Then I tell him about my encounter with Sammy Abrams. Omar agrees he doesn't sound much like a killer, either. But unlike Benny Wolf, Sammy at least would have a good reason to plug Al; also, the drive from Culver City to Beachwood Drive isn't so daunting. We go over a list of names, other people in show biz that Al mistreated, and I say I'm going to pass them on to Malloy to see if he's interested.

"So, where does that leave us?" Omar wants to know.

"Nowhere, I'm afraid. I think you can stop seeing Yelena, though. Let it go."

"It'll break her heart," Omar says, and for a brief moment I think he's serious. "She really liked the candy I brought. It was a big hit."

"Bring a box home to Lourdes," I say. "That's where your attention should be right now. Lourdes likes candy too, doesn't she? And last I checked, she was your wife."

CHAPTER 6

The Devonshire Community Police Station on Etiwanda Avenue in Northridge is a pleasant, red-bricked square fortress of a building with clusters of dwarf palm trees out front and user-friendly signage. It services a wide swath of outlying areas—places like Canoga Park, Chatsworth, Northridge, Porter Ranch, Granada Hills. So when the phone rings around noon and I hear that Benny Wolf has been locked up there in a room with two detectives for the past four hours and needs me now to come rescue him, well, what can I do? He's footing the bill, after all.

Jason and Remo are sitting across from him when I enter. They're both wearing dark sport coats. Remo's red tie is loosened at the throat, and he's unbuttoned his coat so his gun is visible in the leather shoulder holster. He gives Benny the thousand-yard stare—the one where you don't blink. Like he doesn't believe a word he says. Jason is playing with a pencil, drumming it periodically on the table. Jason told me once that he used to be a drummer—long ago, when he was a teenager, before he let Jesus into his life. Now he half-closes his eyes and holds the pencil lightly between two fingers. Maybe he's pretending to be back on stage, I think. Who knows? Maybe there's a small part of him, a private part he never talks about, that still misses the stage.

"What took you so long?" That's the first thing Benny says. He's wearing a white tracksuit and orange running shoes. It looks like he hasn't shaved since the last time we met; his eyes are downcast, and he looks pale and haggard. A little shaky, too.

"Sorry," I say, grabbing the only other vacant seat at the table, "traffic." Traffic is the answer to all things deplorable in Los Angeles. It explains our shortcomings, why nothing works, why marriages fail, why doctors' fees are through the roof, why homelessness goes uncontrolled, why Johnny can't read, why no one says please or thank you anymore.

"Mr. Wolf here was gracious enough to avail himself of our questions," Remo says. "We never realized it would take this long. You know how it is, Parisman: one topic leads to another. But we've already apologized for that, haven't we, Jason? And Mr. Wolf has been so gracious, such a gentleman, you know, like the star he is."

We're in a dull, gray, airless, nondescript room. It's hard to think in a place like this. That's the point. That's where cops like to hold interrogations. Remo is gazing steadily at me now, ignoring Wolf.

Benny Wolf clears his throat. "Are you saying . . . are you telling me I am free to go?"

"You were never under arrest, Mr. Wolf. Never. You came along voluntarily, remember? To help us with our case."

"I—I always want to assist the police," he says, not very convincingly. He turns to me. "They asked me a lot of questions, Parisman. I tried to answer them."

"Yes, you did," says Jason from the far side of the table.

"Do you recall what you said?" I ask.

Benny gives me a blank look. "I told them as much as I could about the night Al died. That I went to see him, but—"

"You were in his house the night he died? What? You never told me that."

"Well," he says defensively, "you didn't ask me, now, did you?"

"I asked him," Remo says. "And he was kind enough to tell the truth. Now, just because he admitted it, that doesn't mean much, right? They were partners. Why would it matter that they talked?"

"You've placed him in the room where it happened, that's why," I say. "And it was one of his wine bottles that killed him."

"For your information, Parisman, we knew he was in the living room all along—even before he opened his mouth. See, he left his fingerprints on a glass in the kitchen. There was no trickery. We just reminded him of that fact."

Remo has a little smirk on his face; I don't know whether it's because he thinks he's put something over on me, something rich, or what. We've always had a rocky time getting along. My guess is it's jealousy on his part. Remo is a good soldier; he's loyal to the institution, period. He works for Malloy, and somewhere in the back of his feral brain he thinks Malloy should be similarly loyal. But the thing is, Bill Malloy isn't someone you can pigeonhole. He studied with the Jesuits. He respects the LAPD, but he's also friends with me. We talk; we take each other to lunch. He asks about Loretta, how's she doing these days, and I want to know about his Jess and her crippling arthritis.

"And now he's free to go," I say.

"Exactly," Remo says.

Benny pushes his chair back and rises. "Maybe you could give me a ride back to my house now, Mr. Parisman. I'd appreciate it."

"Thanks for your cooperation," Jason says, glancing up at him as he goes by. He does a final little drumbeat with the pencil, then slaps it down on the table.

Wolf heads for the door, and I follow. Outside, the sun is beating down relentlessly. We cut diagonally across the parking lot to my Honda. I make him stand outside for a minute while I brush all the schmutz off the passenger seat and toss it in a nearby trashcan—old wrappers from In-N-Out Burger, little leftover packets of ketchup and salt, paper napkins, petrified pumpkin seeds, a plastic toothpick, and a couple of business cards I can no longer identify. "Okay," I say, "it's all yours."

I drive three blocks until we come to a red light. Benny hasn't said a word. He's leaning back in his seat, his eyes are closed, and his hands are resting on his knees.

"Well," I begin, "are you planning to tell me what happened back there?"

He shrugs his shoulders. "They appeared at my front door, showed me their badges, and wondered whether I'd mind accompanying them down to the station. What was I supposed to do? You tell me."

"I don't mind that you went with them, Benny. I knew they wanted to talk to you, but I sorta thought they'd hold off a bit longer. I asked them to."

"You knew?"

"They're like moles—they just follow their noses," I say. "The evidence leads them this way, that way—that's all they care about. I'm sorry, though, that they put you through the wringer."

"They said they found one of my wine bottles."

"I knew about that. What I didn't know was that you went to see him. Why?"

"He owed me money, Parisman. He's owed me money for years. I was going broke."

"Okay," I say. "You went to see him. And how did that go?"

Benny frowns. "About as I expected. Al's a very cagey guy. Good on his feet. Always thinking. He wanted to see my paperwork. 'Where's the proof?' That's what he wanted. 'Show me something written down, we'll talk.'"

"And?"

"Well, of course, I didn't have any paper." He runs his hand twice through his white silky hair, shakes his head. How he arrived at this place is beyond him; he's lost; nothing is as it should be. I'm no psychiatrist, but I know sad when I see it. And he's sad, he's desperate, spiraling downward. Things are falling apart. That's what's probably going through his mind. He bites his lower lip. How he came to be sitting in this old dented Honda on Etiwanda Avenue, waiting for the light to change, is bewildering. "That's not me. Not who I am."

"So, what happened? I mean, how did it end?"

"We argued. That's what always happens. I reminded him we had an agreement, even after Vegas when we broke up. Everything was spelled out. Black and white. Fifty-fifty. How it was supposed to be." He makes a gentle, slow-motion karate chop with his hand. "Right down the middle."

The light changes to green, and I inch forward behind a UPS delivery van. "This agreement—you have a paper copy somewhere I could look at?"

"Yeah," he says, "yeah, somewhere. In my office, maybe. Why? What good will it do you?"

"Well, if he was really cheating you, that could be important."

"He *was* cheating me! He was robbing me blind. And we were friends, you know—years of friendship. You think that was easy for me? To go up against him? No, that hurt."

"But Benny, you see—don't you—what that says to the police?"

"I told them he was cheating me. I got mad."

"Did you hit him?"

"I got mad, yeah. I said some things. But I didn't touch him. I don't remember touching him. I don't even think we shook hands."

"You're sure."

"Sure I'm sure. It was an argument. The same one we always have. He was cheating me."

"And what did Jason and Remo say to that?"

"Who?"

"The cops you spoke with."

"They didn't react. They just nodded. One of them wrote some stuff down."

When you're in this business as long as me, you think you've seen it all. And for the most part, you have. It's hard not to be jaded. I've had clients who hired me because they were desperate, their back was against the wall, and they needed me to succeed. I've also had clients who, for their own reasons, didn't care about the truth. They just wanted the bare minimum from a rusty old detective. They brought me in to go through the motions, put a Band-Aid on it, and tell them everything's fine. I've had clients who were innocent and clients who looked terrific on paper but ended up being guilty as sin. You don't get to choose your customers, I've found. But Benny Wolf is a mystery to me.

"Maybe they didn't react," I say now. "Maybe they let you waltz out the door. But you're in big trouble. You've just handed them a solid gold motive."

"It's the truth," he says, more intently than before. "Albert owed me money."

"Albert owed you money. You were going broke, so you went to see him. You argued about it. He didn't pay you. You left. The next day, his cleaning lady finds him dead. He's naked on the living room rug. Somebody hit him with a wine bottle. After that, somebody shot him two times. Somebody was seriously pissed. You were probably the last person to see him alive. Oh, did I mention that the wine came from your vineyard in Sonoma? That it's impossible to find in LA?"

He is silent for a while. "They didn't arrest me," he says, looking up. He seems to find some comfort in that fact. "They let me go. They told me I was just a person of interest."

"Oh, they're interested, all right. I'd give them a week, and they'll be pounding on your door again. I wouldn't be surprised if you're not under surveillance right now."

"You think so?"

"I'll bet you a hundred dollars."

We turn onto Montague Court. I pull up at the curb beside his house, reach for the key, and switch off the engine. Manuel Morales, the happy gardener, the one Omar made friends with, is busy edging the lawn next door. He looks over and smiles at us, then returns to his task.

"What am I going to do?" Benny asks mournfully. Since it's just the two of us sitting there, I guess he's asking me, but the way he says it, it could be anyone in the universe. It could be God.

"Well, they haven't come for you yet," I say. "Which is good news. But if I were you, I'd find myself a criminal lawyer, someone who knows his way around a courtroom. I'd sit down with him and tell him everything you can remember about that night." I lay my hand reassuringly on Benny Wolf's knee, give it a pat. "You had your problems with Al Pupik, okay, but so did a lot of folks. And you know what else? I still don't think you did it."

"You don't?"

"No, I don't."

"Why's that?"

"Well," I say, "for starters, because you're an honest man, Benny. Old, but honest. And secondly, even if you're a little dotty, you'd still remember something like that. It's not easy to kill someone. You'd think it would be—people kill each other all the time—but it's not. Especially like that. With a bottle and a gun. My God, that's brutal. It stays with you. Ruins your sleep. Believe me, I know."

"I didn't kill him," he says then.

I stare at him. He's a genial old soul, and—God love him—sincere enough, but sincerity is not what keeps you out of the slammer. Does he understand that?

"And I sleep pretty well, Mr. Parisman," he added. "Just so you know."

*　　*　　*

Bill Malloy didn't plan on seeing us today, I can tell; he's listening, he's apologetic. We're back in his office, Omar and me. The fans are rotating overhead, it's another June scorcher, and he's saying all the things a police officer should say, all the things a good police officer has to say, when he's been caught in a lie. "I know, I know," he says. "I told you we'd hold off another week."

"You promised, actually."

"Right. It was a promise. But I don't run the whole show. I have my little bailiwick. And bringing Wolf in was not my idea."

"Whose was it, then?"

He wags his head derisively, lifts his thumb toward the ceiling. "People upstairs. The DA, for sure. They gave the green light. They looked at the evidence we developed; that probably tipped the scales."

"Yeah," I say, "but do they really believe they can make it stick? It's all pretty sketchy, you ask me."

"A Hollywood case." He rubs his hands together thoughtfully. "You know, big glitzy names splattered all over the front page—the Department always has a hard time with that. Reporters, TV news crews. I don't know for sure, they may be looking to just—just put it to bed."

"Then why don't you arrest him?" Omar asks. "What are you waiting for?"

"We're getting closer. I'm holding out, I'm still open to other possibilities, but that could change if something else surfaces. Wolf's not a flight risk. That's a plus. We're keeping an eye on him, of course, but for now it's just as easy to leave him where he is."

I consider offering up the name of Sammy Abrams about now, as well as Jay Wilder and Bud Cornelius; that might give him some perspective, help widen the lens. "You know, Bill, Benny Wolf isn't the only comedian Al Pupik abused. Just ask around at the clubs if you want to learn what a schmuck he was. He stepped on a lot of folks over the years. He had a reputation. I could give you a list."

Remo walks in just then from one of the adjacent cubicles, followed by Jason. He hands the lieutenant a thin blue manila folder, whispers something earnestly in his ear. Malloy nods several times. The two officers give us the once-over, then make a beeline for the stairs.

"And I hope you will," Malloy says to me. "A list of suspects would help. Like I say, anything's possible. Grist for the mill."

"You bet." I stand up then, and so does Omar. He wants to leave, and I can't say I blame him. Talking to cops—even smart cops like Malloy—always makes him antsy. He's good for about twenty minutes, max. The lieutenant takes the blue manila folder and, without opening it, adds it to the considerable stack of papers already on his desk. Our meeting with the LAPD is over, apparently.

"Stay in touch," Malloy mumbles as we walk out the door and head for the elevator.

I push the button for the parking garage, fold my arms in front of me, and wait. Another thought comes to mind. "You know something, Omar? Benny didn't hire me to find Al's killer," I say. "He was very specific. He hired me to prove he was innocent. It's almost like he knew the cops would be zeroing in on him."

"Well, he had that right," Omar says. "Now they're just sitting there waiting to pounce if he ever tries to leave town." The elevator starts to hum and descend then, and even though we're alone, we fall into a solemn silence, the way most people do whenever elevators start to move.

I drive him to Hacienda Heights; his brother-in-law, Santiago, has a small two-bedroom house there he's fixing up to sell or rent out, and Omar needs to help him with the sheetrock. On the Pasadena Freeway, before the off-ramp at Avenue 42, I turn to him.

"How about this for a theory: Benny Wolf's telling us the truth, as far as he can remember. He went to see Albert, but he doesn't think he laid a finger on him. I can believe that. It makes sense. Benny's a scrawny little guy. Albert's much bigger."

"And David killed Goliath, didn't he?" Omar reminds me. "Hit him with a stone."

"Lucky shot," I say. "Anyway, he went to see him. They had their perennial disagreement, what they always say, and he left. A short time after that, somebody else walked in, bonked him on the head, and shot him."

"Maybe so. But you're forgetting one other big thing," Omar says.

"What's that?"

"He was naked. You'd think Benny would have noticed that. Even if he is like—like you say—dotty. You can't ignore a naked man."

"Yeah, you're right. That's a head-scratcher. So, let's play this out. How would something like that happen?"

"You have ideas?"

"Sure, I do. Either he started taking his clothes off when he first met his assailant, which suggests something amorous, or he just happened to be naked—getting ready to hop in the shower or in bed maybe—when the doorbell rang."

"I'm sorry," Omar says. "That's just wrong. There's a knock at the door, late at night, you don't know who it is. And even if it's someone you're expecting, you're not going to show up naked. If he had a girlfriend, maybe—"

"Boyfriend," I correct him.

"Fine. If he had a boyfriend and later on something went wrong, a fight, then you'd think he'd be found in the bedroom, not the living room. It just doesn't figure."

I trust Omar's instincts. The world he comes from is harder, more conservative, more hemmed in by tradition. Family and Catholicism gnaw at his heart; even though he's here now, in neon LA, where it's sex, drugs, and muscle cars, where stars are born overnight, it doesn't matter. He can't shake himself; he can't cross that bridge and leave the truth—the raw truth he understands—behind.

"Maybe the fact that he's naked," he mumbles, upon further consideration, "maybe that's what's hanging the cops up too. It looks like there's something else going on. Maybe that's why they're waiting before they bust Benny Wolf. I know them. They like things neat and tidy."

I drop him at his destination. He reaches into the back seat for his tool belt, slings it over his shoulder, then climbs out.

"I like the way you think, Omar." I lean forward so I can still talk to him through the open window. "I'm going to follow up with Malloy. But in some neutral place, you know, not downtown. He was acting just a little too formal in there. For my money, at least."

"Why's that?" Omar asks.

"I dunno. He's under pressure from somebody. The DA, others. These things take on a life of their own sometimes."

I watch him wander off across the parched yellow lawn toward the unfinished house. He waves to his brother-in-law. Santiago waves back. A couple of other workmen in T-shirts and baseball caps are unloading sheetrock from the rear end of a rusty Toyota pickup. They're lugging it step by step into what will one day be the living room or the dining room, I can't tell. I don't know where Omar is going with this business. I would love for him to continue on with me; he has what it takes to make it someday as an investigator, I'm sure of it. But he also has a wife to feed and children down the line. Also, he plainly enjoys the camaraderie of his brother-in-law, the hammers and nails and saws, the balancing required and the sheer weight of the physical universe.

*   *   *

Mara made plans a month ago, so it shouldn't surprise me now. She and her granddaughter Violet are heading to the East Coast to look around at colleges, see which ones make sense. She even told me the time and date and that I would have to drive them both to LAX, but somehow, when Al Pupik died, it slid off my radar. Lucky for me, I'm pretty good at shifting on the fly. Now we're all in her Lexus and stuck in southbound traffic on 405. Mara's looking down at her watch and telling me how to drive. I'm too close to the car in front of us. I should get over one lane. I should do it now while it's still clear.

Violet sits in the back seat with her eyes closed, listening to God only knows what on her iPhone. She's a seasoned traveler, calm. Or at least she's used to the stomach-churning noise that accompanies her grandmother at the start of every trip. Violet knows full well that she wants to go to college. All her friends at Foxboro are going, and she has never been one to buck the crowd.

"How long do you think you'll be gone?" I ask Mara.

"A week," she says, "maybe two or three, all depending. We want to visit Smith and Vassar, for sure. I'm thinking it might be smart to check out Brown in Rhode Island, and I think she should talk to someone at Middlebury in Vermont. That's a lot of ground to cover."

"It's New England."

"So?"

"New England is not Texas. It shouldn't take you that long."

We haven't talked much about the Albert Pupik matter. Often, when I'm working a case, she'll bring it up, ask for a few gory details, especially if she's anxious about me. She hasn't bothered this time around, so I'm guessing she's not. Two old courtly comedians. I dunno, maybe it seems quaint to her. But I've also been quiet. I didn't tell her about all the people I've been interviewing lately, or that Benny Wolf was this close to being busted, or that his memory is *farblunget*—shot to hell.

I glance in the rearview mirror. Violet still has her eyes closed. We've never been particularly close. We treat each other with kid gloves. She accepts me as an equal, at least for who I am. I'm the guy who's *shtupping* her grandmother, which, because she has an American Express card and was raised liberal and free, is fine, just fine. Violet lost her mother when she was an infant. Whether she even remembers Meghan now is something we've never talked about, and maybe it doesn't matter much anymore. What happened to her shouldn't have happened to anyone—that goes without saying—but it had to have shattered both her and Mara, ripped through them all like a torpedo. I know because long after I heard about it, pieces are still floating around in my brain: the stiff bloated corpse in the trunk of the stolen Chevy; the needle marks up and down her arms.

Mara did the best she could. She stepped in at that point; made sure her granddaughter had lots of therapists and tutors and play-mates around her; threw lavish birthday parties and took her to Broadway musicals and art museums. She showered her with books and toys and clothes and whatever else she could buy. Now that I think about it, it was Mara's problem even more than Violet's. Her way of grieving over Meghan, always trying to find peace where there was none, was to redecorate that hellish landscape, make it livable—which was how Violet received so many bright, shiny objects and came to be who she is.

"Give me a call when you arrive, okay? Just so I know where you are."

"Of course," she says. "And not that I'm worried, but I've left a week's worth of frozen dinners for you in the fridge. Just take the plastic off and stick them in the microwave."

"Thanks," I say. "But you didn't have to. I can fend for myself in the wild. People tell me I'm a wonderful cook."

"Who told you?"

"People. I'm not going to name names. I don't want to embarrass them. They say I'm very inventive."

"I've seen your inventiveness, Amos. Leftovers, that's your forte."

I shrug. "Okay, so I wasn't raised to waste things. My mother always told me, 'Remember the starving Armenians.'"

"Nothing wrong with that. Only they haven't starved in years."

I see the green sign for Exit 46 up ahead and slide expertly into the right lane. "You don't know the same Armenians I do."

I stretch my hand across the front seat. She takes hold and gives it a short, loving squeeze. "I just want you to be safe," she says. "That's all."

*   *   *

There's a pick-up softball game in progress at Roosevelt High—lanky teenage boys with buzz cuts and tattoos, also a few girls and a couple of older men in T-shirts and baggy shorts. They've got the right amount of people to form teams, but not enough for an umpire. The sun seems caught between two huge white billowy clouds; still, it's going to be another blistering day. I've just come from grabbing a snack at King Taco on Cesar Chavez, and I'm running late, which I'm sure Malloy won't appreciate.

He's sitting in the bleachers near the third-base line. This may be the first time I've ever seen him out of uniform—no coat, no tie, not even a pair of polished wingtips. A civilian. He's wearing jeans and leather topsiders, and he's got on a dark blue Cubs cap, a relic from his salad days in Chicago. He's leaning back on his elbows, holding a large paper cup of something in his hand, studying the play through a wire-rim pair of sunglasses.

"Hey," I say, plopping down beside him.

"Hey," he mumbles, without turning.

"I know what you're going to say, Bill."

"Oh, yeah? What's that?"

"You're going to tell me I'm twenty minutes late."

He glances at his watch. "You are."

"And then you're going to say that in your vast experience, Jews are never late."

"So I heard."

"And then, if you're really still upset, you're going to say that I was the Jew who told you that."

He looks at me, shakes his head. "That's great thinking, Amos. Only, you know what? It's my day off. I don't give a damn if you're late."

I nod, check out what's in his paper cup. It looks like ginger ale with ice—something bubbly, anyway. "So, who's winning?" I ask.

"The ones at bat. But I don't think they're paying close attention to the score." He takes his shades off, rubs the space between his eyes, and puts them back on again. "I can't remember the last time I watched a ball game in person. On TV, of course, but it's different then. You have to listen to the sportscasters, let them tell you the last pitch was a slider or a curveball—as if you care, right? Listen to them goof off. It's like sitting next to a couple of drunks. No, I prefer this."

I wait a moment before launching into what I'd really come here for. The teenager at bat slaps one down the third-base line into left field. Everyone cheers, and he ends up with a stand-up double.

"So, I wanted to talk with you about our meeting the other day at your office," I say. "Omar and I both got the feeling you weren't being straight with us."

"I don't know what you mean."

"Just a feeling, Bill. I could be wrong. I just sensed some office politics going on."

"That's always the case," he says.

"Anyway, we talked afterwards, Omar and me. I know you're looking hard at my client. I get that. And there may be good reasons to charge him."

"Oh, there are," he says.

"But there might also be some damn good reasons why you shouldn't."

He continues following the game, where the next batter has popped out to the first baseman beyond the foul line. "I'm listening," he says.

"I'm not a DA, but it just seems to me that you haven't put this baby to bed yet. There are too many loose ends."

"Such as?"

"Well, for instance, there's the circumstance of Al's death. How he was found. Even by Hollywood standards, you have to admit it looks weird. And I wonder, you know, what you make of it."

"You mean, that he was naked?"

"Bingo."

Malloy lifts his cap briefly and runs his hands through his hair. "Well, that does conjure up all kinds of fascinating possibilities, doesn't it?"

"What we thought, yeah."

"And you want me to speculate?"

"No, Bill. I want you to tell me what you can actually infer from the evidence. I'm the speculator here. I haven't even been allowed in the house, so I'm guessing. I'm asking for your help. What do we know? Do we know the time of death? Have your guys figured that out yet?"

"Roughly," he says. "They think—and the science is pretty good on this—between nine and midnight."

"Okay," I say. "And I'm assuming, for the moment, that he died from the bullet wounds, not the conk on the head."

"We're working on that. He bled a lot, but there were no arteries severed. He could have had a heart attack. In which case, maybe he never felt a thing."

"And the blood on the carpet. Was it all Al's? I know you found Benny's prints, but not on the bottle."

"The blood belongs entirely to Al."

"And the prints?"

"We did find Benny's prints on the counter and on the door, but not on the bottle itself. In fact, the bottle was wiped clean, which is odd. There were some other sets, but we haven't been able to make a match yet." He turns to me. "Was that it, then? Have I told you everything?"

"The clothes. He wouldn't just be wandering around with his pants down. No jury will buy that. What happened to his clothes?"

"Good question. Al either showed up naked to talk to his visitor, which would be strange, outlandish—"

"Ridiculous, actually—"

"Or," he continues, "the killer somehow forced him to drop his drawers, then killed him, or stripped him after he killed him."

"None of which makes much sense."

"Agreed. But that's what we're looking at."

Another batter has grounded out, moving the kid on second to third. A teenage girl with long hair braided in a ponytail takes a few practice swings and settles in, waiting for the pitch. The team in the field seems to be in agreement that she's an easy out. They all move in closer.

"Come on, Bill," I say. "If you bust Benny now, with what you've got, it'll be a circus. Worse, you're gonna lose."

"You think I don't know that?" He's not angry, but there's a world-weariness in his tone; he's pissed at himself, at the police department, at the media, at the whole situation. He feels trapped, I imagine. As if he's already sitting in the courtroom, watching the judge pound the gavel, listening to the chuckles in the gallery, listening to the blarney, as he would put it—coming out of the prosecutor's mouth.

The girl at the plate strains and swings hard, she connects and loops a ball surprisingly high over the head of the older paunchy man in left field. A delighted cry goes up from the ragtag bunch on the bench, and the teen from third scores.

Malloy takes off his sunglasses and tucks them quietly in his shirt pocket. "I don't want to charge him, Amos, I don't. Unless we can break him down, unless he confesses and we can back it up, there's not enough evidence. And I agree with everything you've said. But you know what else? I'm just one man. And right now, I'm up against it. I'm standing on the tracks and I'm staring at a freight train. You tell me how to stop it."

CHAPTER 7

After that Sunday at Roosevelt High, I thought they would wait. In fact, I was sure we had more time to make them reconsider. That's what my gut said. But maybe in the end I was betting too much on Malloy. Maybe I was wrong to assume he had magical powers. He told me he was just one man. Still, it caught me off guard when I opened the *LA Times* the next morning, and there was a mournful Benny Wolf in handcuffs on the front page of the City Section.

The story in the paper was short; it didn't offer a whole lot of detail. There was no discussion about why or how he might have done it. It only said he was taken into custody yesterday evening without incident at his ex-wife's home in West Hollywood. He was being arraigned this morning and, because of his frailty and age, was expected to be released on bond.

I put my coffee cup down and call Malloy's office. It's early, but I figure he'll be there. Yesterday at the ballpark he couldn't talk about it, but I realize now he was practically waving a flag at me that they were going to bust him. How blind can you be?

After three rings, Remo picks up. "I sorta thought we'd be hearing from you. You're right on time, Parisman. Only the Lieutenant is in a big powwow upstairs, if that's who you're looking for."

"How'd you guess?"

"Intuition." There's a pause. "You know what else? He probably won't want to talk with you when he comes out."

"Oh, yeah? And why's that?"

"I really should keep my mouth shut," he says, "but just between you and me, well, they're reading him the riot act right about now."

"Why, Remo? What'd he do?"

"Am I in the meeting? No. But I'm guessing they have a problem with the way the Lieutenant does his job. He doesn't always stay put in one lane, if you know what I mean."

"He's a damn good cop, Remo." I'm trying to restrain myself. It's a good thing we're not in the same room together, because I'd probably punch him about now. "Tell me this—is it because of me that he's in hot water?"

"Oh, you're part of it, I'm sure," he says. "When he goes around sharing information with the hoi polloi, evidence we've developed, evidence we need for prosecution, well, it leaves a bad odor in the room. DAs are tidy people. They like their bread buttered a certain way. They—"

"I hear you," I say. "Just tell him I called, will you?"

"You bet," he says. "But don't expect a callback."

I start to hang up, then at the last second I say, "Hey, Remo, one other thing. Can you tell me if Benny Wolf made bail?"

"Are you kidding me? He had a lawyer there ten minutes after we brought him in."

"You remember his name?"

"*Her* name," he says. "Petra Allison."

"Isn't she the one who defended MGM in that big sex-discrimination suit?"

"If memory serves. I think she won, too."

"Thanks, Remo. Much appreciated."

"Hey," he says. "You didn't hear it from me, pal. I stay in my lane."

*   *   *

Benny Wolf must have used the same whimsical method when he chose Petra Allison that he did with me. Maybe he just liked the classy lilt of her name. She couldn't have come cheap, I figure; but from everything I've heard, she knows her stuff.

I make some sourdough toast and coffee, then phone her office in Westwood. A secretary, or maybe it's a receptionist, someone named Jennifer, a brisk, no-nonsense lady, says she's not in. I say yeah, I kinda thought that might be the case, but see, I'm the private investigator working for Benny Wolf, and she and I should probably talk. When I dress it up that way, tell her who I really am—*detective for the stars*—that gets her attention.

"Actually," Jennifer says, "she's meeting with Mr. Wolf this afternoon."

"That's great," I say. "I was going to drive out to his place in Granada Hills. I'm guessing he made bail. He's back home by now, right?"

"Um, I think their meeting was at his wife's apartment. You know where that is?" There's a sudden hesitancy in her voice, like she's biting her lip. That's when I realize she's queasy about giving confidential information out over the phone to a perfect stranger. I want to tell her she can trust me. I want to say no, you've got it all wrong, I'm not perfect, but I'm also not a stranger—not to Benny Wolf, at least.

"She's on La Cienega," I say instead. "I've been there before. And just for the record, it's his ex-wife. Alma'd be pretty upset if you got that wrong."

"Thanks for the heads-up," she says. Then she whispers that I ought to arrive by two, and that she'll let Petra know I'm coming. "She hates surprises, you know."

We leave it there. I do a quick search of Petra Allison on the internet, see what it says. Then I place one more call, this time to Omar.

"You saw the news?"

"What? I haven't seen a paper, man."

"They busted Benny."

"He's locked up?"

"No, he made bail right away. He's got a good lawyer, I think, but I'm worried about what kind of a case they've got. They must have more than that wine bottle and the fact that Al Pupik was doing him wrong."

"Al did a lot of people wrong, sounds like."

"That's what I plan to tell his lawyer this afternoon. She hears what a schmuck he was to everyone, then we can at least expand the number of plausible suspects."

"Good idea."

"But there's something else we should do. Benny was picked up at his ex-wife's apartment in West Hollywood. He's back there now. But he told me he barely leaves Granada Hills these days, that he's terrified to be in Hollywood."

"Yeah, I remember you said that before. So what's it mean?"

"So he's lying, that's what. And if he's lying about that, he's probably lying about other things too. It means we need to keep a much closer tab on him. I want you to meet me at Alma Wolf's place, say, ten minutes before two. What kind of car does Benny drive?"

"In Granada Hills, it was an old green Alfa Romeo. That's all I ever saw. I imagine it's still sitting out on La Cienega somewhere."

"Probably with a parking ticket by now." I give him Alma's address then, and he says he'll be there.

*   *   *

Benny's Alfa isn't hard to spot. I was wrong about the parking ticket, however. Either that, or he lifted it off the windshield when he arrived back at Alma's apartment from his brief incarceration. Omar finds a convenient place for his Camaro three cars away. He promises to keep a sharp eye on him.

When I press the buzzer of Alma's apartment, it's Benny who comes to the door. "Come in, come in," he says, looking around apprehensively in all directions. He leads me into the living room, where Alma and Petra are seated on her couch with their legs crossed, each holding a glass of white wine. There's also another woman in a blue work shirt and capris, who Alma says is a friend of the family, Margaret Mooney. Maggie was once an aspiring comedienne, she says; that's how they met.

Benny is all in black—tight black pants, black long-sleeve shirt, black sneakers. He's like a wiry old ninja; there's a grace and solemnity to him that's remarkable. If I'd just been hustled off in handcuffs, fingerprinted, photographed, strip-searched, and locked up, if I were facing a murder rap that would keep me behind bars the rest of my life, I don't know if I'd be so calm, so self-contained. He folds effortlessly into a leather chair and points to a similar one for me.

Petra, who's been absorbed in some documents, finally turns in my direction. "Hi," she says, extending her hand, "I'm Petra Allison."

"So I've heard," I say. "Amos Parisman." I hand her my business card, which is sorta pointless because she knew I was coming, but so what? It's the kind of thing I do by instinct, especially with lawyers. They like to swap official scraps of paper; it puts them at ease.

She smiles, sets it down on the coffee table without really examining it. Petra Allison has short, clipped strawberry-blond hair and pale, icy-blue eyes. She's carefully put together. Her earrings reflect the same design as her necklace. Her blouse and pants match, too, or at least she didn't get them off the discount rack at Ross. I don't know how I feel about her. She's all clarity and purpose. The internet told me about her hotshot education at Columbia. Then Yale Law. Not to mention parents who could never do enough for her. She stares at me for an extra second or two, like she's sizing me up, pricing me, putting me cautiously back in a box where I belong.

Alma offers me a glass of chardonnay, but I shake my head.

"We were just going over the preliminary charges, Mr. Parisman," Petra says. "They're talking about Murder One, but I've worked with David Cimino's people at the DA's office; I'm sure that will be reduced to Murder Two long before it ever goes to trial."

"How do you figure that?"

Another quick smile. This time she's humoring me. Just walked in and already I've shown her what a rube, what a *grine kuzine*, I am. "First-degree murder requires motive, planning, anticipation," she says. "The DA has to prove that Mr. Wolf went to Al's house that night determined to kill him. I think that'll be relatively easy to knock down." She glances over at Benny, who is paying close attention. "First of all, while he admits going to the house on Beachwood, it clearly wasn't to commit murder. Benny just wanted his fair share. Al was nickel-and-diming him. That's what he's told the police. That's what they'd been arguing about for years. Am I right, Benny?"

Benny nods.

"It was a partnership," Petra continues. "Fifty-fifty. Supposed to be, anyway."

"Not that I believe he did it," I interrupt, "but I have to ask you—if Al was stiffing him, isn't that a motive for murder?"

"He *was* stiffing me!" Benny says. "I have the contract!"

Margaret nods at this. Petra nods too. "And what I'm saying is that the fact that you went there to talk to him, to confront him with proof, to ask for your money—that was legitimate. That doesn't show any intent to kill. Quite the contrary."

"Okay," I say. "So it's second-degree murder, then. Fine. How are you planning to make that disappear?"

"I haven't seen all their so-called evidence," Petra says. "Not yet. We know that Al Pupik was hit with a bottle and later shot with a gun they haven't been able to find. The bottle came originally from Benny's winery in Sonoma, it's true." She takes a small sip of wine, then fixes me with those cold, blue, piercing eyes. She's calculating, weighing every word the way a judge or a jury might. "In my book, it just doesn't amount to much."

"My friends, Sergeants Jason and Remo, spent four long hours grilling him down at the Devonshire Station. Didn't they also get a confession?"

She sets her wine glass down. She's only had a small sip; I get the feeling she accepted it just to be polite. "Benny didn't confess," she says. "Not as far as I can tell. I don't have the transcript of that interview yet. But I think I can show the court that Benny sometimes has problems remembering things." She nods in his direction. "Benny is a poet. He has a great imagination. That's how he succeeded in life. He doesn't always see the world the way it really is. He talks about how he might like it to be."

"Which includes murdering his partner?"

She raises an eyebrow. "Between what he said and what they heard, there's a world of difference."

I tell her how I've been looking into other folks who might have wanted to see Al dead—other comedians he's routinely insulted and ruined, for example. A list, in fact. Petra likes that idea. "I'd appreciate all those names," she says. "And whatever stories or anecdotes they have to tell you, Amos. Can I call you Amos?"

"No problem," I reply.

"Wonderful. I don't know that they would ever rise to the level of suspects, but it'll certainly help muddy the water for Benny here. That'll be part of our defense." She reaches into her purse and offers me her business card. "Meanwhile, I'm going to push the trial date back as far as possible. The more distance we have, the less of a circus it'll be, right? So when you come up with useful material, Amos, just drop it off with Jennifer or Maureen. Anyone at the office can handle it, really. I look forward to working with you."

I stand up then. I don't know why, but in a matter of minutes I feel like she's managed to reduce me to another one of her flunkies. She seems to have more to talk about with Alma and Benny, things I don't need to hear, things that don't include me.

I stuff her card into the side pocket of my sport coat. "Well," I say, "it's nice meeting you. I guess I'll be on my way." I pat Benny on the shoulder. "Glad you're out of the slammer. We'll be in touch, huh?"

"Sure," he says. "Sure, you bet."

Alma Wolf rises. Maybe because it's her apartment and she's still an old-fashioned North Dakota girl, she has some deep primal need to walk me back to the door. "Thanks for coming by, Amos," she murmurs under her breath. "I can't tell you what an awful time these last two days have been. Poor Benny. Well, you see for yourself. He's a wreck."

"I heard they picked him up here, Alma."

"Yes, that's right."

"How'd that happen? I mean, it's a schlep from Granada Hills."

"He drove out to see me late last night. I was in my pajamas. Believe me, I had no idea he'd show up."

"He just rang the doorbell?"

She nods. "We're not married, but we still talk now and then. I guess they followed him."

"Yeah, but why was he here? He told me he never comes to Hollywood anymore. Made a big *tzimmes* about it, in fact."

She rolls her eyes. "And didn't I warn you not to rely on what he says?"

"No, you told me he was crazy."

"Same thing," she says.

*   *   *

That night, Mara checks in with me from their hotel in Boston. She'd already called me once the day before from Logan to let me know they'd arrived safe and sound. I think the East Coast agrees with her: all that humid summer air; the lush greenery; rivers with water in them, water deep enough to drown in; historical markers everywhere you turn. Her voice is amped up, and she sounds more efficient. "I'm taking Violet to Faneuil Hall for lobster. We've been shopping for clothes all day, and she's tuckered out, but Durgin Park is calling me. I hope they're open. Otherwise, we'll go to Legal Seafood."

She wants to know how I'm faring without her around, mainly: am I eating, what am I eating, and why don't I eat more vegetables. These are all terrific questions, but not what I'm thinking about. I feel like telling her that the way to my heart doesn't pass directly through my stomach—nowhere even close. But that would only rub her the wrong way.

She asks what I'm working on; she calls it the "dead comedian case," as in "how's the dead comedian coming along?"

"He's still dead," I say. "Hasn't moved a muscle lately. They did arrest my client, though. That's a problem."

"Didn't you tell me he didn't do it?"

"He probably didn't."

"So why'd they arrest him?"

"Benny and Al were friends once upon a time. They made a ton of money, then Al took over keeping track of things and began screwing Benny out of what was rightfully his. That's how Benny sees it."

"So?"

"So the cops see it that way too. Which gives him a good motive. Good motives are like—I dunno, they're like drawing an inside straight. Like snow leopards."

"What's that supposed to mean?"

"Hard to come by, that's all. Omar and I are looking around for other villains."

"That's fine," she says, "as long as you stay safe."

"Don't you worry," I tell her. "Now that you're gone, I sleep with my gun under my pillow every night. And even then, one eye's always open. Nothing's gonna happen to me, sweetie."

Mara doesn't reply to this. She doesn't like it when I make light of things. Partly because we're both new at this business of starting over. We've only known each other a year or two, and there's not enough time left on Earth to put together the long, complex narrative Loretta and I had. Mara and I both know this.

My cousin Shelly, who had three wives of his own, told me once that he understood how I ended up with Mara. "You did it out of loyalty to Loretta, boychik. I get it."

"No, you don't," I said at the time. "I love Mara. We're different, sure, but I don't know what I'd do without her."

"She's walking you back home," he replied. "And you're doing the same for her. And that's okay, you know. It's necessary. It's a beautiful thing—a mitzvah, in fact. You're a lucky man, Amos. I envy you."

Now, on the phone with Mara, I think about Shelly's words. They're true and comforting as far as they go, but I can't bring myself to say them to Mara. Not yet. She's in Boston, lost in a whirlwind, living the good life and introducing her precious granddaughter to the wider world. For her, it's art. A project. She's working on the improvement of Violet. Me, I'm all about a dead comedian.

*   *   *

You never meet anyone by chance in LA. Oh, now, I shouldn't say that. Maybe once in a hundred years it happens, yeah, but this is a car culture—everything's always in flux. People live and eat and spawn and die inside their vehicles. We always have our foot on the pedal; our eyes are always on the road. We think we know where we want to go. Not everyone gets there, though; that's just how it is.

The morning after the meeting at Alma's, when I stop by Jamal's magazine stand on Third near the Whole Foods to grab a copy of *The Nation*, I'm surprised when I turn around and see Bill Malloy with his hands in his pockets.

"Did you follow me, Lieutenant?" I ask. "Or is this where you always buy your lottery tickets?"

Jamal looks at me, then Malloy. "You two know each other?" He readjusts the white cotton yarmulke he habitually wears on his head. I call it a yarmulke. He calls it a kufi. Same thing. Jamal and I are buddies from when I used to live at Park La Brea a few blocks away. He and his wife came here from Ramallah. This was his very first job, selling magazines and cigarettes and lottery tickets at a different stand, Rick Sherman's. They were penniless back then. That was twelve years ago. Now he's a genuine success story. He's studying hard to become an American citizen. He's a homeowner, and the proud proprietor of Jamal's Magazines and Tobacco. He still does a thriving business in lottery tickets, although personally he believes those who gamble are idiots.

"We work together now and then," Malloy tells him. "I don't buy lottery tickets, but you can give me a pack of Marlboros."

"I thought you quit, Bill," I say.

"I did. That was last week." He lays a crisp twenty down on the counter, and Jamal pushes a little box toward him. "I thought I might find you at Canter's. I know you like to eat breakfast there when you're on your own, but then I spotted your Honda coming down Fairfax. Guess I got lucky."

"No, you're right. I *was* going to Canter's. But I thought I'd pick up something to read first, and I remembered Jamal, so here I am."

We walk back toward my car, me with my magazine under my arm. I unlock the door and toss the magazine onto the passenger seat. He peels open his cigarettes, tears off the cellophane, pulls one out, and lights up. The smoke, which is faintly sweet, drifts out over the parking lot.

Before we get in the car, he says "Remo told me you called the other day while I was upstairs chatting with the boss."

"I did. He said you were in hot water with the powers that be."

"I'm always in hot water."

"Well, for what it's worth, I don't want to be the cause of it."

"It's not about you. We've got a new captain, Brad Mason. Young guy. Younger than me, anyway. My guess is he's temporary. He didn't come up through the ranks, and he's a real martinet about rules and regulations. Doesn't like it when we share dope with people like you. Or anyone outside of LAPD, for that matter."

"How does he think you learn anything in this town?"

"My point exactly. I told him we share what we know with a few select informants. Not everybody, just people we trust. That's how it's always been. That we couldn't do our job without them."

"And that didn't fly with him."

"He's from Buffalo; he doesn't understand California. They have a different notion of community policing back there. But yeah, basically he said I shouldn't be talking to you."

"Only here you are."

He takes another drag on his cigarette and frowns, shuffling back and forth from one foot to the other. "Right. And I'm here because I want you to hear this in person. I'll do my best to stay on Mason's good side. I've been around long enough—I get how the game is played. But I also need folks like you. We don't have ties to comedians or their agents, we don't know that world, and I'm sure the studios don't appreciate the bad publicity when we come nosing around. You know what we really need to crack this open? We need an insider."

I rub my palm incredulously across my mouth. "I thought you've already done that, Lieutenant. Cracked the case, I mean. Whatever happened to Benny Wolf?"

"He *could* be our guy." Malloy shrugs. "I haven't made up my mind. Yet. The Captain has."

"Sounds like he's looking to put a feather in his cap."

"He's ambitious, yeah," Malloy says. "But you know as well as I do that we're holding a weak hand. That could always change. We'll be talking to Benny some more; maybe he'll cough up what we need. And they've been poring over both men's financials, of course. Funny how much you learn from numbers."

"You ever get a copy of the agreement he had with Al?"

"We did. But not from Benny. It was tucked in a drawer at Mr. Pupik's place."

"And?"

"And it seems pretty straightforward. It also seems like Albert Pupik was a whole lot richer than Benny at the time of his death."

"Yeah, because he'd been cheating him for years."

"Maybe. Or maybe Al could simply hang on to a dollar, and Benny never could. But I'm no banker. I leave that to others."

Then he asks me not to call him at work anymore, at least not until Captain Mason has moved on to greener pastures. "Call me at home, after eight, that's fine. And we can always make arrangements to meet, do lunch, whatever."

"How serious is this, Bill? Are you being watched?"

He wags his head. "I'm being cautious, that's all. Remo and Jason are interested in office politics," he says. "Remo especially. He likes me, but I think he'd be just as happy to take my place someday if it ever comes to that."

"I've never cared for that guy."

"Don't be that way, Amos. Remo's a decent fellow. It'll be fine in the end."

*   *   *

I'm finishing up breakfast at Canter's, about to close my copy of *The Nation*, which now has a large, lovely coffee stain on the cover, when my phone rings. It's Joey Marcus.

"I forgot to tell you," he says. "I thought of one other person who knew Al Pupik, somebody you maybe should talk to. His name's Lonny. Lonny Dreyer."

"And who is Lonny Dreyer?"

"Al Pupik's writing partner. He and Lonny were working on a show. It was supposed to be a rehash of Al's best bits—all the stuff he did in nightclubs back in the Pleistocene, and later, on TV."

"And why am I supposed to talk to him? I mean, I'm happy to go see him, but what's he gonna give me?"

"That I don't know, my friend. But Lonny Dreyer was probably the closest person Al had at the end. You gotta realize: Al was a weird guy. Especially as he got older. He kept most people at arm's length."

"Not Lonny, though."

"No, Lonny was like his muse, his ticket to permanent stardom. That's what I heard at this party I went to the other night."

"His muse, huh? He wasn't anything more than that, was he?"

"Whatta you mean—like a boyfriend? Nah, Lonny's a straight arrow. Far as I know. But you should really check him out, man. They were working up to a big show. People were starting to talk about it. I got that direct from Charlie Teitelbaum, so it must be true."

He gives me Lonny's phone number and address. I scribble it down on the napkin in front of me. "Okay," I tell him, "okay, I'll look into it." Joey thinks he's doing me a great favor, of course, but still I can't help but feel a dull weight pressing down on me. It's not reluctance, no—more like I'm slowly losing control of this thing, like I'm wading into deeper and more uncharted water. Maybe that's what it is. Or maybe it's the matzo brei and black coffee churning in my stomach. The only person in the world who'd give a damn about Al Pupik staging a big comeback would be Benny Wolf, and Benny's got enough *tsuris* as it is. Why would I want to add that into the mix?

"Do that, why don't you," Joey says now, pleased with himself. "Go see Lonny. You got nothing to lose, right?"

*   *   *

Lonny Dreyer has a studio apartment in an old rundown Spanish-tile building on Franklin, a stone's throw from the Church of Scientology. I consider calling him up first to see if he'd be open to seeing me. That's polite; that's how you're supposed to do things. But then I think no, better to surprise him. If he's on Al Pupik's team and I'm with Benny Wolf, how much of a welcome can I really expect?

I park the Honda in a spot near an all-you-can-eat Chinese open-24-hours joint, shove every quarter I own into a meter, and walk a block and a half to the building. Dreyer is in apartment 14C. Just past the fresh paint of the lobby, there's an interior wooden stairway. Every time I see him, Dr. Flynn advises me to walk more—"You wanna live? Stretch your legs"—but today I figure I'll take the elevator. When the doors open, I find myself in a narrow, dimly lit hallway. The carpet is industrial gray; years of transient tenants' feet have worn it down to the nub. Beyond that, there's an odd cloying smell in the air; it's like a mouse or a rat died somewhere within these walls, and rather than hunting it down, management has chosen to spray the hell out of it with Lysol and wait for nature to take its course.

I take a few steps toward 14C, which is located toward the far end. At the door, I press the buzzer and wait. There's no response. A radio, or maybe it's a boom box, is spinning out blues on the other side of the door. A woman's voice from another vintage era—someone like Billie Holiday or Lena Horne. I press again. Still nothing. That's when I knock. I hit it hard because I want him to hear me over the singing, and when I do, the door magically opens a few inches.

"Hello?" I call out. "Anyone home?" Now I see the music is coming from a turntable next to his desk. Billie Holiday is singing "Strange Fruit." I step cautiously into Lonny Dreyer's studio living space. There's a bed with a Mexican blanket in one corner, which doubles as a couch. A narrow but clean and modern kitchen with a built-in two-person table and a nice collection of copper pots and pans hanging from the ceiling. There are no flowers, no obvious touch of femininity anywhere; but for a bachelor, it's organized. Lots of dog-eared, well-read books on the shelves, stacks of records, tapes, CDs. Above his bureau there's a small gold-framed watercolor with a Paris street scene—a souvenir, I'm guessing, from a trip long ago. His laptop is on. Looks like he was reading through his email when he stepped away from his desk.

The only room left is the bathroom. I knock on that door too, but it's just a formality. He would have heard me by now if that's where he was hiding. I turn the handle and open it.

Lonny Dreyer looks perplexed. Stunned. This is beyond his understanding. That's what's written on his face: *This is ridiculous.* His eyes are wide, his clothes are disheveled. He's barefoot, his arms are splayed at weird angles across his chest, and he's staring straight up at the plaster in the ceiling. It's like he's asking anyone who'll listen, how the hell did this happen? The bathtub he's sprawled out in is splattered with blood. I lean over for a closer look. It's easy to see what did him in—three dark red splotches, the size of golf balls, one near his shoulder, the other two in the stomach area. His face has lost most of its color. I'm no genius, but I'd say he was forced in here at gunpoint. That he was petrified. That his hands were raised at the time he was shot. That he collapsed, fell backward, landed on his head and came to rest in the bathtub. All very neat and convenient, in a way, except for the blood.

I pull out my cell phone and dial Malloy's office. He picks up.

"I know I'm not supposed to call you here," I say, "but we've got a problem."

"Oh, yeah? What's that?" He seems irritated that we're talking so soon after we agreed to keep radio silence.

"Al Pupik had a writing partner. His name was Lonny Dreyer. I'm standing in Lonny's bathroom right now."

"Okay," he says, "so what's the problem?"

"The problem is Lonny's dead. He's lying here in the bathtub. It's a hot mess. You should come take a look."

His tone kicks up a notch. He's on high alert. "Don't touch anything, okay? Where are you? We're on our way."

I give him the number on Franklin; five minutes later, the first uniformed officers arrive—two very nice, very nervous young cops who jot down my name and address before they pat me down and decide to take my gun away, just as a precaution. Then they also tell me not to touch anything. Malloy, along with Jason and Remo, show up twenty minutes after that, and the two junior cops are dispatched downstairs to the lobby to interview the super.

Malloy pokes his head in the bathroom. Then he turns back to me. "Well?"

I tell him what little I know, and he nods.

Remo can't resist smirking. He wonders how I came to be inside this apartment.

"I knocked," I say. "The door opened. Maybe it was never locked, I dunno."

"Yeah, but then you walked in?"

"I said hello as loud as I could. No one answered. The music was on. It was weird. What can I say?" I look over at Malloy, then back at Remo. I can almost see the words forming in his head. Remo's not dumb; he understands exactly what happened. If he'd been in my shoes, he'd probably have done the same thing. Still, breaking and entering is a crime, no matter how you slice it. That's what he's thinking.

"Give it a rest, Remo," Malloy says. Then he sends Remo and Jason out to quiz the nearby residents, see if they heard anything suspicious like any yelling or shots being fired. See what they know about Lonny Dreyer, he says.

I wait for them to leave. The two of us are just standing there. Okay, three, if you count Lonny in the bathtub. The crime-lab people are en route, and the two nice cops have returned my gun to me; it's safe in my shoulder holster. But I still have my hands in my pockets. "You know, Bill, I could be wrong, but this changes things."

"How do you mean?"

"Well, I've thought it was unlikely all along that Benny killed Al Pupik. I mean, it was a long shot at best. And now it seems like there's a link between Al's murder and this one."

"You don't know that."

"No, I don't. But the fact that they knew each other, they were close, and they were working on the same project together—that's big news. And now they both turn up dead inside a couple of weeks."

"So?"

"So, isn't it strange? Doesn't that pique your curiosity?"

"Sure, but it doesn't let Benny off the hook. Maybe he knew about this. Maybe this just fueled his anger even more."

"Except he has an air-tight alibi for this, I'm sure. Hell, that body in there can't be more than a few hours old. And Benny—I'll bet you a dime, I'll bet you anything you like—he's sitting at home right now in Granada Hills."

"Wonderful," Malloy says. "Then it won't be difficult to bring him in again for a little chat, now, will it."

I shake my head. "You're one stubborn man, Lieutenant."

"I go where the facts lead me, Amos. That's all. But don't get me wrong, I'm glad you walked in on this—this situation. Another man dead, hey, it adds a whole new wrinkle. Doesn't change the case against Benny Wolf, though. Not yet, at least."

"Really?"

Malloy folds his arms in front of himself. "No. I say let's wait until we hear back from forensics. We'll get a better fix on the time of death. We'll have fingerprints. DNA. Who knows? Maybe there's even a witness next door."

"You're saying these cases aren't related, then? Is that it?"

"I'm just saying hold your horses. We'll find out soon enough, one way or another."

"And you'll let me know?"

"For sure," he says. "I'm happy to. Only next time, call me at home, okay?"

CHAPTER 8

I take surface streets over to Boyle Heights to talk it over with Omar. We sit on the concrete steps of his front porch, staring at the lawn, which hasn't been watered since Reagan was in the White House, watching cars go by and sipping big mugs of coffee. The mugs are porcelain, and there are primitive yellow flowers painted on them. I can't say he's as frustrated as I am, but he agrees: Lonny's death is no coincidence.

"I don't believe it, man. No fucking way. And you know what else? I don't think Malloy believes it, either. He's putting you on."

I nurse the steaming coffee in my hands. The lonesome, bewildered image of Lonny Dreyer staring up at the ceiling sticks with me. I feel numbed by what I've seen. He was a young man—well, young by my standards, only in his late thirties or early forties. This writing project, if they'd pulled it off, might have done wonders—not just for Al Pupik in the twilight of his life but for Lonny's career as well.

"Malloy's just buying some time," I say. "His new boss and the DA made a mistake charging Benny Wolf. They didn't have a solid case then, and they sure don't have one now. Benny was nowhere near that apartment on Franklin. It's like my mother used to tell me: you can't be in two places with one behind."

"Yeah," whispers Omar, rolling his eyes. He thinks he's got the drift of what I'm saying, but he's not a hundred percent sure. Two places? One behind?

"Let's back up a step," I suggest. "Let's pretend that whoever killed Albert Pupik also felt a deep need to shoot Lonny Dreyer. Now, why would that be? That's what's hocking my *chinik*."

"Huh?"

"*Hock mir nisht kein chinik.* That's something else my mom used to say. It's Yiddish. It's like, don't bang my teapot—don't give me a headache. This is giving me a headache, Omar. I don't get it. What the hell difference would it make?"

"Maybe this show they were working on was a really big deal. Maybe they knew it would leave somebody like Benny in the dust."

"Okay, but that only adds fuel to the DA's charge against him. Gives him even more reason to do what he did."

"True."

A thought occurs to me then, and I lower my mug. "Maybe we're looking at this from the wrong angle," I say. "What if this is all a giant setup? What if they killed Albert, not because they hated him, but because they wanted to frame Benny?"

"Now you're giving me a headache, *vato*. You better explain."

"Well, think about it: somehow, Benny's prints are found at Al Pupik's house. Who knows when they got there? And one of the murder weapons—a wine bottle from Benny Wolf's exclusive winery in Sonoma—is sitting in plain view in the kitchen, even though Al has been on the wagon for decades. Benny and Al had their disagreements, sure. And Benny's mind is going a little soft, and maybe, if they grill him, they can get a confession. But the case is still circumstantial, still shaky, still hard to prove. They might be able to get past the grand jury, but the DA doesn't want the publicity; he just wants to get this behind him. My thought is they don't have the goods, which is why they're leaning toward Murder Two, or, more likely, Manslaughter."

"So? What's wrong with that?"

"Nothing. Nothing at all. Except that the killer's not dumb; he knows it too. And in his mind, it's not good enough. So what does he do? He ups the ante. He blows away Al's writing partner."

"That's one way to keep the cops interested," Omar says. "No doubt."

"Yeah, and it also says something about him. That he's a calculating sonofabitch. That he's still fuming. That he's ruthless."

Omar yawns and stretches his brawny arms high above his head. He has to go to work later on for his brother-in-law. He seems to enjoy the physical labor, being outdoors, much more than I ever did. But he also has a brain, and he likes to flex that muscle too. "How'd you find out about this dead guy, anyway?" he asks. "Joey Marcus? That little jumping bean? Maybe he knows a few other interesting things."

"No," I say. "Joey always has his ear to the ground, that's all. He heard it from Charlie Teitelbaum. Charlie's the one I really should talk to."

"You still want me to keep an eye on Benny?"

"I do, Omar. He may not have killed anyone, but he has a pretty lyrical relationship with the truth."

"You talking Yiddish again? What's that supposed to mean?"

"He lied to us. Said he never comes to Hollywood anymore. But they found his fingerprints at the house on Beachwood. And the cops tracked him to his ex-wife's apartment. So what else has he lied about? That's what I wanna know."

*   *   *

I figured it would take a small miracle to get an invite to one of Charlie Teitelbaum's parties in Laurel Canyon. When I sat down again with Joey Marcus, he wasn't sure he could get me in the door. He had *glat*, sure, but influence only goes so far, right? Not that he had to explain it. There's no Oscar currently sitting on my living-room mantel. I'm not young or gorgeous, I'm no celebrity, I don't tell jokes, write best sellers, sing songs, make movies, or have my own daytime quiz show. That makes me precisely nobody in his world.

"Hell, you probably couldn't even sneak in as part of the catering crew," Joey says.

"That's okay. I'm too old to walk around with trays of little shrimp on a stick."

Joey nods. "I'll see what I can do," he says.

So I'm mildly surprised when, three days later, he calls and tells me to meet him at Charlie's place that evening.

Teitelbaum lives at the top of Alto Cedro Drive. It's got a pretty fair view of the city, with lots of sliding glass panels that give the illusion of space—like he owns the great outdoors. I don't walk through every room measuring the square footage. You don't have to, however. It's not nearly as big or extravagant as you'd imagine, not for the head of a major network. The house itself is fine and modern; there's plenty of art on the walls and a well-stocked bar. But I don't get the feeling that he lives here, that it's really his home. Charlie's a widower, Joey told me. He was married to the same woman for thirty years, and in his mind I'm not sure he feels like he has a home anymore. He trudges off to work every day, and he sleeps here at night. Joey says he bought it because he felt like he had to move on from Norma, find a girlfriend maybe, give himself another chance to breathe. And it didn't hurt, I suppose, that it was attached to an enormous rectangular heated swimming pool out back; that's where he throws all his parties, where he puts on a happy face now and entertains the world.

There are a couple dozen people milling around the lighted pool when I arrive: an older balding fellow brushes past with a Hawaiian shirt and flip-flops; a young starlet who's surrounded by adoring male stares—she'd neglected to wear a bra for her very revealing blouse. But everyone is dressed casually. It's a hot night, and this is California, as my cousin Shelly once told me, where rules were made to be broken. Three young long-haired guys in shades, their jeans rolled up to their knees, bare feet in the water and laughing at some private joke, are passing a joint between them. Near the diving board, a saxophone, keyboard, and guitar—all of them female— are working their way through a medley of Brazilian tunes. They're pretty good, I think—better than this inattentive crowd deserves, anyway. Two waiters in white coats circulate continuously back and forth from the kitchen, bearing silver trays. I don't see any shrimp on a stick, but maybe that comes later.

One woman in tight lemon pants and high heels has brought her two boys, who are maybe eight or nine. They are splashing around in the shallow end, while their attractive mother is nearby with a cocktail in hand. She looks vaguely familiar. I stare at her for a few seconds before I realize she's Beth Crawford, the news anchor I see every morning on Channel 4.

"Bobby," she cautions, "please stay out of the deep end. You see that big black number 4 on the wall? That's as far as you go. And keep a close eye on your brother. Don't make me yell at you." She flashes me a sheepish look; I've caught her in the act of being a mother, which is awkward for both of us. She came here, presumably, to be a celebrity. Now she grins, hoists her drink in my direction. "What can you do, huh?"

I grin back. Joey Marcus said he'd meet me by the pool and my name was at the bottom of the guest list, but I don't see him anywhere. This is a problem because I have no clue what Charlie Teitelbaum looks like, and I'm relying on Joey to introduce us.

I find my way to the bar and ask for a beer.

"What kind?" the bartender asks. "We've got lots of German and Dutch."

"That's it?"

"You want something else? There's Mexican. Dos Equis. Corona. Bohemia."

"Bohemia will be fine, thanks."

The bartender beams at me. He uncaps a bottle and pours it neatly into a glass. The name tag on his jacket reads *Miguel*.

I turn toward the pool, thinking I'll just look around more, when a sturdy Japanese man in a black suit and tie taps me on the shoulder. "You're Amos Parisman?"

I search for his name tag. He doesn't have one. He also has the air of someone who doesn't require a name tag, not in this house at least. "Amos Parisman. Look right here," I say, pointing to the stick-on square on my chest.

"Mr. Teitelbaum would like to see you."

"Hey, that's why I came. To meet him. I thought Joey Marcus was gonna introduce us, but I guess he's a no-show."

"Mr. Teitelbaum is in his office. Why don't you follow me?"

I look him over. He's an inch or two shorter than me, short, clipped black hair. Eyes that never learned how to blink. Small moon-shaped scar high up on his forehead. Wonderful posture. He looks solid, like a tree planted in the floor. When he asks me would I follow him, it's not a question. "Okay," I say. I take a quick sip of my beer and set it down in front of Miguel. "Can you hold this for me, amigo? I'll be back."

I trail him down a hallway, through a door, and into Charlie Teitelbaum's office, which has a big bay window that looks out on the lights below. It's a substantial arrangement: dark wood-paneled shelves filled with books and tchotchkes and framed photos of famous people. There's a silver laptop and a stack of papers on the desk.

Teitelbaum is hunched over, skimming them, shifting them slowly from one pile to another. My first impression tells me he's sad. Sad or lost, like that proverbial marble rattling around in a pail. A handsome, slightly paunchy fellow in his late fifties. He's got on a lavender silk shirt that could use a fancy tie to go with it. Instead, it's rolled up at the wrists and open at the neck. I sense a weariness in his deep brown eyes, or maybe it's just tragedy, leftover grief on account of his wife. He also has a splendid shock of gray-and-white hair that makes him seem like he's searching for his inner Einstein.

He waits until his assistant leaves and the door closes behind him, then he points me to a cushy chair opposite. "Thanks for accommodating me, Mr. Parisman. I had thought about doing this out in the open, you know, by the pool. But this is Hollywood, and unfortunately some of my guests have big ears."

"I thought that's why people go to parties in the first place," I say. "To hear what's going on."

"I suppose." He runs his fingers through his gorgeous crop of hair before he speaks again. "But there's information. And then there's misinformation. Joey Marcus doesn't always hear things correctly; and even when he does, well, he's a publicist, right? You can't rely on a publicist for the straight skinny."

"Are you saying he got it wrong? Benny didn't tell you how pissed he was at Al? That he was gonna take him to court?"

"Benny mentioned getting a lawyer, going to court, of course, but that was much later, after I'd calmed him down. People are always suing somebody in my world. Every other person you meet is a gonif. In fact, when he threatened to take him to court, I have to tell you frankly, I was relieved; I thought that was when he'd recovered his sanity. But in the beginning, he was all wound up; scary, like a spring."

"What do you mean?"

"Well, he'd had a few drinks. He was a little tipsy, which may account for some of his attitude, but he started rambling, and he said he had a gun. He had a gun and, if he had to, he was prepared to use it. That got my attention."

"LA's lousy with guns. I could walk out the door, bring you a gun in five minutes."

"Yeah, but coming from him, it was just so—I dunno, out of character."

"And you didn't mention this to Joey?"

"I didn't talk about the gun." He puts his hands together, rubs his fingertips as though he's deliberating on some very weighty matter. Is there a God. Who gets Best Picture of the Year. "You have to realize something, Parisman. I've known Benny Wolf forever. He and Al came to my wedding, for Chrissake. Before they were a comedy team. Benny's a dear friend. When a friend makes an offhand remark like that—"

"Okay, then, maybe you can tell me this. Are you familiar with a man named Lonny Dreyer?"

He pauses. He has a nimble mind; he's not easy to trap, which doesn't surprise me, exactly. You don't get to be head of a major television company without knowing how to think your way out of a ditch. "I don't believe I've ever met him, but I heard—I mean, I read the other day in the paper, that is—he was Al Pupik's writing partner. Is that who he is?"

"He was. They were working on a show together. That's what Joey said. It was going to be a collection of Al's greatest comic bits. You know, a tribute."

He lays his hands flat on the desk. "And according to the *Times*, he was found dead in his apartment."

"I read the same article," I say. "Actually, there's more to it than that. I'm the one who found the body. I called the police. He was lying in his bathtub."

"Oh, gee," he says, without much affect. "That must have been awful. I can't—I can't imagine."

I ignore this. Something tells me he's quite capable of imagining a murdered man in a bathtub; he's in television, after all. "The paper didn't mention it," I go on, "but Lonny Dreyer was shot three times at close range. And Benny Wolf was out on bail. And now you're telling me he had a gun. Curious, huh?"

He purses his lips. "Benny says a lot of things. It's a common disease in this business, Parisman. He likes to hear himself talk. He lives in a world with heroes and villains and who knows what else. But what comes out of his mouth at any given moment? Well, let's just say I wouldn't bet on it."

"So that's why you didn't tell Joey about the gun?"

He nods. "Mostly what people do in this town is talk. It's all about probabilities. I told him what I thought was *probably* going on. Joey's a one-man rumor mill. So I pared it down, edited it, you might say. Tried to keep it in bounds. Benny's got plenty to deal with as it is."

"All right, I'll buy that. But you said you were friends with Benny and Al. Both of them."

He taps the desk lightly. "No, I think what I said was: I'm friends with Benny. I knew Al."

"So you weren't friends, then?"

"I wouldn't go that far."

"How come?"

"Al was a funny man in front of the camera, but he could be hard to like. I remember Carl Reiner once called him an arsonist."

"Meaning?"

"Meaning he burned his bridges. If you didn't agree with him sometimes, he'd burn the whole house down. That's not what you do in Hollywood. Not if you want to succeed."

"He had enemies, then?"

He smiles ruefully. "I'm sure. But you know, I didn't keep count. You'd have to get in line, take a number."

I stand up. I've heard this story before. Albert Pupik was a user, a schmuck. Okay. Then I think: maybe it's like *Murder on the Orient Express*. Maybe everybody hated him; maybe he deserved what he got. And maybe, if you follow that train to the station, Benny Wolf was just doing the world a favor. But can someone's death be a mitzvah? A good deed? How evil do you have to be before that makes sense? "All very well and good," I say, coming down to Earth. "But if the cops find this fictional gun that Benny owns, he could be in a whole bunch of *tsuris*."

"Are you going to tell them about this conversation, Mr. Parisman? I hope not. The publicity could make things . . . difficult."

"I don't know. I don't have to, I guess. Not part of my civic duty. The DA's office has already decided he killed Al Pupik, and I'm sure they also see the value of linking him to Dreyer's murder. That would be all they'd need, right? That's the ribbon on the box. But don't be surprised if you get a call." I turn to go again.

"Oh, Parisman? There's one more thing we should perhaps clear up," he says.

"Really?" I say. "What's that?"

He tilts his head and squints his eyes, like he doesn't know how to proceed, like he's about to wade into slightly deeper water. "You may not realize this, but I've been at CBS for nearly twenty years."

"Mazel tov. You're a survivor."

"Yes, I am. And there's a reason I've survived so long. It's not because I'm talented."

"No?"

"No. I'm meticulous. People tell me I'm thorough. I do my homework. So when Joey begged me to spare time for you tonight, I asked my assistant, Akihiro, if he would make some inquiries. I didn't know you, you see, and the fact is, I don't like surprises."

"And what did you learn?"

"Akihiro called the LAPD. His contacts there said you're not on their team. You're freelancing, is what they said. Then he looked into your background with other colleagues of his at bars and clubs. Some of them are a little rough around the edges. And it turns out, you're a private investigator. Licensed and everything."

"Joey didn't tell you that?"

"He said you were a detective, yeah, but who knows what that means? Joey—he thinks you're working both sides of the street."

"Somebody's paying me, Mr. Teitelbaum, that's so."

"And who might that be?"

"I'm not at liberty to say. But in the end, it's not so important. I just want to find out who did this."

"Even if it's your client?"

"I don't think it's my client," I say, reaching for the door knob. "But yeah, I'm not going to lie or trample all over an investigation to protect anyone. That's not how I roll."

He nods, then scratches the back of his head. "You know what, Parisman? The remarkable thing is, I believe you."

My beer is still waiting for me untouched when I return to the counter. Miguel smiles. I say a few choice phrases in Spanish, smile back, and for a few minutes it's a Pan-American solidarity we both share. I stand there and work the glass down. The band is playing "Corcovado." All's well with the world. That's when I see Joey Marcus inching toward me through the crowd.

He grabs my hand. His is cold and clammy at the same time. "I got stuck behind a three-car pileup on Wilton and Third," he says. "Sorry I'm late. Some joker tried to make a quick left at the light without waiting. People like that shouldn't be allowed to drive, you ask me."

"It's all right, Joey. I got to chat with Mr. Teitelbaum."

"Good, that's good, I'm glad. What'd he tell you?"

"Not much. He just backed up what I've been hearing all over town. Al had a long list of people who hated him. Even Charlie wasn't all that keen on him."

Joey is wearing a white linen sport jacket with a deep-blue polo shirt underneath. He's got high-top orange sneakers on, which would be acceptable if he were eighteen or twenty years old maybe, but that was a long time ago. Now he's making what they call a fashion statement. He sees me staring at them. "You like the shoes?" he says. "Nikes. They cost a fucking fortune."

"Oh, yeah?"

He nods. "I won't tell you how much, but between you and me, I could sell them tomorrow and live very comfortably after that."

"Yeah, it could be part of your retirement package."

"No, it's true, man. These shoes cost some serious coin. I shouldn't even be wearing them out in public. Somebody might try to cut my feet off."

"I think you're probably safe in Laurel Canyon, Joey."

I finish my beer, ask for another. The conversation meanders back to Charlie Teitelbaum, who Joey doesn't regard as particularly diplomatic. "I've seen him blow up a time or two. He's not so even-tempered, believe me. He likes things a certain way."

"He ever have a run-in with Al?"

"Not that I heard. They traveled in different worlds, mostly. Al was always pushing the envelope, trying to get on Carson or Leno or Kimmel. He had a bunch of agents. One after another they got fed up, quit. Benny wasn't as driven, somehow. He was the dreamer."

"You heard they charged Benny with Al's murder?"

"It was on the news, yeah."

"And that Lonny Dreyer was found dead in his apartment?"

"I missed that headline."

"Somebody shot him. So what do you think?"

Joey pulls his polo shirt out, lets it cover his belt. He looks at me and shakes his head. "You're the detective, man. It's not my problem."

"No," I say, "you're right. It's Benny's."

CHAPTER 9

I'm halfway home, just starting up the hill on Gower, when I glance in my rearview mirror and notice I'm being followed. It's not for sure, of course, but something weird about the vehicle behind me—the way he keeps pace, the way he stays close enough but not so close as to reveal who he is, the smoothness of it all— well, it trips a wire in my brain. He's driving a large car, dark and classic and powerful—a Mercedes or a Lincoln—but I'm not about to pull over and admire the hood ornament. Also, I didn't bring my gun to the party in Laurel Canyon; now I wish I had. I swerve onto Temple Hill. Ordinarily I'd take a sharp right on Vasanta Way, but this time I keep going straight until I'm heading back down. Left on Primrose, left again on Argyle. He tries to stay with me, but this is unfamiliar ground, and the twists and curves are rattling him. I speed up. When I hit the incline down to Franklin, I look back. He's gone. At least I think he is.

I veer over to the curb then, in front of another parked car, kill the engine, drop down in the seat. Wait. Breathe. Count slowly to ten. One Mississippi, two Mississippi. Give him a chance to roll on past. It takes a very long time to count to ten in the dark, it turns out—you have no idea. An eternity. Finally, I decide it's safe. I wheel around and head back up the narrow streets to my house. Is he behind me? I dunno, but I'm not going to slow down to check.

When I get inside, I go straight to our bedroom and pull out my old Glock 9mm from the underwear drawer. I leave all the lights off. The sheets are thrown every which way, but that's only because I'm a bachelor. I prop my back against the pillows. I need to make the bed. Mara's coming home tomorrow, and I want to tidy up before she can confirm every lazy, good-for-nothing thought she has about me. But first I call Omar.

"Things are getting complicated," I say. I tell him about the gala at Charlie Teitelbaum's, then how I was followed by a suspicious vehicle.

"You sure they were following you?"

"Pretty sure. They may not know where I live, though. Otherwise, why were they tailing me if they could tell where I was going all along?"

"Maybe they're trying to spook you," Omar says. "Or maybe you're just spooking yourself over nobody." He doesn't sound moved by my plight.

"I'm sitting in my bedroom right now in the pitch dark, Omar. I've got my gun next to me, and I'm a little tense. So if they wanted to scare me, well, they succeeded."

"You want me to come over?"

"No," I say. "Just stay on the line for a while. Keep me company."

We talk some more—or, rather, he talks and I whisper, while I listen to the wind in the trees and the occasional dog barking outside. He asks me if there was anyone suspicious at Teitelbaum's party.

"The only one who caught my eye was his assistant, a guy named Akihiro. I got the feeling he was moonlighting as Charlie's personal bodyguard. We didn't hit it off, but hey, good help is hard to find."

Omar doesn't like where I'm going with this. "Why would someone you've barely met go to all the trouble of tailing you home? What's he care?"

"I don't think he'd do it on his own," I say. "But if Teitelbaum said, 'Follow him,' well, that's another story."

"And why would Teitelbaum care?"

"Dunno," I say. "He doesn't want what he told me to get back to the cops. He's scared of the publicity, he said, getting his name mixed up in the whole sordid circus. Which makes sense, I guess, from a business point of view."

"Then why'd he tell you in the first place? He knew who you were."

"Yeah," I say, "but he didn't know who I'm working for. He tried to worm that out of me. It was important to him, somehow." Then I hear a faint noise coming from the direction of the driveway. An engine shutting down? A car door closing? "I'll call you back, Omar. I've got company."

I move silently from the bedroom through the kitchen into the living room. The only light available comes from the moon filtering through the blinds.

If someone were positioned just right, there's a small chance he could see me, so I drop down on the carpet and crawl forward on my belly toward the front door. There's no sound coming from the other side; but I figure if someone's standing out there fixing to come in, the first thing he'll do is shoot the lock off, then walk in, straight ahead, guns blazing. It'll be pitch-black in the foyer, he won't know where the switch is, he'll be nervous, and he'll spray the whole room with bullets. But he won't be expecting anyone squatting down on the floor where I am. I wait there for six minutes. I stare at my watch. My knees begin to ache. I'm too old for this, I say to myself, but I stay put anyway. A car revs up and drives away, and a zealous dog starts barking in the distance. Then silence. I wait another five excruciating minutes, then get back on my feet, take a deep breath, and gently turn the knob.

Out in the driveway, it's just my Honda sitting there in the cool night air. I hold the Glock by my side and amble slowly into the street. There's no one around. Pat and Phil, my two retired gay neighbors across the street, have their lights on in the living room, and though I can't quite hear it, they're plainly curled up on the couch watching television.

I turn around, start walking back to the house. Maybe I was wrong. Maybe there was nobody there. Maybe Omar was right and

I dreamed the whole thing up. Then, as I'm passing my car, my eyes glance down and I see it: the right rear tire seems remarkably low; the same for the other three. Someone, it seems, has punched a bullet hole in all of them.

I go back to the bedroom, call Omar, tell him what happened.

"How're you gonna get around?" he wants to know. He sounds devastated. Like most Angelenos, a car is a matter of life and death.

"Oh, it's okay," I say. "I'll call Triple-A in the morning, have them tow it to that tire place out on Pico. Four new tires won't take long. Meantime, I can drive Mara's Lexus. I have to pick them up at LAX tomorrow night anyway. But this is news, Omar."

"I don't get you."

"Well, I just think it's bananas that someone would do that. Follow me back from Laurel Canyon. Shoot out my tires. What's the point?"

"Yeah, what is the point?"

"And not only that, he must have had a silencer on his gun."

"How'd you figure that?"

"I didn't hear a thing, that's how. And my neighbors across the street, they're still lounging around watching TV. You'd think four gunshots in the middle of the night would get them up off the couch. That didn't happen. Therefore, he had a silencer."

"Or maybe all of you have gone deaf up there," Omar says. Then he goes into a long spiel on how sorry he is about my car, not that it's his fault, but we're friends and a man needs his vehicle, especially in this goddamn town, and if there's anything he can do, if I need a ride somewhere, well, of course, *por supuesto*, I can always count on him.

"It'll be fine," I tell him. "We'll talk tomorrow."

Then I hang up and call Malloy at his home number.

"You still awake?"

"Apparently," Malloy says. His voice is subdued. "I'm in my pajamas, and Jess is fast asleep beside me. What can I do for you, Amos?"

"I thought you might be interested to know about the meeting I had with Charlie Teitelbaum this evening."

"Maybe I would," Malloy says, "if I knew who he was."

"He runs CBS here in Hollywood. Or some section of it. But that doesn't matter. What matters is he's pals with Benny Wolf. He also knew Al Pupik."

"And?"

"He said Benny came to one of his parties not long ago, right before Al died. That he was upset with the way Al had been treating him, and I guess he'd been drinking, and somewhere along the line he mentioned that he had a gun and he knew how to use it."

"Oh, yeah?"

"Now, of course, talk is cheap, right? People—drunks—they babble about everything under the sun. It probably doesn't amount to much, and they don't remember it in the morning."

"That's true. Idle chatter."

"Then the conversation took an odd turn. He knew I was a detective, and he wanted to know who I worked for."

"You tell him?"

"No. I said I couldn't do that. I said I was looking for truth and justice."

"How did that go over?"

"I'm not sure. He was afraid I'd tell the police about this. He had concerns. My impression was, he didn't give two red cents about protecting Benny, he just didn't want to have his name dragged into the case."

"And now you've gone and done that, haven't you. How inconvenient. You want us to interview him? Is that why you called?"

"Not entirely," I say. "You can do that. I don't expect you'll get any more from him than I just told you. But it doesn't end there. Somebody followed me home from that party. And while I was inside, crouched down with my gun and waiting for them to come in and try to kill me, guess what? The *mamzer* shot out all four of my tires."

"*Mamzer?*"

"Bastard," I say. "I keep forgetting, you're not a Yiddish linguist."

"Somebody does that, you can call him anything you want. But I don't understand. How's this all connected?"

"Maybe it's not, Bill. But if the bullets that flattened my tires come from the same gun that snuffed out Lonny Dreyer—"

"You're right," he says. "That changes everything."

*   *   *

The forensics team arrives early the next morning. I've met them before—their faces look familiar—but we've never actually sat down and talked. Forensics guys don't talk, in fact, not to people like me. They're all business; they just unpack their equipment, unspool the yellow crime tape, let the science speak for itself. While they're poking around my tires, Malloy drives up in an unmarked car.

"Hey, Amos."

"Good morning, Lieutenant. I hope we're allowed to meet here in public like this."

"Oh, we're allowed," he says. "In fact, I left a message this morning with the DA. Told him what happened to you, how it might complicate the whole investigation."

"Did you tell him to put Benny Wolf's trial on the back burner for now?"

"I can't tell the DA anything. He knows what he's doing, though. Cimino's not stupid. I'm sure he'll wait and see what we come up with here." He walks all around my vehicle with his hands jammed in his jacket pockets. The photographer is on a short stepladder, snapping pictures. Another fellow with plastic gloves on is down on one knee, flat against the pavement. He's using some fancy metal tool and trying, like a dentist, to extract a gnarled slug from my right front tire.

Across the street, my neighbors, Pat and Phil, have come outside, only half awake in their slippers and matching white terry cloth bathrobes. They're holding mugs of coffee. It smells good. Pat and Phil know everything there is to know about coffee. Coffee, sushi, ramen. The finer things of life. We nod amiably at one another, but they stay at the edge of their yard.

"So, where does this go from here?" Malloy wants to know.

"My opinion? I'd like to leave the authorities out of it for now. I want to go back there and have a heart-to-heart chat with Mr. Teitelbaum."

Malloy bites his lower lip. The old cop in him rejects this approach as walking back into the lion's den. "I can't see that," he says. "What if he's the one who tried to kill you?"

"First of all, let's back up. We don't know it was him. We don't. Maybe he had a hand in it, but I'm a hundred percent sure it wasn't the great Teitelbaum standing outside my door."

"Somebody who works for him, then?"

"Maybe. There's a guy named Akihiro. Or it might have been somebody else at the party. Less likely, but still possible. I suppose it could also have been a perfect stranger, too, but then you're talking about a coincidence. And you know how I feel about coincidences."

"No, not exactly."

"There are none. God doesn't shoot dice, right?"

"That would make more sense if you believed in God."

"Okay, you win. Still, nothing happens by coincidence; that's my experience. And whoever did this wasn't trying to kill me. He was sending a message. Stay back. Stay the hell away. I can't let that stand, Bill."

He pulls out a pack of cigarettes, reaches in, then thinks better of it, and shoves it back in his pocket. "All right," he says, "we won't follow up with Teitelbaum then. Not until we hear from the guys in the lab, anyway."

"I appreciate that," I say. "And if I learn anything more from him, I'll pass it along, just like old times."

He smiles. "I'm looking forward to old times."

After the guys with the white coats pack their gear and leave, I call Triple-A. Half an hour later, they show up with a tow truck, and my sad little Honda is headed for the shop. I spend the rest of the day researching Charlie Teitelbaum's illustrious television career on the internet, which doesn't tell me much I don't already know. He's famous. Fine. He's the reason we have so many sitcoms and police dramas to choose from. Our minds will never want for entertainment, thanks to good old Charlie.

On the personal side, he grew up in New York, the only son of a corporate attorney and a therapist. He studied literature at NYU, graduated Phi Beta Kappa. His parents rewarded him with a ticket to London, and he milked it into almost a year hitchhiking around Europe. He lived on espresso and croissants; he slept on friendly couches and in open doorways. Then, when his money ran out, he moved back to California and went to work at Disney, writing and editing scripts. That's how he met Norma Elizabeth Zack, who became the love of his life, at a Christmas party in Pasadena. They were inseparable after that. Norma Elizabeth Zack, who never changed her name, recently lost her battle with breast cancer and died. Thirty-three years of wedded bliss. No mention of children. He's squeaky-clean, it looks like. Untouchable, at any rate.

After a while, I give up on him. I'm more interested in his friend Akihiro. He's harder to track down, but, after several phone calls, I reach a friend who knows him. Henry Yamada worked the vice squad unit in Little Tokyo for a long time. He retired ten years ago, and now he spends his days playing tennis with his buddies in Monterey Park. We don't see each other much anymore, but he still recognizes my voice on the phone.

I ask him how his tennis game is coming along, and he says he's been reduced to doubles and his elbow is really beginning to ache. Also his knees. They hurt, in fact. But only when he moves. And the heart? Well, he doesn't want to talk about his heart.

"Why do you keep playing, then? Sounds like you're killing yourself."

"Shh," he says. "Don't tell my wife. She needs the life insurance."

I tell him I'm following up on a Hollywood case and I'm looking for information about a ninja named Akihiro.

"Does he have a last name?"

"How many Akihiros in your Rolodex, Henry?"

"None. And guess what? I don't own a Rolodex. Not anymore. But a last name would help."

"I'm sure he's got one. We just don't know each other that well. He's about five seven, five eight. Forty years old, maybe. Handsome

fellow, well built. Like I say, a ninja. There's a tiny scar on his forehead. Seems to match his personality. Doesn't talk much. He has
friends at the LAPD, and he spent time working the clubs back
in your day; I'm guessing as a bouncer. Right now he looks after a
television executive."

"Doing what?"

"That's what I'm not sure of. Protection, probably. Making bad
things go away."

Henry Yamada mulls it over. "There was a guy like that, yeah,
used to keep the lid on at Lolita's on Hill Street. And maybe his
name was Akihiro, but don't quote me, man. That's another thing
that's starting to slip away—my memory."

"Are they still open? I thought your boys shut it down when they
started trading cocaine in earnest."

"We did, but then they sold the business. It was under new management about the time I retired. That would coincide with your
friend being there."

"Thanks, Henry. I'll give them a call."

Lolita's doesn't open until nine at night, which makes sense for
a strip club, I guess. I get fresh clean sheets and tuck them into the
bed, add the blankets and the extra pillows, empty the garbage, run
the dishwasher, and tidy up around the rest of the house. Then I
back the Lexus out of the garage and take La Cienega down toward
LAX instead of the 405, which, surprisingly, takes less than an hour.
Mara and Violet aren't there. Their long, bumpy flight from Boston
is delayed—a band of thunderstorms in the Rockies—but I have to
think they're even happier to see me now when they finally step off
the plane.

We get home very late. For some unknown reason, they didn't
touch the delicious peanuts and pretzel snacks the flight attendants
offered them, and now it's eleven o'clock at night and they're raven-
ous. I whip up a batch of scrambled eggs and throw some sourdough
slices into the toaster.

"I've decided to apply to Smith in the fall," Violet says, between
bites. "That is, if they'll have me."

"Why?" I ask. "I mean, how'd you make up your mind?"

"It's so bucolic," she says, waving her fork around. "I don't know—the buildings, the teachers, the trees, even the air—it just felt like I'd come home. It's the kind of place I always imagined going to school."

"That's a two-dollar word you've got there—bucolic," I say.

"They were very welcoming." Mara nods. "They spoke our language—let's put it that way. After half an hour, we both knew."

"And I could totally see myself there," Violet says. "I mean, I haven't even thought about a major, but they have so many different programs to choose from. That'll happen later. Right now it's just this nice warm gushy feeling I'm having." She taps her chest for emphasis. "A hunch, I guess. But you've gone with hunches before, haven't you, Amos?"

"I trust my gut, yeah."

Violet's come a long way. She's not the moody, nail-biting freshman I met a few years ago—the kid who barely spoke to anyone, who walked around the halls of Foxboro with her eyes averted, who never laughed, who had no friends or outside interests.

They clean their plates, then they head for bed. Violet wants to get back to Claremont as soon as possible to talk to her girlfriends, tell them what she's learned, what's next. I stay up an extra fifteen minutes to catch the news on television. When I come back into our bedroom, the light is on next to her pillow, but Mara is sound asleep. It's two in the morning where she is. I click off the switch, pull the covers up around her shoulders, and give her a kiss on the forehead.

We don't talk much over our coffee the next morning. Maybe she's still sleepy, or maybe she's anxious to get Violet back to her dorm. She doesn't think it's at all strange that the Honda isn't sitting where it usually does in the driveway, and she doesn't press me when I mention that I dropped it off at the garage on Pico to have four new tires put on.

I think about telling her the whole truth, but I know how Mara is wired. She's smart, cosmopolitan. She went to a good school, and she reads the *New Yorker* from cover to cover every week. She doesn't like surprises. What sets her apart from other rich people is that she doesn't try to hide behind her checkbook. She feels responsible to everyone. I'm investing in paradise, she told me once. Well, what does that mean, you might ask. So I'll tell you: she's never forgotten to vote, she gives to food banks and homeless shelters, to foster kids and suicide hotlines—all the right causes. She wants the same lovely world I want, in other words—a bucolic world, to borrow from Violet—and she doesn't for one second believe she's vulnerable.

And that's where she's dead wrong. I'm a *luftmensch*, too, a dreamer, but I know better. It would crush her if she heard that some thug had just driven up here with a gun last night and emptied it into my car. I don't want that to happen. That's why I keep my mouth shut.

After they leave, I phone Omar and ask him to pick me up and drop me off at the tire place on Pico.

"You aren't going back to Teitelbaum's, are you?"

"That was the plan, yeah."

"Well, you're not going back without me, buddy. And not without some weapons."

"You're welcome to come along, Omar. In fact, I was going to ask you anyway."

"Good. In that case, I accept your invitation."

*   *   *

Omar rides with me back to Laurel Canyon. In his jacket pocket he's carrying the Glock 9mm I gave him when he went off briefly to the Police Academy. I've got mine strapped to my chest, though I tell him I don't think we're going to need them.

"This'll just be a chat," I tell him. "Charlie Teitelbaum believes he's nothing if not a civilized human being."

"Even if he hires a gorilla to work for him?"

"Wait, Omar. Let's let that be a bridge when we cross it."

The house hasn't changed from two nights before, although it looks larger and more defended by the five-foot-high plaster walls and the heavy slatted wooden gate near the curb. We push through the gate and press the doorbell. An old bald fellow in a red tie and black vest and a sallow expression answers it.

"Is Mr. Teitelbaum in?"

"Why, er, yes," he says. He has a British accent, and he seems a little perplexed to see us. Or maybe he's puzzled that anyone would just show up at the door without an appointment. "Are you expected?"

"He'll want to see us," I say. "Tell him it's Amos Parisman. We met at the party here the other night."

"Good to meet you, sir. My name is Wendell." He bows ever so slightly, which I chalk up as a genetic memory from his time in merry olde England. Then he recedes down the hall. When he returns five minutes later, he looks even more perplexed. "Mr. Teitelbaum is engaged in a project at present," he says, "and he wonders whether you might reschedule your visit for another time. Perhaps you could call beforehand?"

The anteroom we're standing in is glassed in on two sides. The window on the left points to an elaborate sloping garden; the one on the right looks out on the swimming pool. I glance over at the pool and see Charlie settled into a chaise longue near the diving board. He's got his trunks on. There's a yellow towel draped around his neck and a bottle of suntan oil on the table, and he's holding a paperback. I guess that's the project he's engaged in.

"Tell you what," I say to Wendell; "I know he's a busy man, but we're gonna go out to the pool and say hello for a minute. Since we're in the neighborhood." I turn quickly down the hall, followed by Omar. Wendell makes a startled noise and a half-hearted waving motion with his arms as if he were a basketball player trying to stop us, but we push past him. I get the feeling he was hired merely to answer the door and take visitors' coats.

"Mr. Teitelbaum will not be pleased," he calls after us.

I open one door, which I think leads to the pool, but it turns out to be just a linen closet. By the time we step out onto the patio, Charlie has been joined by Akihiro, who must have heard the commotion in the hall. He's got a white long-sleeved shirt on, but I can see a slight bulge in the waistband behind his back.

Teitelbaum remains seated on the chaise longue. "I don't believe you were invited in, Mr. Parisman. What's going on?"

We close to within a few feet. Akihiro steps between us. "You heard the man," he says. "Why are you here?"

"We need to talk, Charlie. After the party the other night, one of your dwarves followed me home. I thought they were going to bust into my house, but instead they shot out all four of my tires. Not exactly civilized, wouldn't you agree?" I give a sidelong glance at Akihiro, then back at him. "Any idea who could have done that?"

"Not offhand," he says. "But if somebody really wrecked your car, you should take it up with the police. Talk to them before you start coming here. This doesn't make sense. I can't see how I'm responsible for your little . . . mishap."

"I think you two better go now," Akihiro says. He's staring at me directly, but I can tell he's already taken the measure of Omar, and he's determined that if push comes to shove, Omar is the one to watch.

"Here's the thing, Charlie," I say. "When we talked at the party, it didn't go so well. You wanted to know who I worked for and I wouldn't tell you. You didn't care for that. You're a big man. You've been a big man for a long time, and you're not used to people telling you no. And who knows? Maybe you've got a dog in this fight. Maybe you're trying to protect your old pal Benny, and you imagine I'm out to get him. Maybe truth and justice aren't as important to you as friendship and loyalty."

"As I said earlier, Mr. Parisman, I don't believe I invited you here today. Your problem is not my problem."

"Get the fuck out," Akihiro says. He's squinting now, and his tone is far less cordial than before, not that anyone would ever mistake him for a diplomat.

Out of the corner of my eye, I notice his right hand sliding quietly behind him. Omar sees it, too, and in the same moment Akihiro pulls a pistol out and waves it in my face. "Out!" he says forcefully. "I'm not gonna tell you again, motherfucker!"

Omar grabs at the gun. The two of them wrestle with it, but Omar is taller and stronger. He covers Akihiro's hand with his own and manages to point the gun down. But Akihiro is wild; he squeezes the trigger, and a bullet ricochets over the concrete. Then he throws a punch with his free left hand. He's aiming for the throat, but it hits Omar in the shoulder. That's when Omar finally yanks the gun away. It sails high into the air and splashes down in the pool near the ten-foot marker. Without a weapon to brandish, Akihiro shrivels up like a morning glory. Omar grabs him by the lapels, slugs him hard twice across the face, and shoves him roughly into a vacant chaise longue. He doesn't move after that.

Charlie Teitelbaum gazes into my eyes, shaken. This was not on his calendar today. "All right, Parisman, you're here. Now, what do you want?"

"First," I say, "I want some answers. I want to know what you thought you'd accomplish by that bit of vandalism the other night. I want to know why I'm a threat to you. I want to know who you're protecting. If you know anything about who killed Al Pupik, I want to know that too. And when we've settled all those things, I want you to pay me back for the four new tires I had to buy. They weren't cheap. Do we understand each other, Charlie?"

CHAPTER 10

Teitelbaum doesn't know who killed Al Pupik—that's what he says. But he wasn't sad when he heard about it. "Man lives his whole fucking life stomping on other people, he got what he deserved, in my opinion."

"I take it you don't feel quite the same about Benny Wolf."

"Benny's always been sweet. A little too soft in the head for his own good, sometimes—a babe in the woods. But you couldn't dislike him."

"The cops think he's a murderer."

"The cops can think whatever they want. Benny Wolf wouldn't step on an ant."

"Weren't you the one who told me he had a gun?"

"That's what he told me, Mr. Parisman. He was drunk and angry at the time. I wouldn't put much stock in it."

"All right," I say, "so let's talk about something else. Why would you have Akihiro follow me home? What was the point of his messing with my car like that?"

He holds up his hands in a don't-blame-me gesture. "I don't recall my specific instructions. I don't think I told him to do anything. But frankly, I was worried about you."

"Me?"

"Well, not you. But where your snooping around was going to lead. I couldn't be sure. You wouldn't say who your client was; and if you turned up more material, material that was harmful to Benny, you know, I—I just couldn't tolerate that."

"So you tried to—what? Slow me down? Is that it? Why would you go so far out on a limb like that?"

"Benny Wolf didn't kill him. I keep telling you." He frowns, wags his head.

"I agree with you, Charlie."

His eyes widen incomprehensively. "You do?"

It's not a rule so much as an old habit, a fetish of mine: don't reveal who you work for, not if you don't have to. People hear you're a member of Team A, they automatically start assuming things. They clam up when you talk to them, they flat-out lie, or they tell you only what they think you want to hear. Information withers on the vine. Of course, it can also backfire: Charlie Teitelbaum, for example, who doesn't appreciate surprises, couldn't handle not knowing where I stood. Oh well, I figure, maybe I should make an exception of him, just this once.

"I'll let you in on a little secret, Charlie. I wasn't going to, but now I've changed my mind. Benny Wolf is my client."

"You could have mentioned that the other night," he says. "It might have saved you a lot of trouble."

"Tell me something," I say. "Do you always go to such extraordinary lengths for your friends? I mean, you didn't give Akihiro instructions. You just let him have at me. So what if he'd tried to send me a different message? What if he'd decided to kick down my door the other night instead of attacking my Honda? What then?"

"I dunno," he says. "What then?"

"I would have shot him," I say. "He'd be a dead intruder to the police. And they'd be the ones who are here right now chatting with you, not me."

In the chaise longue beside him, Akihiro blinks, looks around, stretches his beefy arms, and starts to come back to life. He wasn't ever really out so much as just jarred by the sheer force of Omar's hand.

Omar gazes down at him sternly. "Don't get any dumb ideas," he warns. "Not unless you want to end up in the swimming pool."

"You're right," Charlie says. "I didn't think that through. My fault. I'll be straight with you, Parisman. I'm fond of Benny. But we also have a business relationship; I need to protect that. If Benny ends up going to prison, well, I could lose a substantial investment."

"You want to tell me about that?"

"Travesty Vineyards. Just outside of Sonoma. It's an expensive lot of acreage he owns."

"So what's the problem?"

"The problem is, the money came from me."

"You loaned him the money?"

"Something like that. Only it wasn't strictly kosher, what we did. We just, you know, shook hands. There's no contract, no paperwork."

"And why not?"

Akihiro is staring hard at his boss now. "Don't talk about this, boss," he says.

"We just shook hands," Teitelbaum continues, ignoring Akihiro, "and he agreed to start paying me back in a few years with interest, when the winery was on its feet."

"Is that how you always do business?" Omar wants to know.

"No, not usually," he says. "But it seemed like an opportunity. When my wife died, I got an unexpected windfall. Three and a half million dollars she had in life insurance. All these years, I had no idea she was such a capitalist. Anyway, around that same time, Benny came to see me, looking for a loan. Said he wanted to start over, get out from under the shadow of Al Pupik, redefine himself. Well, I said I'd help him, naturally. There was this rundown little winery for sale. Benny thought he could raise it from the dead, turn it into a combination winery and entertainment center. Bring in rock bands and theatrical groups, comedians, folk singers, whatever. But it had to look like it was all his idea, his money. I thought it sounded great. He had the name and the personality to pull it off."

"So you just gave it to him under the table, three and a half million dollars, no questions asked?"

Teitelbaum runs his hand through his hair, glances up at me, moistens his lips before he answers. "It was a gamble—I knew that. But I didn't get to where I am in life by always playing it safe."

"That's all well and good," I say. "It may not even be illegal. But the cops are going to take a hard look at his finances, Charlie. They're not stupid. They already know how he feels about Albert screwing him out of his rightful share. They can see he's living a less-than-princely life out there in Granada Hills. They know the bottle that killed Al came from his winery. Don't you think they're gonna raise an eyebrow when they find out the money came from you? Three and a half million? In cash?"

"I'm not worried," he says. "I can explain that to them when the time comes."

Omar shakes his head. "They're gonna think you're some kind of drug dealer, man. You're gonna have a lot of explaining to do."

*   *   *

Omar and I stop at King Taco near Pico to grab a bite afterwards. It's a bare-bones joint with new, uncomfortable metal chairs, cool white walls, and recessed lighting. What your typical Mexican chain restaurant will resemble maybe a hundred years from now. When I look around, it also feels kind of listless and unloved. There are more flies than customers, but who cares. The hostess gives us each a menu, says we can sit wherever. I've got six crisp hundreds tucked in my wallet from Teitelbaum to cover the tires. They didn't cost that much, but Charlie is a free-wheeling, generous sort when he wants to be. He's also the sort who has a wall safe full of cash, so I wasn't about to turn him down. Omar and I crouch at a table in the corner. Another girl comes and takes our order.

"I still think he's hiding something," Omar insists. "Nobody drops that kind of money on another person—not without wanting something back, and soon. You don't lay down three million dollars out of love, not where I come from."

"He's a businessman, Omar. People like that take risks all the time. And three million to him might not mean quite as much. You have to keep it in perspective."

"He said it meant a lot," Omar says. "He was worried enough that he sent his goon Akihiro out after you."

"That's true."

"And I'll tell you something else that bothers me. That low-life goon of his? There's more to him too. We should have kept his gun, at least, as a souvenir. Lieutenant Malloy would love to know where that gun's been."

"You're full of great ideas, Omar. You really should be a detective."

"I thought I was."

"You are when you're helping me out. Just not when you're pounding nails for your brother-in-law."

"Hey, man, I got rent to pay."

Over tacos al pastor we wonder some more about the real nature of Charlie Teitelbaum's interest in Benny Wolf and why a man in his eminent position would go out on a limb like that. They're gamblers, I insist. Neither one probably knows a goddamn thing about growing grapes or making wine, but with enough money Benny could have hired people to take care of those matters. And finding big-name entertainers who'd be happy to spend a weekend in Sonoma wouldn't be too difficult. Omar and I agree on that much.

"And hell," I continue, "they'd already started bottling on a small scale."

"You mean, the one bottle that killed Al?"

"That, plus a few others, I imagine. We should check a few liquor stores around town. See how many carry the Travesty label."

"I can do that." He puts a paper napkin to his mouth, then lays it down on the table and smooths it out. "Are you planning to tell Malloy about Charlie's little investment?"

"Why not? Don't you think I should?"

"I wouldn't," he says. "Malloy isn't letting you in on what he knows, and—"

"That's not his fault. He has no choice. His captain is riding him hard."

"I get it," Omar says. "Only you just made a friend out of Charlie, remember? He thinks you're both on the same side. But if the cops start knocking on his door now, asking him about this money thing, how's it gonna go down?"

"I dunno," I say.

"I'll tell you," Omar says. "He'll feel set up. Angry. Like he can't trust you. The last time that happened, you had a little run-in with Akihiro."

The waitress comes by with the check. I take it from her and wait till she's out of earshot. "And you think he might do that again?"

Omar gets up from the table, pushing his chair away. It makes a hard scratching noise on the tile floor. "He told you up front, didn't he? He doesn't like surprises."

*   *   *

When you're a child, there's a whole lot that rushes past you, stuff you can't possibly grasp, stuff that doesn't have anything at all to do with your life. The world of adults, what they do, what they think about all day and why, is a mystery. Flotsam and jetsam, ideas tucked away, slowly ripen like apples in the treetops. You don't care about it, of course: the news out of China, the bill from our cousin who is also our dentist, the nosy next-door neighbor; but eventually you realize that that's what you're going to end up thinking about too.

When I was six or seven, I first saw Wolf and Pupik on the Ed Sullivan Show. That's when it dawned on me. My parents were laughing at something they'd heard, sitting on the couch in the den, holding their sides, and I didn't get it, not a word. But I knew *they* thought it was funny. So what's a kid supposed to do? I wanted to be part of the family, so I started laughing along with them. To this day, I'm still not sure what Wolf and Pupik said. How earth-shaking could it have been? And now I think: maybe it wasn't the words. No, it was how they said it. The way they just bounced off each other, how their faces turned to rubber with every new line.

Three guys jump out of an airplane.
A Catholic, a Protestant, and a Jew, right?
Hey! How'd you know?
I know them. They're friends of mine. Tom, Dick, and Herschel.
No, not them. Three other guys.
What're their names?
How the hell do I know?
Not Tom, Dick, and Herschel?
It could be them, I suppose. It's just three guys, you know.
So Tom, Dick, and Herschel, then.
Yeah.
And they get in a plane.
Yeah.
There's only one problem with that. Herschel hates to fly. Makes him nauseous.
How am I supposed to know that?
Well, it's your joke. Don't you know anything?

An hour later, I'm sitting next to Loretta's bed at Olympic Terrace, holding her hand. The television is on, but the sound is turned off. It's a vintage movie from the thirties. Ginger Rogers and Fred Astaire, who can do no wrong, glide across a stage. The room feels cold to me. I make a mental note to tell the nurse to crank up the heat when I leave. There's another bed behind the folding screen, with nice starched white pillows and sheets, but it's empty. The last time I visited, Rosie, the old woman in it, was babbling to herself. Now it's just the two of us.

Loretta wants to know where I've been. Her long white hair is all combed out, her cheeks have some color, someone has painted her nails pink, and she's wearing what looks like a new silver nightgown with ruffles. She's been missing me, she says. She speaks softly, but I can hear the irritation. "Where have you been?"

"I had a little car trouble, Loretta. Somebody shot out my tires."

"I don't know why they'd do that," she says. Her eyes widen in disbelief. "That's not polite."

"No. Well, at least he didn't take a shot at me. Better to aim at the tires, right?"

"Were you in the car?"

"No, no, sweets. I was inside the house. I was safe. He just did it to warn me off."

She squints at me. "I don't like the kind of business you're mixed up in, Amos. It's not kosher. I want you to find another line of work, you hear me?"

"What should I do?"

"I dunno. How about a bookstore? I can see you there. You like to read, don't you?"

My expression says maybe yes, maybe no. "You don't get to read nearly as much as you think, working in a bookstore. It's about schlepping, really. Books are the heaviest things in the world."

"They are?"

"Except for bricks, and they're always schlepping them back and forth. They're always shelving books. It's about alphabetizing."

"You could do that. You know the alphabet."

"More or less," I say. "I'm good all the way to M. That's what I'm stuck on now."

"M?"

"M as in murder," I say.

"Oh yeah, that's what you do. You told me before."

When she says that, something clicks inside me and I'm tempted to spill everything then, the whole enchilada. To unburden myself the way I used to in the olden days, when we were together back in Park La Brea. It hasn't been that long, has it, Parisman? No, not so many years. There was a time when she moved about, when she wasn't always resting in bed, a shadow of her former self, when no nurses fluttered in and out, plumping her pillows and giving her pills in tiny white paper cups. When she wasn't patiently waiting for them to revive her again like a bunch of cut flowers in a jar, a withered bouquet. I can still remember what she was like. Energetic. Upright and cheerful, a responsible woman with a strong voice and a head on her shoulders; she had a job and a purpose and a future. I was proud of her then; dammit, I loved her.

I open my mouth to speak, and the words tumble out. I'm not trying to protect her. I tell her about the grisly photos of Al Pupik—but somehow, maybe it's the way I explain it, him sprawled out on the living room floor with his pants yanked down around his ankles, the haplessness of it all, the buffoonery, even at the end, she smiles, her cheeks turn red, and in spite of herself she starts giggling. No, don't, I say, come on now, this is serious: *a man died.* When she gathers her composure again, I move on to Lonny Dreyer in his blood-soaked bathtub. That sobers her up. Then I throw in Joey Marcus and Marv Rich and Darius Shapiro and Charlie Teitelbaum. She furrows her brow, it's too much for her, she can't possibly keep the cast of characters straight in her head, she's juggling them all at once. She gets that they're important, that they play a part. But what?

"I'm sleepy," she blurts out suddenly. "I'm tired. You're wearing me out with all this."

"I'm just telling you what I'm up to these days, honey."

"I know, I know. I love you. But now I need to rest." She squeezes my hand with affection. I squeeze back. She has thin, cool, delicate hands, and you squeeze them at your peril. "I need my own time. Is that okay?"

*   *   *

I grab an early dinner at home with Mara—take-out Thai food. She's had a long day unpacking, bickering with her lawyers on the phone (some lingering trouble over the estate), and sifting through the mountain of magazines and mail that greets her whenever she goes away. It's only a little after five when I get home, she hasn't drunk a single glass of wine in twenty-four hours, and already she has a headache.

"How about I pick us up something tasty from Jitlada?"

"Fine. Whatever you like. I'm planning on turning in early. I love Violet, but she's so young, so intense, and ten days on the road with her—well, ten days with anyone is a bunch."

"You know what? For a person who has everything, you've got a complicated life. I don't envy you."

"You shouldn't envy me," she says. "I don't enjoy it much myself. It's really a job, like anything else. It's taken me a long time to figure that out."

We dine on crispy spinach, crispy morning glory salad, crispy honey duck. Oh, so many wonderful crispy things at that Jitlada on Sunset. After dinner, she pops two aspirins, throws on a fresh nightgown just this side of transparent, and settles down in the bedroom with the *New Yorker*s she hasn't yet had a chance to read. She doesn't require my company, so I kiss her cheek goodbye and drive over to visit with Bill Malloy.

He lives on Berendo, in a plain but, in this market, priceless little bungalow just off Franklin in the heart of the Los Feliz district. And he's expecting me; this is how we've agreed to meet without jeopardizing his job at LAPD. It takes more time than I'd like to find a parking place. I have to circle the block twice, in fact; and while I do, I consult the rearview mirror. No one is tailing me. Still, old habits die hard, and I glance around one more time just in case as I walk up the narrow stone path.

His wife Jess answers the door. I haven't seen her in months, although her name comes up regularly in conversation. "Amos," she says, hugging me gently, "what a pleasure."

She's a handsome woman, almost six feet tall, but since the arthritis started chipping away at her knees and back, she seems to have shrunk some. She's dressed in comfortable stretchy charcoal running pants and a light blue top, which makes you pay greater attention to her red hair. She used to have long luxurious red hair, that's what I remember. Only she's cropped it back recently and also probably stopped dyeing it, so now there's a gray mist forming around the roots that gives her an otherworldly look. "My wife the space alien" is what Malloy called her not long ago.

Bill is waiting for me in a big cushy living-room chair. He puts down the worn copy of Seamus Heaney's poetry he's been reading. There aren't very many books in the house, but almost all of it is Irish plays and poetry. You can tell right away he's off duty. His face is relaxed, and he's smiling, and he's got a brown cardigan sweater on. He's got on his slippers too. The only thing missing is a pipe.

I take a seat on the couch opposite. "We have to stop meeting this way," I say.

"Oh, we will," he says. "Sooner than you think, actually. Rumor is, Mason has put in for another job in San Jose."

"What's so great about San Jose?"

"His wife's family is from there. She's pining for her brother and sisters. Desperate to go home."

"Can't argue with that."

"Neither can Mason," Malloy says. He taps his hand on the chair rest. "That's all I care about."

Jess comes in. Did I want a cup of tea? Coffee? Something stronger?

"No, no," I say. "I'm good. I've just got a few tiny state secrets to pass on to your husband. Then I'll be on my way."

"Secrets?" she says. "Oh, I assume you're talking about police matters, then. I'm not allowed to hear those kinds of things."

"No," Bill agrees, without missing a beat. "That's right, you're not."

She rolls her eyes—a wife can put up with only so much malarkey, after all—and heads back to the kitchen.

"So, what do you have?" he asks as soon as it's just the two of us.

"Well, Omar and I got together with Charlie Teitelbaum yesterday."

"He invited you over?"

"No, not exactly. But I needed to be up-front with him. You know, clear the air."

"Meaning?"

"I asked him why he thought it was such a brilliant idea to send somebody over to shoot up my car."

"And he didn't just flat out deny it?"

"At first, yeah. Come to think of it, he never got around to actually admitting it. Not in so many words. But he did reimburse me for the tires."

"Money counts, I guess. Still, you were taking a risk."

"Oh, I'd never go in there alone. Especially if his man, Akihiro, was on duty. And he was."

"So, what happened?"

I start to talk with my hands then—which, like Benny himself, is what I do whenever I get excited. My dad did too. Maybe all Jews do, I dunno. "Akihiro went on autopilot," I say. "He's not the most artful guy I've ever met. Told us to get lost."

"And you didn't, right?"

"I don't like it when somebody points a pistol in my face. I mean, come on. That's not what you do to a senior citizen, right? It's just rude."

"So?"

"So Omar roughed him up a little, okay? He had no choice. Tossed the guy's gun in the swimming pool. But that's not what I came here to tell you about."

"There's more?" Malloy used to be incredulous when I told him what I'd been up to; tonight, he's had his dinner and he's taking it in stride.

"Sure, there's more. I found out why Charlie was so eager to slow me down. Turns out he's trying to protect Benny Wolf. It's Charlie's money that's behind that winery in Sonoma. Charlie loaned him three million in cash to get it started. There's no contract, no paperwork, no nothing. Charlie's wetting his pants. He figures if Benny goes to prison for killing Al, there goes his investment."

"Where'd the money come from?"

"He said his wife left him an insurance policy when she died. Maybe that's true, maybe not. Interesting, huh?"

"Fascinating," Malloy says. "Only I don't see how it adds to our case."

"It doesn't," I say. "But Charlie's a gambler."

"Meaning what?"

"Meaning he plays by his own rules. He wants to win, and he always goes for broke. And what he did up at my house the other night—that was a distraction. He didn't know how it would turn out; still, he rolled the dice. And if he's capable of that, maybe he's also capable of eliminating Al Pupik's writing partner for the same reason."

Malloy nods. "It's true—we didn't have any luck linking Benny to that guy in the bathtub. There were no prints, no witnesses, and you were right—he had a solid alibi."

"Maybe you should check the slugs they took out of my tires, see if they came from the same gun that killed Lonny Dreyer."

"We can do that," he says. "But I have to tell you, we're miles away from knocking on Teitelbaum's door, certainly not with an arrest warrant. Why would he bother to have Dreyer killed? What's the point? Just to prop up Benny Wolf somehow? We're spinning in the wilderness here, Amos. None of this'll ever get past the DA, let alone a judge and a jury."

I ask him about Benny's case, when it might go to trial.

"Probably not for another month or two," he says. "There's still different theories that need to be sorted through."

"Such as?"

"Well," he says, "the sequencing, to begin with. I mean, did he die from getting whacked with a wine bottle? Or did he have a heart attack from the trauma of the home invasion plus getting hit with a bottle? Or was it the loss of blood from the gunshot wounds afterwards? What was the cause?"

"What difference does it make if you're sure Benny's your guy?"

He shrugs. "Benny admits to being there that night. He says he came to talk about their contract. He even admits to bringing the wine—says it was a peace offering."

"Didn't he know that Al wasn't drinking anymore?"

"Says he forgot. Or by the time he got in the door he remembered, yeah, but it was too late. He was standing there with a bottle of wine. Nothing to be done."

"That doesn't exactly add up to a crime, Bill."

"No," he says. "And Benny insists he didn't do it. They talked, he said. They had words. They shouted at each other. And then he turned around and left. That's all Jason and Remo were able to squeeze out of him." He frowns, rubs the side of his neck.

"What about the gun Benny said he owned? The one he told Charlie about?"

He stifles a chuckle. "We went through his house, top to bottom. A whole team. Didn't turn up anything. And there's no record he ever bought one, either—no license, certainly. I think that was all just talk. Now he says he's never even touched a gun, doesn't even know how a gun works."

I stand up. It's time to go. "He's a delicate flower, Bill. You have to admit that."

William Malloy looks at me wistfully. He doesn't want this case any more than I do. "Thanks for dropping by," he says. "I can't say you've made my job easier, but I always enjoy your company." He reaches over, picks up his book of Seamus Heaney, cracks it open. "Are you a fan of poetry, Amos?"

"Now and then," I say. "But usually, when I pick up a book these days, it's history. You know, man's inhumanity to man."

"There's a lot of that going around," Malloy says.

"You're telling me."

CHAPTER 11

Omar and Lourdes come over to our place on Sunday for brunch. Omar only has a vague idea about what a brunch really is, but he has tried valiantly to explain it to Lourdes, who has no idea whatsoever. Still, they show up—that's all I care about. Mara has pulled a glorious frittata out of the oven, with lemons and asparagus and red bell peppers and spinach and feta. She's not a confident baker, so she went down to Viktor Benes and came back with a nice spread of pastries; also, berries and bananas and a pineapple from Gelson's, which she chopped up in a big glass bowl and added mint and God only knows what else. The table now has a fresh linen tablecloth on it, as well as our best plates and silverware. My job is to make mimosas.

Omar is wearing a red tie. I'm tempted to tell him to yank it off, he doesn't need it, but since Mara made me put one on, a tan one that goes nice with my black shirt, I let it go. Lourdes and Mara hug each other at the front door. They bond quickly, unlike us males, who've been trained from infancy to stand back and be on the lookout for threats. Mara speaks passable Spanish, and Lourdes is picking up English fast enough that it doesn't matter if one of them trips over the wrong tense or word. From the beginning, it just flows.

Also, they have so much to focus on. Beyond the food, there's the huge excitement of the baby, the rush of the future welling up like an ocean wave. The baby that doesn't yet have a name. That could be a boy or a girl. That will change their lives forever. So much is still unresolved, can't be resolved, and Mara—I can practically feel her heart jumping up and down in her chest—she wants to hear it all.

"Four more months," Lourdes says. "Cuatro meses. Not so long." She fixes her eyes across the table at Omar, and he reaches over and covers her tiny hand with his own.

Later, he and I take our coffee out to the deck to talk.

"She's beautiful, Omar. Radiant. She'll be a wonderful mother."

"Let's hope so. She's got a sister and a couple of cousins who can help out when the time comes. For me, I'm concentrating on bringing home a paycheck. I don't care how many jobs I have to work. It's about the money now."

I ask him then if he's made any progress finding where Benny's wine is sold.

"That's what's weird," he says. "I called all over town—liquor stores, supermarkets, bars, you name it. None of them stocks anything from Travesty Vineyards. Never heard of it, in fact. The older guys, they know the name Benny Wolf, of course. He's famous."

"So it's not sold down here?"

"Not that I can tell. I don't think it's available anywhere."

"But how do we account for that bottle on Beachwood Drive?"

Omar's hands do a short, silent dance in the air. "They must have shipped a sample case to Benny," he says. "That's all I can think. Maybe it's true what he told the cops, that he brought it over to Al's house as a peace offering."

"You know something?" I say. "You could have saved yourself a lot of trouble if you called the winery and asked them point-blank if they've started distributing it yet in LA."

"I did, man. Four times." Omar frowns. "They've got a phone number, but it's just a machine. Nobody ever picks up. And nobody ever calls you back when you leave a message. What the fuck good is that?"

It's a warm, soft, cloudless day. It feels like a gift from the gods. Birds are whistling in the eucalyptus trees nearby. Maybe they're busy nesting. A police helicopter is doing lazy circles in the light blue sky beyond Griffith Park. I finish my coffee and set the cup down quietly on the glass table between us.

"I've only met with Benny two or three times," I say, "but to me, you know, he always looks like someone lost, a guy who got off the bus at the wrong stop. I don't know what's the matter with him; he's damaged."

"I get that too, yeah."

"And he talks like a child sometimes. I want to put my arms around him, comfort him, tell him it's gonna be okay."

"You're not his therapist. That's not what he paid you for."

"No," I say. "He could use one, though." I turn to Omar. "And given that, I just don't see how he could have ever driven over there on his own. Oh, he might have talked about it, he talks about all kinds of things, but you know what? I'm not buying it."

"So where does that leave us?"

I don't respond right away. But what I'm thinking hits me hard. It's so painfully obvious, I should have acted on it weeks ago. If I had, maybe Lonny Dreyer would still be alive. You're slipping, Parisman. Loretta's right, you're in the wrong goddamn business. Benny probably wasn't enough of a mensch to get in a car and drive over to Al's house, not all by himself. He'd had help. Benny'd been a passenger.

"I think I ought to touch base again with Alma Wolf," I say. "Really grill her this time. She knew him better than anyone."

"Except for Al, maybe."

"Maybe. But Al's not talking much these days, is he?"

Omar shakes his head.

"And Benny—Benny's like a homing pigeon; he claims he doesn't ever go to Hollywood anymore. That's what he says, but then he ends up at her apartment on the regular. What's that all about?"

"How long have they been divorced?" Omar asks.

"I dunno. A while. They obviously still get together now and then. Divorce just seems to be a formality."

"You want me to come along with you?"

"Nah," I say. "Not necessary. I think having two strong, handsome men in her small apartment at once would only make her nervous."

"You're lying, right?"

"Have I ever lied to you, Omar?"

* * *

Alma agrees, reluctantly, to see me, but not until two-thirty the following afternoon. I wanted to do it in the morning hours, get it over with when it's a lot cooler, but she insisted she has to be down at the hair salon then. "I've got a business to run. I hope you don't expect me to just drop everything because you've suddenly come up with a few more questions."

"No, ma'am," I told her. "My questions can wait."

The heat is unbearable by the time I climb the stairs at her place and ring the doorbell; I'm already sweating bullets. She lets me in, and I can feel the rush of cool air as I follow her down the dimly lit hallway to the living room. Once again, I'm struck immediately by how graceful she is. Alma Wolf is wearing a sleeveless white blouse and honey-colored jeans that stop just above her ankles. She's barefoot, which is what I'd be, too, if it were my house and I had feet as pretty as hers.

"I just got home a little while ago," she says. "You'll have to excuse the mess." She curls up on the couch. The room doesn't seem particularly disheveled, not by my standards, anyway. In front of her is a tall round glass of white wine with an ice cube floating in it. "Would you like one?" she says.

"Ordinarily I'd say no, but since it's a hundred degrees out there"—I point with my thumb toward the front door—"well, what the hell?"

"I'll take that as a yes, then." She smiles, rises, vanishes into the kitchen, and returns with a similar drink in her hand. Also, with the remainder of the chardonnay, which looks to be about half gone.

"L'chaim," she says, and lifts her glass.

"L'chaim."

She jiggles the ice. It makes a pleasant clinky sound. "So, okay, Mr. Parisman. You're here. What brings you back?"

She tilts her head to one side. A few hairs are out of place, but it's not that. Something about her attitude, something in the way she speaks, a very slight impression, not quite a slur, makes me think she hadn't just arrived home a few minutes ago. She's probably been here for the better part of an hour, drinking steadily.

"First of all," I begin, "it's my obligation, my job, to help my client; but, as you know, Benny's a strange guy. I can't quite figure out what makes him tick."

"Why don't you go ask him?" she says. She takes another swallow of wine. "I've been trying to do the same thing for twenty-five years. Figure him out. A thankless task, let me tell you. But at least you're getting paid, Mr. Parisman. You should be grateful, count your lucky stars. I worked at it a long time, figuring Benny out. The best years of my life. Didn't get a nickel."

"He gave you the beauty salon, didn't he?"

She looks up at me. "Oh, yeah, I guess so. That was sweet of him. But really, he had to. He had no choice. Otherwise I'd—I'd have ended up with so much money. Half his money. That's the law in California."

"He had a lot of money when you two split up?"

She picks up the bottle and adds to the glass. "I don't know," she says. "I like comedians, don't get me wrong, I've always loved comedians. But I try to stay away from their money. That's the dark side, the money."

"So, what did you agree to?"

"We sold the house in Brentwood. That was fifty-fifty. Then on top of that, I got the beauty salon, free and clear. Benny—Benny got everything else."

"And you both thought that was fair?"

She waves her hands dismissively. "Fair? Sure, why not? He was still working nightclubs with Al. Still doing the late-night walk-ons once in a while. He was even in a commercial for life insurance. Maybe you saw it. Me, I didn't want to have anything more to do with him."

"He left you in a comfortable situation, Alma. Looks to me like you got what you needed, wouldn't you agree?"

"I didn't complain at the time. But then, I didn't know about all the dough he and Al were raking in. I was just a simple little girl from Minot when we got together. A country bumpkin, you know what I mean? We lived well, mind you. Money was never an issue. But we never talked about it. I didn't think it was part of my job description."

"So what was your job, exactly?"

She takes a short gulp of wine before she answers. "His job was to make the money. Mine was to spend it. It worked for a while."

"But then, apparently, it didn't."

"His career took a turn," she says. Her eyes dart back and forth. "Not long after he and Al called it quits. Benny wasn't so good at handling things. He's an idealist, as you know. And Al took advantage of him."

"How'd that make you feel, Alma?"

She settles back among the pillows on the couch. "Our marriage was ending by then, Mr. Parisman. Of course I had feelings. But I also wanted to move on with my life."

"So, what happened between him and Al—that didn't affect you? Is that what you mean?"

A telephone rings then in the bedroom, and what happens next startles me. In my family, we were conditioned: the minute the phone rang, you picked it up. We were as trained as Pavlov's dogs. It was automatic; there was never a question. Your Aunt Elsie might be locked out of her house again. Your father could have been hit by a milk truck. You might have won the Irish Sweepstakes. But how would you know? You have to pick up the goddamn phone.

Not Alma. She doesn't say please excuse me; she doesn't leap up to get it. No, she sits there, transfixed, like a Buddha with her wine glass, nestled in the half-light among the pillows. She waits for it to be over, she gives it space, but she lets it go. It rings three, four, five, six, seven times. When it finally stops, that's when she bites her lower lip and turns in my direction.

"Maybe a small part of me was angry then at Benny," she offers. "It was a difficult period. And maybe I didn't mind it much when

I first heard he was getting taken to the cleaners by Al. I told my girlfriends he deserved it. But let me be clear: what Al did to my husband was wrong. Very, very wrong." She blinks, sets her glass down on the coffee table in front of her, and glances over at the bottle of chardonnay, which only has about an inch or two remaining. "Would you like to finish this? There's plenty more in the fridge."

I shake my head. "Nah, I'm still working on what I got. Thanks."

"Okay, then," she says. "It's mine."

Alma Wolf is as big a mystery as her ex-husband, I realize. She has her own demons, dreams, and fears—people from her past who keep her awake at night—and I'm not sure but what I'm opening up an even larger can of worms by talking to her. Oh, well, Parisman. Onward. I lean forward, ask her if she would tell me a little about her relationship with Al Pupik. How well did she know him? Did they have mutual acquaintances? Did she still continue seeing him after she broke up with Benny?

This leads to a long story. "In the house where I grew up," she says, "there never seemed to be much to laugh about. I dunno, maybe it was just too cold. My parents didn't tell jokes, I remember. It wasn't their fault; my mother never knew any, and by the time my father got home at night, he was too beat to talk. So maybe he knew a few but I never heard them. It was just about surviving with them. Putting food on the table, it's what they knew. When I got to LA, that whole landscape changed. I began to go out more. I had a thing for comedians, I guess. Or maybe I was just desperate to laugh." She sips a little more wine, then grabs the bottle by the neck and pours the rest into her glass. "My parents thought I was going to be a fashion designer. And they approved of that. Clothes are basic; everybody needs clothes. But the thing is, six months after I got here I realized I didn't give a damn about drawing skirts and blouses; I wanted to be around people, wherever there was a crowd. That's why I started hanging out at clubs."

"And that's where you met Benny?"

"Benny, yeah, and Al, later on, and a dozen other performers. I was too shy at first to talk to them, but I started doing quick sketches while they were on stage and gave them away afterwards. They liked that. It pumped them up—bolstered their egos, I suppose. Anyway, we all became pals. They called me Picasso. That was my nickname."

"And what happened then, Alma? Are you still pals?"

She sniffs, rubs her neck. "With some of them. A few. That number's dwindled down though, I have to tell you."

"How come?"

"Okay. Here's what," she says, choosing her words carefully. "You wanna know something? Comedians aren't normal. They're not like lawyers or accountants—or even private detectives."

"They're not?"

"Not at all. And you know why? Because . . . because to be a comedian—a real comedian—to force yourself to get up on the stage when you're small and scared and knowing, even before you open your mouth, that you're unworthy—you have to be crazy." She stares hard at me then. "I'm serious," she says. "Take any comic. The more they make you laugh, the louder the applause—it's like a drug, that rush of attention—they can't get enough; it just shows you how sick and fragile they are."

"You want to explain how you figured that out?"

"Experience. Sleeping with this one and that one. Going to parties and hanging on their arms, watching how they talk to other women right in front of you. The way they practice their material on people, the way they use people up, eat them alive."

"They all do that?"

"Well, no. I'm talking generalities. Al Pupik didn't. He didn't use women, that is, not like the rest. Women who came out to see him felt safe, there was never any tension there. If you weren't doing stand-up, he was fine. I mean, he was gay. Women didn't matter to him. They were irrelevant. To them, he was a perfect gentleman."

"But if you were straight? Or another comedian? What then?"

"Anyone competing with Al, he'd come after you—male or female."

"And Benny? Just how does he fit into this grand theory of yours?"

"Benny? He was the exception." She raises her index finger to illustrate. "Twenty years, I never saw him attack. He never stole a joke. Never stepped on another act or made them look bad. Nothing like that. Benny Wolf? He was the kindest man on earth. Too kind, you ask me."

I put down my glass. "So, let's talk about the night of the murder, Alma. Part of their case, a big part of the prosecution, is that Benny was there in the room. He was maybe the last person to see Al alive. That much is plain. They have his fingerprints. The wine bottle. And Benny has admitted that he came out that evening. They also have his statement that he was—what shall we say—*unhappy*—unhappy about their arrangement."

"Al was ripping him off."

"Yeah, I get that. But I also hear that Benny was kind and gentle. Wouldn't hurt a fly."

"He was. He still is."

"And that he almost never drove into Hollywood anymore. Except here. To see you. Hollywood scared him."

She's staring at me steadily now. Her nostrils are flaring. "So what? What are you suggesting?"

"I'm suggesting that he was upset that night and that maybe he was at the end of his rope and that he wanted to drive over and have it out with Al."

"That's true."

"But that's not how it happened. What he did instead—what I *think* he did—was he came to see you. He wanted to talk it over first, get his words straight. I dunno, maybe he thought you could stiffen his spine, give him courage."

"You're very insightful, Mr. Parisman. He did drop by here that night. We talked. I gave him a bottle of his own Merlot to take to Al. Benny had brought me a case for my birthday the month before. He appreciated that idea. Thought it was pretty funny. A peace offering, he called it."

"But you both knew Al Pupik had stopped drinking long ago, right? That he was in AA?"

"Sure, I did. That was the point. I didn't figure he'd open it up and pass it around. But he's a comic. I thought he'd get a kick out of having a bottle from Travesty Vineyards."

"So you sent Benny off with a bottle to give to Al. You told him exactly what to say. And he was fine with that."

"That's right."

"No, it's not, Alma. Come on. You knew how it would go down. You knew Al would talk circles around him, that he'd bully him, that Benny would walk off with his tail between his legs, just like always."

"I—I was hoping he'd show some backbone this time. He was angry. And it was wrong, what Al was doing to him."

"Exactly! And that's why you decided to go with him, wasn't it? Because it was wrong? Because you're a good person with a good heart, and you know how to stand your ground, and you couldn't let Al get away with it?"

She wets her lips, sighs. "Benny needed a spokesman," she admits. "He was living like some feral animal out there in Granada Hills. You've seen his house, haven't you? You should look at it closely. It's a dump. And it didn't need to be that way. Al just had to give him his fair share, that's all."

"So the two of you went out there? And what happened?"

"We talked. Benny gave him the Merlot, which Al did find amusing, at first. He laughed, anyway. But then it went back and forth, you know, got a little heated. I tried to be the intermediary, tried to reason with Al."

"Meaning what?"

"They'd been friends a long time. Longer than we were ever married. I wanted to get him to remember that. Then, in the middle, I got a phone call from a girlfriend and I went outside to talk to her."

"How long did that go on?"

"Oh, I don't know. Ten, fifteen minutes. She was having a personal crisis. But when I looked up, Benny was charging out the door with his hands stuffed in his pockets. 'He's never gonna change,' that's what he was mumbling as he went to my car."

"Did you catch a glimpse of Al Pupik before you left? I mean, was the front door open? Could you see him through the bay window?"

She takes another swallow of wine. "What are you asking me, Mr. Parisman?"

"If you saw him. It's a simple question, really. Was he still alive when you both got back in the car?"

"Sorry." She shakes her head. "I wasn't thinking about Al. I was worried about Benny. He looked so sad. He crawled inside and was all crumpled up like a pretzel, you know, in the passenger seat. He didn't want to talk to me. He didn't want to talk to anyone. He was just sitting there, weeping."

CHAPTER 12

Mara and I go out to dinner that night at Republique on South La Brea. I don't mind, exactly, although it's not my kind of joint—too modern, way too rich for my blood—still, we drive over there because she's all dolled up and in the mood, because she's gone to the trouble and made a reservation, and sure, she's paying for it, so who am I to tell her no?

There's the bluefin tuna tartare, and the wine, of course, and the bread. I could stop right there, but then the entrees land on our table. She's taking apart the Dover sole a la meunière, and I'm about to tack into the bucatini.

"So, how's the dead comedian coming along?"

Something in her tone takes me aback. She sounds smooth and confident, but she doesn't really know what she's asking about, certainly doesn't know what I'm going to tell her. "The dead one's not doing much of anything right now," I say. "He's stashed in a concrete crypt over at West Side Memorial, along with the other celebrities. It's where he's always wanted to be, I guess. Whether he's happy or not, now, that's another story."

She lowers her fork. "What about you? Is that where you'd like to be someday?"

"No, no, just plant me wherever. Loretta likes that place, though. Thinks it's a classier neighborhood."

"How about I bury you right outside our bedroom window? That grassy space between the roses and the eucalyptus tree? It's level, and you'd have a nice view. All of Hollywood down below."

Now I put down my fork. "How about we stop talking about my funeral, okay? At least until we get to dessert."

"Oh, Amos, I'm sorry, I didn't mean—"

"Besides which, I'm not planning to check out yet. I still have another twenty years left on my odometer. You probably won't believe this, Mara, but Dr. Flynn told me I have the genes of a teen-ager."

She frowns. "When did he say that?"

"Last time. When I went to see him about getting rid of my cholesterol prescription."

"That was six months ago."

"Okay, then maybe it was that week my blood pressure started acting up. Or when I had that business with the spots in front of my eyes."

"You had spots in front of your eyes? When was that?"

"I dunno, I forget. I don't have them anymore. Spots, that is. Anyway, I'm not gonna die for a long time. You'll probably go long before I do."

She rolls her eyes. "Well, that's a relief," she says, turning her attention back to the fish on her plate.

I sip my wine and stare steadily at her. Mara has never been squeamish or cowardly. She's had years of expensive therapy, and she's in touch with her pain, all of which means we talk about death more than Loretta and I ever did. Mara doesn't care for what I do and the proximity to danger that I'm sometimes in. I understand. But so what? At our stage of the game, it doesn't carry the same weight anymore. There's a familiar breeziness about it. Death, our old family friend. Or is he more like a nosy neighbor? I dunno. For her, I'm sure it all comes from what she learned when her daughter died and now because she's just lost Gus. For me, it's because of all the guys I knew in Vietnam who never came home, and now, more than ever, it's all about Loretta. I'm on the verge of losing her; I won't deny it anymore. Oh, not today or even next month, but soon. She's getting weaker, more distant. It'll happen. And I can feel myself winding up like a spring inside, anticipating that moment when the mirror finally shatters, imagining the hole in my stomach when I walk into her room and see the bed made up fresh and empty and waiting.

"You really should be asking me about the live comedian," I say. "Benny Wolf."

"He's the one I meant. What did you turn up?"

"Well, you know, there's good news and bad news."

"Oh, I like this," she says. "Tell me the bad news first."

"Okay. The bad news is he was very likely the last person to see Al Pupik alive the night he died. He even admits to being there in the room."

"Opportunity," she says knowingly, taking another bite.

"That's number one," I say. "And then there's the matter of motive. Benny hated Al. For years, Al was systematically screwing him out of what should have been his. Which, in the eyes of the LAPD, gives him a solid reason."

"All right, that's the bad news. Now I'm ready for the good news."

"The good news?" I say. "The good news is simple. Benny didn't do it."

She gives me a smirk. "And how do you know this, Sherlock?"

"Well, the case against him is almost entirely circumstantial. For instance, Al was shot with a .38. Which is great, only Benny doesn't own a .38. He doesn't own anything. In fact, he doesn't know which end of a gun is up."

"Couldn't he steal one?"

"Maybe. It's kind of remote, though, given his age and situation. They've searched his house, scoured his car from top to bottom. Zilch. There are no traces or chemical residues. Not even a suspicious receipt. And another thing: Benny hated Al, but for good reason. And it turns out that every other comic in LA did, too. If there was a Hitler in their world, they'd call him Al Pupik."

"Sounds like you've got plenty of good news on your side."

"I think so, yeah. And there's even more: Al had a writing partner, young guy named Lonny Dreyer. He and Al were putting together a big project when Al died. It was supposed to be a huge retrospective, Al Pupik's greatest hits, the finishing touch on his legacy. People were never going to forget him after that, right?"

"I don't know. I suppose so."

"Trust me, this was gonna seal his place in history. Only Al was murdered, and then, a few days after that, I found Lonny Dreyer in his bathtub on Franklin. Somebody put three slugs into him."

"*You* found the body?"

"Yeah," I say. "But that was just by accident. Joey Marcus gave me a tip. I went over to talk to Lonny about Al. I didn't do anything wrong. Not exactly. The door was unlocked. I stepped inside. It's a small apartment. There was music playing on a turntable. Billie Holiday. I called, 'Hello, anybody home?' Then I peeked into the bathroom and there he was. What can I say?"

She looks at me closely. "You know what? It's amazing. In all my years on earth I've never once found a dead body. I don't have any friends who've found one, either. You? You do it all the time."

"You're in the wrong line of work, Mara. You don't get out enough." I beam at her.

"So what does this guy Dreyer's death have to do with anything?" she asks. "Why couldn't Benny have shot him, too?"

"Well, he could have," I say. "If only he'd been in Hollywood, and not twenty miles away in Granada Hills at the time. He has an undocumented cleaning lady who can vouch for him. That's one problem. And if only he'd known about Lonny Dreyer's existence, which I'm pretty sure he didn't. That's another. There's a lot of if-onlys at play here."

"But what if these murders have nothing to do with each other?"

"That could be. Sometimes things happen by coincidence. It's rare, though, let me tell you. I read a case once where this guy was convicted of robbing a jewelry store in Palm Springs. He wore a ski mask and the clerk didn't get a look at him, but the whole trial hinged on the fact that he drove away in a bright yellow Ford

Mustang. The CHP stopped a car like that an hour later and busted the driver. He had no record at all. Not only that, there was no jewelry in the vehicle. No ski mask, no weapon, nothing. But the jury decided the chances of there being another yellow Mustang in the vicinity at the time were a million to one. He went to prison."

"So that's another piece of good news for the defense? Is that what you're saying?"

My eyebrows go up and down suggestively. I don't do Groucho Marx, except for that. "I haven't seen the forensics report yet, but my guess is that just one gun killed both men. That's a thorn in the DA's side. Benny's attorney will kick up a huge cloud of doubt if that happens. She'll blind the jury."

"You're a smart man, Amos."

"Why don't you say I'm cute, too? I'd rather be cute."

"You're cute enough. It's the smart part I care about."

"I'm just following the bread crumbs, that's all. And at the end of the day, you could still be right: it's dimly possible somebody gunned down Dreyer independent of Al Pupik. It's also possible we faked the moon landing and the Kennedy assassination."

"Possible, but you don't buy it."

I shake my head. "And neither do the cops, but you don't want to rule that out. Not completely. People drop dead all the time. Some of my best friends."

"So I hear."

* * *

Early next morning, I drive down the hill and take Franklin east. I pass the Scientology Center on my right and the apartment building where Lonny Dreyer used to live on the third floor. It's weirdly cool and overcast. The guy on the radio was talking about a rogue weather front sneaking up from Baja; he didn't say the word *rain*, but he hinted at it, which is about as much as you can ever do in Los Angeles in the beginning of July. A few minutes later, I'm in the Los Feliz district. Large, rambling, beautiful, overpriced apartments, with swimming pools and all kinds of amenities like underground parking and saunas. Rich people live quietly in Los Feliz. A handful of new stars and starlets, but also people with a certain pedigree. Entitled people. Self-satisfied people. That's my impression, anyway. I don't know this for a fact; it's just a notion I've toted around for years. You could call it a prejudice, a superstition, a *bubbe meise*, as they say in Yiddish. I also believe that many of them are young and male, that they drive their zippy little sports cars way too fast to get to wherever the hell they're going, and that their vision of success is not mine. I could be dead wrong about all of this, of course. I'm an old man, but I still have an open mind.

Soon I turn in at Griffith Park and head for the pony rides and the petting zoo. Bill Malloy is standing at a polite distance behind the cyclone fence; he's watching contemplatively, his hands behind his back, as a trio of five-year-olds are strapped in and loped around the dusty oval track. He's wearing sunglasses, slacks, and a white cotton short-sleeve shirt, on account of the heat. No tie or sport coat, which I'm guessing he's left behind in the car. The kids are bewildered. One little girl is whimpering. They've been told this is supposed to be fun, but most of them have never met a pony before now. The ponies look bored. They are the pros here. They have old, patient eyes. They shake their heads, their tails flick reflexively now and then at the black flies gathering around their haunches. They know the routine. And eager parents and grand-parents are standing there too, on the periphery with their cameras at the ready, waiting to record it all for history.

I wave to Bill as I approach. He nods, and we move off toward a picnic bench where we can talk.

"How are things at the office?" I ask.

"Better, actually." He gives me a tight smile. "I heard from a guy down at the Hollenbeck Station who's friends with Mason. He's planning on transferring out by the end of the week—his wife leased a condo in San Jose. I even know his replacement, Wayne Kobayashi. We used to work together in the olden days. Should be fun."

"So that means we can talk to each other now without looking over our shoulder all the time?"

"Wayne's no slave driver. He knows we need the public's help to do our job. Hell, I remember he had a whole nest of informants back when he covered Little Tokyo. Half of them were his cousins. It'll be fine."

He turns his eyes toward the kids on the ponies. Their rides are coming to an end. One child is whimpering, but the other two just look confused. One by one they're unstrapped by the attendant and gently lifted off into the waiting arms of exuberant adults.

"Well, in that case," I say, "here's another tidbit you can add to your collection. I don't know if it'll help get Benny convicted, but—"

"You don't want to do that, anyway."

"No," I say, throwing up my hands, "I don't. But not because he's paying me."

"Then why?"

"Honestly? Because he didn't do it."

"I'm starting to agree with you," Malloy says. He removes his sunglasses and massages the dust from his eyes. "So, what's the news?"

"You know how you've placed him at the scene of the crime. What you may not know is how he got there."

"What do you mean? He drove."

"He drove, yeah. But first he went to see his ex-wife, and she ended up driving him to Al's."

"She was there, too?"

I nod. "Alma and I had a long heart-to-heart talk. She knew Benny, what he was made of. Said he wasn't man enough to go there all by himself and face Al. She gave him one of his own Merlots to take over as a peace offering, but even then she realized she needed to come along to support him, tell him what to say. Put some backbone in him."

Malloy taps his fingers lightly on the picnic table. "She never mentioned any of this to us," he says, a little chastened.

"You never asked."

"No," he says, "maybe not. But what did she tell you about the meeting?"

"That it didn't go well. Benny tried to soft-pedal it. He reasoned with him, brought up all their years together. What a shame it was to just toss everything now into the toilet."

"Al didn't care for any of that, I gather."

"No, not according to her. Al had his own ax to grind. He accused Benny of walking away from the team. Abandoning him, leaving him high and dry in Vegas. Even after all these years he was angry, she said; his face turned red. He wouldn't back down. Then, somewhere right in the middle of it all, she got this phone call and had to go outside to talk with a girlfriend. I guess it went on a while. She heard a sound and saw Benny stomping out the door. He looked depressed, she said, broken. He got into her car. They turned around and went home. End of story."

"What time was that?"

"Jesus, I don't know. But I know this: when she walked out the door, Al Pupik was still breathing and he still had his pants on."

"Benny didn't spend the night with her, did he?"

"I doubt it. They're not a couple anymore. I imagine he just drove home."

"That's one scenario," Malloy says. "Or she could have driven them both over to her place, and he could have turned right around an hour later and gone back to Beachwood. She said he looked depressed, right? Well, maybe that's when his depression ended. Boiled over into anger."

"That's pretty far-fetched, Bill."

"Sure, but it might also be closer to the truth. You saw the photographs. Whoever shot him was pissed." He glances at his wristwatch. "I gotta get into the office soon. Mason said he wants to meet with me in private."

"Can he fire you before he goes?"

"No, that's not in the cards. More likely is, he's going to let me in on his future plans." He stands up. "I better act surprised, huh?"

"I would, if I were you."

He smiles. "Thanks for dropping by, Amos. You've been a big help. I think this is the last time we have to keep these little trysts to ourselves." He turns on his heel.

"Bill," I say, "one last thing before you go. You ever get the report back on Lonny Dreyer? The ballistics on those slugs?"

"Oh, yeah," he says. "I forgot to mention. They came from the same type of gun that killed Al. It was a match. A .38."

"What about the guy who attacked my car?"

"Whoever ruined your tires used something else. A nine-millimeter, as I recall."

"Really? That's great about the two murders. That's big news. What's the DA gonna do with that? Doesn't that mean he has to let Benny walk?"

"Maybe." He shrugs. "Maybe not. It's just another wrinkle in my world."

"You're very philosophical, Lieutenant. I like that about you."

*   *   *

Omar has a sudden craving for Tommy's Original chili cheese-burger, so we meet there for lunch the next day. I get the same thing he does, only I bring along a couple of Alka-Seltzer to chase it. The food at Tommy's is good—it's fabulous, don't get me wrong—but it's a joint, you know. There's no other way to describe it, and you can't pretend there aren't consequences. Either that, or you gotta be thirty years younger. We sit in my car with the windows rolled down near the big orange sign on Beverly. It's a warm, sweet day. A bus lumbers by. There's cigarette and marijuana smoke in the air. Omar's Camaro is much roomier than my old Honda, but now, out of deference to Lourdes, he doesn't allow any food to be eaten inside.

"I'd forget about that Teitelbaum guy," he says in between bites, mopping his chin with a paper napkin. "He's on the hook for all the money he put into Benny's winery, and he needs to get a grip on that thug he has working for him. But between you and me, I don't see him as a killer."

"That's not how he's wired, I agree. But he's worried about his investment. He said as much. And if Benny goes to prison, that's probably the end of the line for the winery. It would never survive the bad press."

"Right. That's what I think too. In which case, Charlie Teitelbaum would be the last person to want to kill Al and that friend of his, Dreyer."

"You'd think that, yeah. Unless something else was going on."

Omar stops eating for a moment. "Like what?"

"I dunno," I say. "I'm just guessing. I keep coming back to character. Al Pupik's, in particular. He was a predator, a bully, according to everyone who worked with him. And I'm sure Benny's interest in the wine business wasn't a deep, dark secret, not if he was actively looking for backers."

"Where are you taking this, Amos?"

"Like I say, it's just a guess. But what if Al let his greed get the better of him? What if he decided he deserved a share in Travesty Vineyards? That a nice rolling piece of land in Wine Country was part of his legacy? I mean, he and Dreyer were working on elevating him at the end. He was about to become a god. It sorta fits, if you're a god, doesn't it? To have your own private vineyard?"

"Are you're saying Benny might have warned Charlie about this?"

"He might have."

"And Charlie realized that Benny was too soft? That Al would roll right over him?"

"Charlie Teitelbaum's a banker," I say. "He wouldn't have had any direct involvement. He keeps his hands clean, no matter what. But he knows who to hire."

Omar takes a sip of soda and lowers the paper cup to the floor between his legs. "So, how do we prove this?"

"Well, for starters, It'd be nice to have a look at Akihiro's weapon," I say. "Malloy said the gun that killed Al Pupik was the same one that did in Dreyer. A .38. But whoever shot up my tires, he had some kind of nine-millimeter job. And he also put a silencer on it. I didn't hear a thing that night."

"Maybe Akihiro owns more than one gun. He could be one of those *pendejos* with a whole closet full of guns. You ever think of that?"

"It's a scary thought, Omar. You need to look into that."

"Me?" His jaw drops, and he stops chewing on the last of his hamburger. Omar's lived out on the streets of Boyle Heights for years. He has a keen sense of danger. It's not that he's afraid; although he's seen friends die in difficult circumstances, he doesn't avoid trouble. It's just that his first inclination is never to go searching for it. He's barely out of his twenties, but he acts like someone who's in charge of a great treasure inside, someone with a lot to lose.

"Yeah," I say. "Let's find out where he lives. Pay him a visit. I mean, don't worry: I'll be there, you know, to back you up."

He grins. "I just hope you're not trying to get me killed, old man. I went to a fortune teller once on Hollywood Boulevard. She studied my palm, said I have a long, sweet life ahead of me."

"Then you've got nothing to worry about, now, do you? Just track down Akihiro. Get me an address. We'll take it from there."

*   *   *

Tonight, Mara's on a phone call with Violet. It's a dark, thorny conversation. I only hear one end, but I get the gist. Violet seems to be wavering; she's having second thoughts, she says, about college in general and Smith College in particular. Something about not being quite ready to face the responsibility of the adult world, wanting to take a break from books and tests and academia, wanting to take advantage of the free time she has to explore her inner self. Mara is not amused.

"Listen, kiddo, I didn't pay for your education so you could piss it away playing volleyball at the beach. Do you even know what a year at Foxboro costs? I made that mistake once with your mother. I won't make it again. Do you understand?"

There is a long awkward silence. Mara paces back and forth in the living room. She looks at me, shakes her head, rolls her eyes. This is not what she needs. Violet was always so compliant before she went away to prep school. Everything was mapped out; she knew the plan. The plan was always to graduate with honors and go straight to college.

"Okay, here's what I'm willing to do," Mara says after much back-and-forth. "I don't care which university you choose. It doesn't have to be Smith. But you're a smart girl, and I want you to go somewhere decent. Now isn't the moment to take a vacation. I want you to get a degree, a meaningful degree. I'll pay for that. But if you start at a good school and somewhere along the way you hit a bump in the road—you're still hesitant, and you decide you need a temporary break—well, okay. I could live with that, I suppose."

She keeps talking, even as she wanders into the kitchen. There's a whole lot that isn't said in this conversation, words both of them are deliberately holding back, out of guilt or fear or resentment. Mara's practically biting her tongue. I know her mind is caroming around like a billiard ball: she's worried about Violet; but even more, she's remembering Meghan, how in her own mind she abandoned her daughter, let her vanish for the sake of freedom, let her run with whomever she chose, which of course was the wrong crowd. And even though it's been years, Mara can still be lured back into that same old dance. It doesn't take much, and it doesn't make a damn's worth of difference that it's not her fault. Meghan was always passionate, head-over-heels in love, is what Mara told me. It was one thing or another. Addicted to tennis. Addicted to boys. Addicted, in the end, to heroin. Mara can never let this go. That's why her voice is so shrill; that's why she's pushing so hard now with Violet.

When they finally hang up, she comes back into the living room and curls up with me on the couch. I throw my arm around her and pull her close.

"Problem solved?" I ask.

"Hardly," she says. "That girl wears me out. She has no fucking idea of how I've greased the wheels for her. Her future could be so simple, Amos. She could do it in her sleep if she wanted to."

"Maybe that's the problem right there."

"Huh?"

"If she wanted to. She's eighteen, Mara. Think about it. She has no idea what she wants. Of course not. Nobody does at that age. Hell, that's when I joined the Marines. I thought it'd be a kick."

She stifles a laugh. "You joined the Marines because your cousin Shelly conned you into it. Because he felt guilty that the draft board had turned him down on account of his ulcer."

"Yeah, well, that's true, too. But you get my point. Violet is just drifting. She'll figure things out. Like you said, she's a smart girl."

"So I should just chuck everything and let her go skipping off to have an adventure? That's what happened with Meghan."

"What happened with Meghan was always going to happen. That's who she was. Maybe you didn't pressure her like you're doing with Violet, but it wouldn't have mattered. Don't you get it? She would have found a way."

I hold her even more tightly, and listen to her while the tears make familiar tracks down her cheeks. She doesn't bother to stop them with a Kleenex, they just fall.

We've had this discussion a few times now. It always seems to help, and God knows it's cheaper than the therapy she had in the past. It's just grief. I've given up wondering if there's ever an end to it. Right now she's focused on Violet. Violet is everything. She's determined that Violet will not suffer and die the way Meghan did, that Violet will find her path to success and happiness, no matter the cost. And who am I to tell her no?

*   *   *

The phone rings later that night, as I'm about to climb into bed. I'm down to my underwear, wondering whether to bother with pajamas. It's Omar on the line.

"Okay," he says, "he wasn't that hard to find. All I did was follow him home from Teitelbaum's place. He's got a cute little black Karmann Ghia, by the way. 1966 or '67, has to be. I'm jealous."

"That's nice. But where's he live?"

"East side of town, just off Melrose. 1032 Heliotrope Drive."

"Heliotrope. That's one I never heard of."

"Between the Hollywood Freeway and Vermont," he says. "It's an older area, a mix of houses and new apartments. There's an iron fence around his apartment building, but they're not very serious about keeping it locked. He's in number six."

"Beautiful, Omar. How do you feel about meeting me there around ten or ten-thirty tomorrow morning?"

"How do I feel? How do I feel? You really wanna know?"

"No," I say. "I just want you to be there, in case I need you."

"Oh, you're gonna need me, vato, you can count on that. All right, I'll see you there."

"Hey, Omar. One more thing. Don't forget your pistol, okay? I mean, you took care of him last time without it, but he might not be so friendly when we show up uninvited."

I grab a quick breakfast the next day at the Beachwood Café, right down the road from Al Pupik and the scene of the crime: scrambled eggs and spicy turkey sausage, plus three cups of strong black coffee. That kind of does the trick, though I can't quite seem to stop yawning.

The truth is, I didn't sleep so well, thinking about this morning. Also, I never sleep so well. This is what happens when you get old. I was up and down at least five times in the night. Which was fine, really—I'm not complaining. Sleep is overrated, if you ask me. Anyway, I'm used to it by now. I padded around like an old cat burglar, except I wasn't there to steal anything. I was just making my regular pilgrimages back and forth to the bathroom. Mainly, I was tip-toeing around, trying hard not to wake Mara.

I pay the bill and head over to the address on Heliotrope. I get there twenty minutes early; Omar is nowhere in sight. I lean against the wrought-iron gate, waiting. 1032 Heliotrope is a white, Moorish-looking apartment complex. It seems as if it's been remodeled very recently; there's a coat of fresh white paint and new window frames. It's also pleasant and airy, especially when you compare it to the unloved pink cube sitting beside it. Across the street, three

Craftsman houses from the turn of the century are set back from the sidewalk. Their front lawns have gone dry and brittle; they're waiting maybe for a contractor to come along, knock on the door, and make an offer. 1032 Heliotrope, I think, is the future of this place. A row of stunted palms occupy the apron, and management has added tasteful foliage all around the entrance. I can't see anything that resembles a parking garage, which is puzzling at first. But when I think about it more, it makes sense. Nobody here drives a new Audi or a BMW. Not yet. They leave their car by the curb overnight and still expect it'll be there in the morning.

Omar shows up then. He's wearing a tan sport coat, sunglasses, and a blue polo shirt. We stand by the iron gate, which is closed but not locked.

"How do you know he's in number six?" I ask. "You didn't follow him in, did you?"

"No, but there's a set of mailboxes right by the door. I only saw one Japanese name listed. Trust me, that's where you'll find him."

"Actually, I don't think he's home. I don't see a Karmann Ghia anywhere on the block. Maybe he's gone off to work."

"Maybe," Omar says; "let's hope so. I brought my pal along"—he taps the slight bulge on his right hip—"just in case."

I nod. We push the gate open, which squeals, and head up the gravel path. The front door is thick and sturdy, an oak barrier braced by a heavy metal pair of strap hinges. Even worse, the front door is locked. I'm prepared for that, though. I have a handy little tool for just this kind of occasion. It's something my old pal Jerry Vournas gave me after he got out of prison. Jerry was a gonif, a thief, by trade. We went to high school together, although we didn't have much in common. He liked to get his hands dirty—woodworking, welding, auto repair. Later on, he liked breaking the windows of jewelry stores in Beverly Hills and running off with whatever he could scoop up in a few seconds. I tracked him down, and he did seven years in Chino. I visited him from time to time, brought him books to read. That's when we grew close, and this was how he returned the favor.

I take out the tool and slide it sideways into the keyhole. I jiggle it ever so gently back and forth, feeling around for the tumblers. It's a massive old door, a primitive barrier, and maybe they just let it be when they started doing the renovation. After a minute or two, something shifts within. That's when I twist the handle and it magically gives way.

"You're gonna have to teach me how to do that someday," Omar whispers as we enter the cool, brightly lit hallway, which is covered with a thin blood-red carpet.

"It's not that hard, Omar. Someday, when I retire, I'll give you this. Then, every time you force open a door, you'll think of me." We wander down to the end. Number 6 is the last door on the right. Omar stands off to the side. He's holding his gun flat against his leg, his finger on the trigger, waiting. I knock three times. No answer. Then again, harder this time.

"See?" I grin at him. "Nobody home." I take out my tool, bend down, and start quietly to work.

"So why'd you tell me to come?" he says. "I could be home right now with Lourdes. She complained when I told her I had to leave."

"You need to study what a detective does," I say. "You also need to make money to pay for that baby of yours when it arrives. And I need you to be here, you know, just in case I'm wrong."

A minute later, we're inside Akihiro's apartment. I call out hello, but that's just for show: it's clearly vacant. Akihiro Ohnuki occupies a plain functional space. It feels a little bit like a Zen temple, or what I imagine a Zen temple would look like, if it were in LA and occupied by a thuggish bachelor like Akihiro. The living room has a large Persian rug, on which sits a gray couch and a Morris chair and a silver goose-neck lamp. Beside the Morris chair, there's a stack of manga (Japanese comic books), plus a few dog-eared paperback mysteries. The kitchen has a small television on the counter, but like the living room, it's also excruciatingly neat and clean. No stray forks or knives or dishes. No coffee grounds in the sink. He's placed a clear glass vase with daffodils on the table. The tablecloth is cotton and blue. It has little swirls that evoke ocean waves. He has almost nothing in the refrigerator—a stick of butter, a jar of mayo, a dozen eggs, two bottles of Sapporo beer, a pound of hamburger, half a cantaloupe, three aging Meyer lemons. There's a large open bag of rice in the pantry, some soy sauce, cans of tuna, and a few other items that make me think he could make a meal here if he had to, but more than likely he gets the bulk of his nourishment elsewhere.

We move on to the bedroom, which is also spare and tidy. He's got a small plastic radio by his pillow and a nice collection of boxer briefs folded in his bureau. Several sharp suits and ties. Six pairs of leather shoes, all polished and lined up like soldiers. On top of the bureau, there's a lovely bonsai tree in a jade green ceramic planter and a framed photo of a stern Japanese fellow. He's got a wispy white beard and he's staring straight into the camera. He's all about strength, and you know right away you don't want to mess with him. It could be his father, I think, but there's no resemblance. A teacher, then, from the old country.

Omar is sorting through the upper shelf of the closet, when he comes upon the cardboard box of ammunition. "Hey, take a look at this," he says, handing it down to me.

"Nine-millimeter," I say. "I figured we'd find that. Isn't that what you took away and tossed into the swimming pool the other day—a nine-millimeter?"

"I wasn't looking too close," Omar says. "I just wanted it the fuck out of his hand before he shot me, you know."

I nod, pocket one of the shells. There must be a hundred in there. "Think I'll pass this on to Malloy, see what he thinks. Akihiro won't miss it, that's for sure."

Next to his bed is a small oak desk. It has a stack of bills neatly arranged by their due date. Utilities and garbage collection, plus three hundred dollars a month for his Karmann Ghia, which he financed through Golden State Credit. There's also a shallow drawer. I pull it open and see a dark leather notebook. Inside, Akihiro has scribbled a series of brief, breathless little poems about everyday life in Los Angeles. They aren't cleaned up and slick; there's nothing perfect the way you'd read in a printed version. He has crossed out words and phrases and replaced them with others. What's plain is his struggle for clarity; you can feel the anxiety, the frustration, and the work. That's what makes them beautiful.

> *The young Filipina waitress has no*
> *time for me.*
> *She pulls a stubby pencil out from*
> *behind her ear, takes my order in silence. By now*
> *she knows my name, the way*
> *I like my eggs. My morning coffee. Everything about me*
> *except who I am.*

I close the notebook and put it back in the drawer just as I found it. "C'mon, there's nothing more to see here," I tell Omar.

We retrace our steps, leave his world. In a moment we are standing back outside the iron fence. There's a road crew from Southern California Edison jackhammering at the end of the block. The sun is high in the sky, and already it's heating up.

"Well," he says, "what'd you think?"

"I think Akihiro's not our man. More of a misunderstood poet, really. He may have blown out my tires, but we're never gonna pin a murder on him."

"Just 'cause we didn't find a weapon?"

"That's one thing. But looking at his space, how he lives, what he values, it just doesn't add up to a killer in my mind. I dunno, I can't talk about it."

"A poet, you say."

I start to wander back to my car. Seeing that piece in his notebook has jogged my memory, taken me back to Frederico Garcia Llorca. How they came for him in Granada. How he was lined up and shot by Franco's fascists. Because of who he was. Because he scribbled poems. The tragedy. The waste of a brilliant mind. Akihiro's no Llorca, but they share a common landscape.

I stop, turn around. Omar's still standing there by the gate. "They shoot poets," I explain. "Don't you get it? That's how it works."

CHAPTER 13

A bare stage. An acoustic guitar on a metal stand separates Benny from Al.

Al: Wait, wait! (Putting a palm to his forehead, closing his eyes.) I'm hearing a song. Having a vision!

Benny: A vision, yeah. Great. What do you see?

Al: Well, I'm walking . . . I'm walking on a ribbon of highway.

Benny: A ribbon of highway. Not just a plain highway? (Makes a puzzled face.) Okay, got it.

Al: And I see above me . . . right above me, an endless . . . endless skyway. You know what I mean?

Benny: Maybe. You're looking up at the sky. That's a fancy-schmancy way of putting it.

Al: And I see below me, right below me, a golden . . . a golden valley.

Benny: A valley. Golden valley. Sounds good. Like they're raising wheat. Or corn.

Al: And I'm thinking . . . I'm thinking (grabs the guitar, strums a chord). Oh boy, am I thinking . . .

Benny: What the hell are you thinking? C'mon! Don't keep me in suspense!

Al: I'm thinking that . . . this land was made for you and me.

Benny: You and me? You and me? That's it? Nobody else?

Al: Well, you and me. Yeah. But that means all of us, really. Everybody.

*Benny: No. You and me means you and me. What about the Indians?
What about the atheists?
Al (sighing): Now you're acting like a liberal again. Don't be such an
idiot. You don't get it.
Benny: Oh, I get it. (Furious.) And let me tell you something. On behalf
of all the liberal idiots in America, I refuse to be in this song of yours.
You hear me? This land belongs to you! And you can keep it! (He stalks
off.)*

Sunday morning, before the sun gets too high, Bill Malloy goes for his usual walk down by Frogtown—a scruffy, industrial area of warehouses, hip coffee roasters, and auto repair shops, all sandwiched at random between freeways. It runs parallel with the Los Angeles River.

Nature has to work its way in through the crevices here. This is still the city; and while it's slowly coming back, nature is not in charge. Not yet. There's a well-worn bicycle path and a few paved areas dedicated to children, with swings and climbing structures and rusting metal sculptures of bears and snakes; there are flashes of sycamore trees and brambles and piles of river rock and sudden bursts of birds turning north or twisting south, but Bill isn't interested in any of that. He just likes the silence, is what he says.

He comes here to get lost, to pad around by himself in the morning gray, to gaze down at the river, which, if you listen to him, is not a true river anymore, which is also lost, emasculated ever since civil engineers smoothed it over with concrete. There are seasons, of course, if you can call them that. Last winter, after the heavy rains, he noticed ducks and even a pair of intrepid young lovers in a canoe. But now, in July, it's just a muddy trickle that runs down the center. You can step across without getting wet, and graffiti artists are back on the inclines with their aerosol cans and gaudy messages of hope and despair.

He meets me in Egret Park, and we stop to rest on a stone bench. A couple of bike riders lumber by, men in their fifties and sixties, all decked out in bright neon colors.

"I thought about taking up biking once," I say, after they pass.

"You did, huh?"

"Sure. I got nothing against exercise. I thought about it. But where we were at Park La Brea—the traffic, all those buses everywhere, puffing out poison—it just seemed like I'd be taking my own life in my hands."

"There's that," he agrees.

"Besides which, there's no storage. I'd have to keep it on the ninth floor and lug it up and down in the elevator. People were already giving me dirty looks whenever I got on, you know, even without a bike."

"But now you're in the Hollywood Hills. So what's stopping you?"

"You said it right there. The Hollywood Hills. I could maybe go down, fine, but then what? You think I'm strong enough to pedal back? Are you serious? At my age?"

"That's why I stick to walking," he says. "And only on flat surfaces, like here. There was a time when Jess and I first arrived in LA, we'd go to Big Bear and Arrowhead, rent a cabin for the weekend. Just to get out of the city, but also so we could breathe the fresh air and hike around."

"And how long did that last?"

"Oh, a year or two, I guess. Until I got promoted and bogged down with work, and her knees started acting up. You know how it is."

He hangs his head. He and Jess don't go anywhere much anymore, except to consult with bone doctors and naturopaths. She's not an invalid yet, but her knees have gotten much worse. This is the silent cross he bears.

"Omar and I went to visit Akihiro Ohnuki the other day. Teitelbaum's assistant? That's one of the reasons I wanted to chat with you."

"And what'd he have to say?"

I wag my head. "Well, that's the thing. He wasn't home, but we found something interesting there we thought you'd wanna see." I pull out the nine-millimeter bullet and set it down gently on the bench. It shines in the sun.

He picks it up, turns it over, gives me a raised eyebrow. "What the hell do you mean, he wasn't home? Where'd this come from?"

"An ammo box in his bedroom closet. He has plenty more. I don't think he'll miss it."

"You broke into his house?"

"We didn't break in, not exactly. I wouldn't put it like that."

"So, how would you put it?"

"We knocked first."

"I see. Wonderful. But the door was locked, right? And he didn't leave you a note, didn't tell you to look under the mat for a key?"

"He forgot to do that. I dunno, maybe he meant to. Anyway, the door was locked. But that doesn't mean it can't be opened, does it."

"Apparently not," Malloy says. He's not happy with the way I do business, I'm well aware, but by now we're both too old to change. Or should I put it more diplomatically? That we've reached an understanding? That it's pointless to pretend? He knows I'd never do anything that truly crosses the line. And I'm sure he'd never bust me for letting myself into a stranger's apartment uninvited. At least he hasn't so far.

Neither one of us says anything for a full minute. Then Malloy tucks the bullet in his pocket and says, as if he's reading my mind, "We can check this out. I can tell you right now it won't match the slugs in Al Pupik and Lonny Dreyer, but it might line up nicely with the ones in your tires. You can take him to small claims, I imagine."

"You don't have to, Bill. It's not a problem. Mr. Teitelbaum has already reimbursed me for the damage. In fact, I just wanted to let you know you don't have to fuss too much more with Akihiro."

"No? Didn't you say he was bad news?"

"I may have hinted. He did try to shoot Omar, okay. But they were both caught up in a situation, hard to tell whose fault it was. Anyway, that was before Omar took his gun away and threw it in the swimming pool."

"Sounds like somebody committed a crime. We ought to interview him at least. Give him a warning. Teitelbaum, too, if he's behind all that mayhem."

"You can do that if you want to. But grilling Charlie's not going to get you any closer to the killer. He's a sideshow. Charlie's about one thing and one thing only: protecting his money."

"Maybe," Malloy says. "I've also seen plenty of people kill for money."

"You've been watching too many gangster movies," I tell him.

He yawns. "You know, we can dance around this all day long, Amos, but the truth is your man, Benny, is going to stand trial soon for second-degree murder. It's not that hard a case. And right now, if I was a betting man, I'd say he's guilty as charged."

"Even when you add in Lonny Dreyer? Didn't you tell me that was a wrinkle?"

Malloy crosses his legs, reaches down, and scratches at something irritating his left ankle. It's too late in the season for mosquitoes, besides which, there's still not enough water in the Los Angeles River for them to grow up and make trouble. "I could give you a bundle of ways to explain Dreyer. Maybe Benny hired someone to do the job. Or maybe Benny drove out there and did the deed himself. He was released on his own recognizance, after all. We weren't tailing him. Maybe he put together a solid alibi with his cleaning lady, then hopped in the car. Could happen. He certainly knew about Lonny Dreyer and the big writing project. Joey Marcus told us that."

"So you've stopped looking for the actual killer, in other words."

Malloy frowns. I've seen this look before. It's the look of a man who is worn out, a man who has lined up all the available facts in his head, weighed them carefully one by one, and this is the best he can do. It's not perfect, but it's what he's learned to live with. "According to the DA," he says, "who's a very bright guy, by the way, we've found the killer. His name is Benny Wolf. He used to tell jokes. He lives on Montague Court in Granada Hills. The end."

"I don't understand," I say.

"I realize that," he says. "But it's where we're at. Sometimes the answer is just staring you right in the face. Simple, but elegant, know what I mean?"

"I disagree, Bill. If you stop now—"

"It's not me, Amos. It's you. You're the one who should stop. You've been making yourself crazy. You're like a rat in a cage. Now just give it a rest."

*   *   *

I walk back to my car and start driving slowly up Silver Lake Boulevard, past the liquor stores and fabric shops and Vietnamese beauty parlors, toward home. It's barely nine o'clock. Everything's closed now.

Maybe the lieutenant has a point. Maybe I've been overthinking this. Not all mysteries are blind alleys; in fact, most of them are pretty straightforward. I once worked long distance for a guy in Cleveland named Frank Coolidge. He hired me to track down his only son, Whitney, with whom he'd had a falling out. Whitney had gone off to film school at USC; he dreamed of becoming a director. In his junior year, his mother died suddenly of cancer. That was bad enough. Then his father remarried someone two months later, and the boy lost it. He cut off all contact.

Weeks of silence turned into months. When Frank finally swallowed his pride and dialed his son's number, an automated female voice told him it had been disconnected. He called the university. They informed him that his son had dropped out two weeks earlier. He called the frat house where Whitney lived, hit another brick wall. In a panic then, he called me. I found him three days later. How, you ask? One of his frat brothers mentioned off the record that Whitney had a girlfriend named Sheila Arakalian. She was a senior, he said, studying to be an architect. I checked with the architecture school. Turns out, there aren't that many Arakalians at USC; she wasn't tough to find. And when I walked through her front door, Whitney was standing right there in her kitchen, cooking pasta.

Of course, finding him didn't solve the problem with his dad. Not right away. That knot took months to untie. Frank Coolidge still had to fly out here and go into family therapy. But the case— my part of it, at least—was simple. There was no mystery.

I'm a few blocks from Alvarado when my phone rings. It's Benny Wolf.

"I've made a decision," he says. "I'm leaving."

"Leaving? What? Where to?"

"I can't tell you that," he says. "If I told you, they'd find me."

"They'll find you anyway."

"No, they won't, Mr. Parisman. I'm not that stupid. But I wanted to call you before I left. As a courtesy. You're an honest man, and you've been very kind to me. I just put another check in the mailbox. But it's your last one. I won't be needing your services anymore. I won't be needing anyone anymore. I hope you understand."

"Benny," I say, "you're not a magician. You can't just disappear. Maybe you don't realize the gravity of what you're about to do."

"Oh, you're wrong."

"There are consequences," I say. "You run away, that'll put the kibosh on your defense if it ever comes to trial."

"It won't come to trial," he says wistfully. "That's the beauty. I'll be gone."

"You run away," I say, "and if and when they catch up to you, the fact that you ran away will help convict you. Don't you see?"

"I'm aware of that," he says. "But I spoke with Alma yesterday— and with Alma's friend, Margaret. And they both thought the evidence was piling up against me."

"What do they know?" I say. "Have you asked your lawyer? I'd trust her opinion a whole lot more than them. She's defending you."

He doesn't speak for a moment, and I worry that he's about to hang up. My mind is racing. All at once, the improbable becomes plausible. What if the DA is right? What if Benny *did* kill both of them? And what if he still has the .38? The one the cops couldn't find? What if he's sitting there in his bedroom right now, contemplating killing himself? That's one way to disappear.

"The evidence is piling up," he says again. His voice is strained and contorted, like it's a great effort for him to push those five words out of his mouth. "That's what they told me."

"Did they tell you to run away?"

"No, no; that was my own idea. I thought of it last night as I was brushing my teeth. And now I've made all the preparations. I'm ready to go."

"Are you at home, Benny?"

He pauses. "I can't tell you that, Mr. Parisman. I don't want to be rude, but you understand, I'm sure."

Silver Lake Boulevard is mercifully quiet. That's when I do a one-eighty in the middle of the block and race back down the hill toward the Golden State. "Here's what I'm gonna do, Benny. I'm coming out to see you right now. I'm in my car, and I can be there in forty minutes, maybe less."

"I'll be gone," he says. "Don't bother."

"I don't want you to be gone," I say. "I want you to stick around, for my sake. See, I don't think the evidence is piling up like you say. Not at all. And if you give me a chance, I can prove it. I can. But I need you to stick around, so we can talk it through. Just stay where you are. Can you do that, Benny? For me?"

"Goodbye, Mr. Parisman. Thanks again." And that's where our conversation ends.

I stare at the screen for a second, then I dial 911 and explain to the female dispatcher what I think is happening. That I just received a phone call and that caller sounded suicidal. That he's an unstable personality and awaiting trial for murder. Did he say he was going to harm himself? That's what she wants to know. He said he was going to disappear, I say. Who the hell knows what he meant? Then I give her Benny Wolf's address, and she assures me she'll take it from there.

By the time I reach the on-ramp for the Golden State, I'm back on the phone with Bill Malloy.

"The court didn't think he was much of a flight risk," he says. "I mean, he's been camping out inside our televisions for years. Not exactly a stranger, right?"

"No, but he's trying to become one."

"I wouldn't worry," he says. "There's probably a squad car rolling up to his door right now. They'll handle it. You don't need to drive out there, Amos. You've done your part. I'll call you when this is over. I promise."

"Don't hurt him, okay, Bill? He sounded fragile."

Malloy says he's gotta go then and hangs up. There's part of him, I think, that's pissed to see his Sunday-morning walk by the river ruined; but there's also another part that thinks he's got his man at last. That part, the cop in him, is probably grinning from ear to ear.

CHAPTER 14

When Jews get depressed, they eat. Something basic and prehistoric about chewing, I guess. Takes your mind off the problem at hand. Anyway, my spirits are in my shoes, and later that morning I talk Mara into driving over and meeting me for brunch at Langer's Deli on Alvarado.

She doesn't normally come to places like this, I get that; all the years with Gus have made her more at home in highbrow joints. But once in a while she gives in and we go slumming. She probably doesn't tell her therapist, but this is clearly how she acknowledges her working-class roots. Besides, the food's pretty good at Langer's, even if the neighborhood is kind of *farblunget* (lost). Well, maybe I shouldn't say that. The neighborhood is in flux. Everyone is out on the street, it seems, and there are lots of new arrivals from other lands. English is spoken here, as well as Spanish and Quechua and God only knows what else. And yeah, you usually can't help but run into some homeless folks camped out in MacArthur Park nearby. They're not going anywhere, that's for sure; they're just hanging on.

We're lucky enough to find a booth in a corner. She orders the spinach omelet, and even though Dr. Flynn has warned me time and time again, I get the pastrami and eggs.

"Guess what?" she announces as she sips her coffee. "I just got off the phone with Violet. She's made up her mind. She's going to Smith after all."

"You mean, if they let her in."

"Oh, they'll let her in. Between her brains and my money, it shouldn't be a problem."

"So, why'd she change her mind?"

Mara gives me a sly wink. "I'd like to think I had something to do with it. But I also heard that her best friend, Tara, has decided on Smith as well."

"I didn't know she had a friend named Tara. Let alone a *best* friend."

"Everyone's her best friend. That's not important. What counts is that she's going." She reaches over with her fork and spears a significant hunk of pastrami off my plate. "You're not supposed to eat this," she says. "I'm going to help you live to a ripe old age. You'll thank me someday."

I grin. "How about I thank you now and get it over with? Just in case I drop dead tonight?"

We talk about this and that. I debate whether I should tell her anything about the call from Benny Wolf. He might be clever enough to avoid the police for a while, but sooner or later they'll find him and lock him up. Then what? There'll be a presumption of guilt, not just with the cops and at the DA's office, but all over town. The *LA Times* will have a field day; that's how they handle things like this. And of course, depending on the length of the trial, it will simmer forever on the back burner, filter down into private conversations. Like the O.J. Simpson case, it'll take on a life of its own: women waiting in supermarket checkout lines will scan the lurid headlines. All he did was run away.

"How's your omelet?" I ask.

"Excellent. You want some?" She starts to cut me a forkful.

"No, that's okay. I'm watching my vegetable intake."

"Very funny."

I'm this close to opening my mouth about Benny then, tell her how presumed guilt works, all the various ways it can muck up a case, when my phone rings. It's Malloy. I can tell from his tone right away it's bad news.

"We found Benny," he says. "He killed himself. Bullet to the head."

"Oh, shit," I say.

"You might want to come out here after all. Forensics won't be here for a while, but I could really use your take on the house. Maybe you'll notice something I'd miss."

"I'm on my way," I tell him. I turn to Mara. She hasn't touched her food. She's been watching me all along, and she can read my mood as well as anyone.

"Do you want to tell me what's wrong?" she asks. "Or shall I guess?"

"Benny's dead," I say quietly. "Benny—he shot himself in the head."

"Oh, my God!"

I drop a couple of crumpled twenties on the table, slide out of the booth, and stand. "I've gotta get over there, honey. I'm sorry."

"No, no," she says. "You go on. I'll see you when you come home."

*   *   *

You never know what you're up against in this business. I guess that's what I love about being a detective. It's also what I hate. You have to keep your balance, stay in the moment. Oh, there are patterns, sure, scenarios that repeat themselves. A man gets bored with his marriage, cheats on his wife. One night, she's had enough. She snaps. She confronts him. Tries to kill him. With a gun. A knife. Rat poison. Whatever she has at hand. It's a pattern, but you can't just follow the pattern every time and expect it to always pan out.

The two uniformed officers standing guard at Benny Wolf's door both have their thumbs dug into their belts. They're young and gawky and white, and their shoulder patches tell me they're from the Chatsworth station. I don't recognize them, but they've been instructed to let me in, which is all I care about. There are four other squad cars parked along the block at various angles. Their emergency lights are all blinking merrily, bouncing off the windows of nearby houses. If you didn't know better, you'd think it was Christmas around here. Across the street, a clot of curious neighbors in T-shirts and khaki shorts and swim trunks has gathered on their front lawns.

Malloy is poking around in the entryway. He's wearing blue plastic gloves and paper booties; so are Jason and Remo, who are off in the kitchen. He hands me these items to put on, and I do.

"Where is he?" I ask.

"Follow me," he says.

We step carefully into the den. It's the same as I remember from that first day—the long black leather U-shaped couches, the glass coffee table, the empty walls. There are two stacks of art magazines on the carpet. The coffee table is bare, except for a gorgeous blue Japanese vase containing three white lilies.

"This is as far as I ever got in the house," I say. "We sat over there. He never gave me the grand tour."

"And does anything strike you as different?"

I shake my head. Nothing seems amiss; but behind the middle couch, almost to the archway that leads to the kitchen, that's where Benny Wolf is sprawled. His hand is the first thing you see. His cell phone is nearby. It looks as if he might have been sitting down with his knees up, bracing his back against the couch and facing the kitchen when he opted to pull the trigger. The bullet slammed into the right side of his head, just above the ear, and exited diagonally at the top left. He fell over then and dropped the gun. All around him, the carpet is soaked through, a reddish lake; ringlets of his soft white hair are thick with matted blood. I bend in closer. His right eye is shut tight, as if the impact of the shot made him wince. But his left eye is still partly open, and his eyebrow is strangely raised. It's like he's puzzled, like he was chewing on something imponderable, a big important question. That's when he threw up his hands, said fuck it, and decided to end it all.

I look down at the gun. "There's your .38," I say.

"I noticed that too," he says, biting his lip. The presence of the weapon seems to confirm at last what he's been telling me all along; but even so, it doesn't make him happy.

"He told Charlie Teitelbaum he had a gun. That he knew how to use it, too."

"Yeah," Malloy mutters, "and believe me, we looked all over for that goddamned thing. Tore this house apart. Remo checked—it's not registered to him. I don't know who it belonged to originally. Or how he got his hands on it."

"You know what's weird, Bill? I swear he's wearing the exact same clothes he had on the first time I met him. The gray silk suit, the white shirt, barefoot."

"Yeah. Well, it's a fashion statement, isn't it? I guess if you're gonna die, you wanna look your best for people like us."

"Speaking of statements," I say, "did he leave one behind? A note? A short story? Anything?"

Malloy rubs his forehead. "We haven't found one. Not unless you count that last phone call he made to you."

"But he never said suicide. Never. He was going to disappear. Like, you know, run away. Did he pack a bag?"

"Again," Malloy says, "we haven't found it. Not so far. It's early, though. Maybe he put it in his car, then changed his mind." He frowns, gazes down at the body. "This is one sure way to disappear, I suppose."

We both stare down at the rumpled corpse. It's hard to think. He was a complex little man. A *luftmensch*, okay. Lost in the clouds. I wonder what people will find to say when the time comes to bury him.

Remo and Jason amble in; they have a little white dog squirming on a leash. It could be a Pekinese, but I'm not good with breeds.

"Her name is Greta," I say, scratching her under the chin. "We never met before."

"How do you know her, then?" Jason asks.

"My man, Omar. He followed them around for a time. Benny was pretty devoted; he took her out every day. She belongs to the neighborhood."

"Well, she shouldn't be here," Remo says resolutely, toting her out in his arms. "Not now. We have to find her a home. I'll get animal control on it."

There's a commotion at the door then, and the forensics team fills the entryway. Malloy waves them over—five serious guys with gloves and paper booties. The last one is Fong, the photographer. I've known him forever, and we nod at each other. He's got three cameras draped around his neck and an aluminum stepladder for better angles. We move politely out of their way. Outside, two lads from the Chatsworth Police Department are busy unspooling yellow crime tape around the perimeter. An old gardener next door, maybe the one named Manuel Morales, the guy Omar befriended, is squatting down in the dichondra with an edger in his hand. He's got an Angels cap on and he's gazing at us. There's bewilderment in his eyes. That, and maybe a hefty dash of fear. America's a crazy goddamn country, is what he's probably thinking.

"So, what happens now?" I ask, even though I can kinda guess what he's going to say.

"Now?" Malloy says. There's resignation in his voice. This is not how he wants it to end. I know. He likes to think about the finer points of law. The process is what he's always been drawn to. He prefers arresting people and bringing them to justice; it makes him cringe whenever he's forced to be a janitor. "Now we do what we can to clean up this mess. We hunt for evidence. A suicide note. A coroner's report. Whatever. And the scientists inside will take the gun back to their lab and do their tests. They'll dot all the i's, cross the t's. And I'll bet you my next paycheck it's a match with Al Pupik and Lonny Dreyer. That's what's now."

"Yeah," I say, "probably. Maybe so."

He tilts his head then, like a dog who's heard a high whistling noise that none of the rest of us could. "What? You're still having doubts?"

I shrug. "I dunno, Bill. I'd like to agree with you. I can't put my finger on it. But even now, something still doesn't feel right."

"I don't know what you're talking about," he says. "Let me spell it out one more time. Here's how this will be remembered: Benny Wolf killed his partner in a rage because Al was cheating him. You buy that?"

"It's possible," I admit. "But then why'd he kill Dreyer? He didn't know Dreyer. Not really. Maybe he'd heard of him. You hear lots of things in this town. Did that also happen in a moment of rage?"

"I'm not a mind-reader," Malloy offers, raising his hands. "Maybe he went over there just to threaten him."

"But why?"

"Why? Because he was still pissed. Because he realized the show they were cooking up would have written Benny out of existence. It was all about Al, right? All about Al, like always. And Benny wanted equal billing. Hell, he'd just killed a man who'd been denying him his place in the sun. Why stop now?"

"Which brings us here," I say, "to his sudden and inexplicable suicide."

"That's maybe the easiest part," says Malloy. "We don't have him around to ask anymore, but I can guess what was going through his mind. Benny felt the walls caving in around him, pure and simple. You said yourself he was fragile. He even half confessed, the first time we sat down and interviewed him." He points with his thumb back to the house. "We may not find a suicide note in there, but it doesn't take a shrink to figure this out: the idea of going to prison for the rest of his life weighed on him. He knew he couldn't take it. When push came to shove, he just cracked."

*   *   *

I pass an ambulance from the Fire Department on my way back. The two guys in the cab are relaxed; their lights aren't flashing and they aren't moving at breakneck speed. They're just gonna pick up the body and drop it off at the morgue. My mind drifts back to the last thing Malloy said while we were resting on the bench this morning in Frogtown—that it's over. That I should give it a rest. Maybe for once I ought to listen to him; he could be right. You're always such a stubborn sonofabitch, Parisman. But what's it ever done for you, huh?

I come to a red light, scan the perpetual mess on the passenger seat beside me—another thing I've let go for too long. It looks and smells like a college dorm room. There are toothpicks and wrappers and empty cardboard boxes from In-N-Out, packets of salt, the stale remains of a glazed doughnut, half a bottle of aspirin, receipts from my dry-cleaners, even a couple of ancient French fries embedded on the floor mat. No wonder Mara refuses to ride in it.

About an hour later, I'm standing in a smooth, silent elevator in Westwood, gliding up to the sixth floor to chat with Petra Allison. I don't have an appointment with her; but once I tell her what's going on with Benny, I'm sure she'll want to see me.

Petra is in Suite 3A. It's a large, airy corner of the building with a view that probably goes all the way out to Hawaii. A couple of fancy designer couches and a splash of modern art on the wall—nothing too flamboyant: just, you know, perfect. A short, energetic blonde with red-framed eyeglasses is working the reception desk. She's the only one there, and, unlike the young punk who ran the show for Joey Marcus, this one's not reading magazines. She has things to do. There's a stack of manila folders next to her computer.

I lay my business card on the table. "I'm here to see Petra."

She glances at the card without touching it, then apprehensively up at me. "Do you have an appointment, Mr.—Mr. Parisman?"

"No," I say. "Just tell her it's about Benny Wolf. Tell her it's important."

That doesn't do the trick. I've spent a lifetime trying to get past people like this, and I can tell right away that she's not about to budge. "You know what?" she replies coolly. Her eyes flicker up at me. "I hate to break it to you, but everything she does is important. She's on a conference call at the moment, so perhaps if you grab a seat over—"

"Tell her Benny Wolf is dead."

Now she drops the pencil she's holding. She chews on her lower lip. Her face moves in three directions at once. This *is* out of the ordinary. "Oh. Oh, I see." She rises from her leather contoured chair and darts quickly for the doors to the inner office. "I'll try to interrupt her," she says as she twists the handle.

A minute later, I'm plopped down with Petra.

"What do you mean, he's dead?" she says.

"I just came from his place in Granada Hills. He committed suicide, looks like." I make a make-believe gun out of my right hand, and point it at the spot just above my ear. "You know, bang?"

"Dear God."

Tears, or something that approximates tears, well up then, and she reaches for some Kleenex in her desk drawer. I look around at her office. There's a cluster of family pictures on the desk—Petra smiling with her husband or boyfriend on a ski slope, an eight-year-old Petra in a tutu, a teenage Petra with her brothers and sisters, laughing and roasting marshmallows around a fire, Petra with her arm around some handsome devil in a tux, who I'm sure is a famous movie star, but which one? She has a nice, thick oriental carpet, which lends the room a sense of tranquility, but the rest of her office is strictly business. There's a trio of tall metal filing cabinets in the corner, a side desk with an imposing computer and all sorts of modern printing and scanning devices, and right behind that, a somber bookshelf with titles like *Black's Law Dictionary* and *Torts and Contracts*.

"Funny thing," I say, "he called me just this morning. Wanted to thank me, to say goodbye, I guess."

She puts her hands out on the desk, cups them in front of her. "When he was on the phone, did he tell you—did he indicate somehow, that he might—"

"He said he was going to disappear. That was how he put it. But I didn't figure that meant suicide, would you?"

"No."

"Not that I could have stopped him, either way. I told him not to run, though. Pleaded with him, in fact. I mean, I knew that was the surest way to screw up his case. He wouldn't get far. And they'd use it against him."

"It wouldn't have looked good for our side, you're right."

I stare coldly at her. She glances back at me for a while, then averts her eyes. I realize I don't know her very well. Or rather, the little I know of her is just what I've read online. The tabloids have her as self-assured, this bright shiny wind-up toy. And she acts like a tough cookie, I think, but maybe in the end, that's all it is: an act. Now all the bluster is gone. Now, at least it points to a human being underneath.

"What I don't get"—I say now—"what's still rubbing me the wrong way, is why?"

"Why what?"

"Why would he kill himself? You said yourself the evidence against him is flimsy. He admits he was there that night to talk to Al. Oh, by the way, I assume you know that he didn't go by himself. Alma was there, too. She drove him."

"She did? No, I hadn't—I hadn't heard." She combs her hands through her stubby blond hair, blinks as though trying to get a handle on the situation. "I would have thought she'd say something. To me. As his attorney."

"Yeah, it would have helped his case maybe if the cops knew they went together. I mean, two people can get together and shoot somebody. I've seen it happen, but it's harder. Takes planning."

She stares at me then. Her blue eyes widen, her face contorts. Maybe she's trying to reimagine this in a whole new light—Alma and Benny, knocking on Al's door late at night. Arguing with him over money, money that was rightfully theirs, years of money denied, then losing all control, smacking him with a bottle of wine, gunning him down. "It doesn't make sense," she says finally.

"Oh, I agree," I say. "They're not killers, neither one. Benny's frail. He's a poet. And Alma? Alma's a drunk. She went there just to back him up, you know, give him enough courage to make his case. That's all that happened. They talked, but it didn't go anywhere."

"So, back to your question," she says. "Why did he kill himself? Why, when the truth is we had this case won? My God, I thought I'd spelled everything out!"

She probably had, I think. How's that for irony? People rarely listen, especially when it counts. I go back to the last day my dad and I argued years ago, how he tried to talk me out of joining the Marines, how—although he'd never put on a uniform—he refused because he knew better, he knew the toll war took on men's lives. It's all a hoax, he said in that gravelly voice of his. A goddamn fucking hoax. He was on his soapbox, but all of a sudden he started coughing up phlegm, and after that he started raving, chewing his words, wandering off like a lunatic in no-man's-land. He called it a machine that would crush my soul, turn me into a killer, or even worse. He wouldn't say what "worse" meant. I asked him, but he stopped talking, leaned his head back on the starched, pristine pillows, and closed his eyes. He was in the hospital by then, at Cedars, in the same bed he'd eventually die in. I held his hand as long as I could. Then I kissed him on the forehead and left. I drove down to the recruiter's office the next day. I was eighteen years old. I told myself I'd make him proud.

Now I rest my hands on my knees. "He wasn't convinced of that, I'm afraid. Alma and some friend of hers named Margaret said he was in deep trouble. That the evidence was piling up."

"What evidence?" she asks sarcastically. "What the hell are they talking about? The DA was playing a weak hand. He had a motive, sure. Al was robbing Benny blind, and Benny couldn't take it anymore. Benny hated Al. Well, pardon me. Everyone who had anything to do with him hated Al by the time he died. You hated Al Pupik? Take a number, buddy, get in line. I had witnesses, Parisman. I was set to call a half dozen failed comedians to the stand, people he'd trampled all over, people with promise, people you probably never heard of because he ended their careers. You gave me a couple of names, but there are plenty more. And they were all willing to testify."

"Yeah, well, that's not gonna happen, is it?" I clamber to my feet. She's still sitting there behind her big slick desk, trying to take it all in. I can't tell if she cared about the case, really; it was over so abruptly. There would be other cases with this kind of noise around them, other Hollywood stars who'd fall from the heavens, sleep with the wrong man's wife, take too many pills, go bananas and shoot up a bar. There would always be more madness and running amok, especially with people like that. She'd never have to scrounge around for billable hours.

I walk out the door, nodding goodbye to the secretary. As I step into the air-conditioned silence of the elevator and press L for the lobby, I'm thinking that, like me, she must have formed a bond with Benny over all these years. He wasn't simply a client; he'd spoken to her from inside a television set, from late at night and far away; and he'd lived on through summer reruns and comedy specials. Benny Wolf might die. But the one who made her laugh? Never.

Before she moved into Olympic Terrace, Loretta used to tell me that the folks she watched on TV were her friends. At first, she said this casually, and I didn't think she was serious. But then as time went on, and her condition slowly worsened, and as our real friends found excuses to stop coming by and dropped off the radar, she became more insistent. *These are my friends.* She meant it.

CHAPTER 15

There's no time like the present.
Yeah, well, it's better to be present than absent.
You can't be absent. No one can be absent. Not without an excuse.
I had an excuse, once upon a time. But that's all it was. A poor excuse,
you ask me.
I didn't ask you. I DID NOT ASK YOU. I try not to talk to you.
You don't want to talk to me?
No, not so much. I have to, though. It's just you and me, and this desert
island.
I know what you mean. The two of us. And we've been here forever.
Forever.
A long time.
How long?
I don't wanna think about it. I stay in the present.
Good idea. There's no time like the present.

Omar is just about to knock off early from work on the house he's helping his brother-in-law remodel in Lincoln Heights. I tell him Benny Wolf is dead, and he agrees to meet me at La Chuperia on Mission. I'd never been there before. I don't care for bars as a rule, but this one, even though it's dark inside and in a sketchy neighborhood, has a good selection of beer and appetizers. They specialize in micheladas,

I find out right away, which is a concoction of beer, lime and tomato juices, salsa, and a few other choice ingredients I'd rather not know about. Omar likes it because it's only a few blocks from where he was taping sheetrock in somebody's future living room.

He's been sitting there for half an hour when I show up and has already emptied three bottles of Modelo Negra. He's got on a soiled wife-beater T-shirt, black Levi's, and a pair of work boots that might have been tan when they were new. "What the hell do you mean, he's dead?" he asks, looking up from a half-eaten plate of nachos.

I explain briefly what happened—or what I think happened. How the body looked, all crumpled up behind the couch. The gun, the .38, which in all likelihood will prove to be the weapon that did in Al Pupik and Lonny Dreyer. I leave out some details. I don't talk about the little dime-sized hole he put into the side of his head, just above the ear, or the blood that ruined his carpet, but Omar's got a powerful imagination.

"The point is," I say, after a long summing-up, "the cops think this is over. They've got their man. He's lying on his back in the county morgue. And they're breathing easier, now that they don't have to bother putting him on trial."

"You really think they would have lost?"

I take a long, pensive sip of the Dos Equis I'm nursing and turn to him. Omar's not a plodder; he's not a by-the-book kind of guy, like Lieutenant Malloy. He's always been brave, a flexible thinker. He didn't find his way to Los Angeles until he was thirteen or fourteen; he arrived very late to this party. He came in off the desert, a newcomer who couldn't speak two words of English. All he had was the strength in his body and the knowledge in his bones, knowledge that was never allowed to shine in a classroom. Maybe that's the difference. Like a mountain goat, his mind takes wild leaps of faith sometimes; I admire that. But now I wonder whether in this case, at least, he's starting to side with the establishment.

"They would have had a tough time. The evidence wasn't there. I just talked to his lawyer. She says she would have mopped the floor with them."

"So, why'd he kill himself?" Omar says. "Makes no sense." He signals to the waitress for a fourth beer.

"You sure you want another one, buddy? You're gonna get in the car soon and drive home like that?"

"I can drive fine," he assures me. "Only thing, I just gotta remember to pee before I leave."

Norteño music is coming out of the ceiling, not too loud, but a pleasant thumping in the background. We listen in silence for a while. Then I bring up the real reason I came.

"He may have killed himself, yeah. I can bring myself to believe that, but I would have felt better if he'd left us a note."

"Why?"

"I dunno," I say. "You leave a note behind, explain why you did something awful like that, it's a courtesy. Maybe it doesn't ease the pain, but at least everybody's clear. They know what's behind it. There's closure."

He looks at me uncomprehendingly, like now all of a sudden I'm speaking Greek.

"I hate that word, too," I say. "Closure. Some New York shrink dreamed that one up. Probably charged extra for it."

A fourth icy beer is set down before Omar, and he takes a long meditative pull. "He didn't leave a note," he says, "so maybe that tells us what? That he didn't shoot himself? That he was framed?"

"Unlikely. Just thinking over my last chat with him, and looking at how he was positioned behind the couch, I'd say he shot himself. The forensics guys will make the final call about that. But *why* he killed himself—now that's the head-scratcher."

Omar puts his hand over his mouth and stifles a burp. "I'm guessing you have an opinion about that, too," he says glumly.

"I have an opinion about everything, amigo. But I keep coming back to something he said on the phone. The evidence is piling up, he said."

"And was it?"

"Not according to his lawyer. Not the way I saw it."

"So he just dreamed this up on his own?"

"No, not at all," I say. "Alma, his ex-wife, and a friend of hers named Margaret, they talked to him, evidently. That did the trick."

"Still," Omar says, "didn't you tell me he was innocent? If you thought he didn't do it, and his lawyer was sure all along she'd win, why the hell would he even care what Alma said?"

"That's the question, isn't it? The thing is, he didn't just care. It went way beyond that. He cared enough to kill himself."

Omar shakes his head, then goes back to polishing off the nachos on his plate. As he swallows the last morsel, he raises his fork like a baton. He has an idea. "Maybe you should go talk to Alma."

"Somebody probably should do that, anyway. Just to let her know about Benny, before she reads about it in the paper." I finish my beer and set the bottle down gently on the table next to Omar's budding collection.

*   *   *

Once in a blue moon the police get it right. Well, maybe more often than that; I mean, crime—real crime—is not like they show in the movies. It's not as complicated and nowhere near as romantic as it seems. It's all about people. And here's the thing: most people, if they've had a balanced, decent upbringing, don't commit crimes. Oh, they cheat on their taxes, or play fast and loose with their best friend's wife; a few of them go overboard now and then, drinking and doing dope. And some of that stuff can lead you down the drain, but I don't count it as criminal. More like foibles. Peccadilloes. Bad habits. Everyone has one or two. Me, I have a weakness for sour cream herring and hot pastrami, which is short of criminal, but probably suicidal. Most people, when you sit down with them and unwind in their back yards, with the sun shining and the kids playing tag and the dog rolling the fleas off his back in the grass—most people are kind and generous and law-abiding. And maybe a little boring; but you can't have everything, can you?

Late that afternoon, I'm mulling over these notions, thinking I've missed my calling in life, as I roll up behind Alma Wolf's hair salon on Doheny. They're piping in samba music at A Cut Above. It's a big glass establishment with eight black leather swivel chairs and mirrors everywhere you turn. Every chair is occupied. The eight seated women, all older, wiser victims of gravity, are chatting amiably back and forth, while eight other women (younger and frenetic) hover over them with scissors and towels and sprays and gels and blow-dryers. There's a cloying sweetness in the air that makes it hard for a guy like me to breathe. I stop at the reception desk, where a pretty, sad-eyed Asian girl with long black hair that she touches constantly sits with her legs crossed on a metal stool. She's been gazing at me steadily ever since I pushed through the glass entrance.

"I'm looking for Alma Wolf," I say. "She in?"

The girl smiles faintly; I've answered her most pressing question, I guess, and she points to the rear, where there are a series of cubicles. "I didn't think you were dropping by for a trim," she says. "And we're booked for the rest of the afternoon. But maybe you should make an appointment."

"Thanks," I say, slipping past her. "I'll take it up with my barber, Antonio. He's the only one I let near me."

Alma Wolf is in the last cubicle on the right. She's leaning back behind her desk. She's got a frilly white blouse on and tight lavender pants, and she's talking to someone on the phone—well, not talking so much as listening to some endless rant on the other end. She waves me silently into a chair on the other side, holds up a finger to tell me she'll just be another minute.

"Listen, I've got someone here that needs to talk to me," she says. "Let me call you back, okay?" She nods several times to concede or acknowledge something the caller is saying, then says okay, fine, goodbye, and hangs up.

We sit silently together for a couple of seconds. It's not much of an executive office she has—really just your basic proletarian cubicle. A laptop computer, half a plastic bottle of Evian water, a cupful of pens and pencils, a yellow legal pad, that's about it. No frills or family photos. Not even a view, unless you count the private parking lot behind the building.

"So, Mr. Parisman," she says. There's a hint of surprise in her voice. "What brings you here? I take it you're not looking for a haircut, are you?"

"Funny," I say. "That's just what your receptionist asked me a minute ago."

"Noriko's always trying to drum up business," she says. "What can I do for you?"

I hesitate then, wonder what's next. Sure, she's his ex-wife and she had her reasons for leaving him—good reasons, too, I'll bet—but twenty years is a long chunk of time to be connected. And it doesn't matter how smooth you are, Parisman, you're still going to open your big fat mouth now and shatter her feelings. Sometimes there's nothing to be done. *Ein breira*, as they say in Hebrew. You plunge ahead. I wipe a speck of imaginary dirt from my chin. "I've got some sad news for you," I tell her then. "I was just out to see Benny this morning."

"And?" Her eyebrows go up apprehensively.

"And I'm afraid . . . well, I'm afraid he's no longer . . . Alma, when I got there he was dead."

"What?" She doesn't weep, not immediately, but I can see she's stunned. Her brown eyes widen and for a second, maybe to distract herself with pain, she bites down hard on her lower lip. Her face freezes, and she sits up straight in her chair. "What?" she says again. The tears are there now, ready, waiting to fall. "What are you saying? I—I don't understand."

I keep talking and pretty soon it dawns on her, what I'm saying. And she stops sobbing, more or less. Her face is drawn, her eyes are bloodshot, and she's gone through a dozen Kleenex. She's still in shock; it's hard to get a coherent sentence out of her. I tell her about the morning phone call, how Benny said he was going to disappear, how I pleaded with him not to run. I tell her what I found at the house. The blood on the carpet. The gun. She seems to want to hear what I have to say, all of it; it's as if every bit of information, no matter how small or insignificant, helps her form a new skin, helps her heal.

"He used a .38 caliber pistol, Alma."

"Yes. Yes, you mentioned before. That he shot himself."

"Was it his? Did you know he had a gun? I mean, did you ever see it when you two were still together?"

She looks at me, makes a grimace. This is clearly a curveball. She's taken aback she didn't expect to be interrogated. "Why do you want to know?"

"Well, at one point he told the cops he didn't own a gun, didn't even know how they worked. And here he is with a .38 right beside him. It's just curious."

"The gun belongs to me, Mr. Parisman. Benny gave it to me when we split up. For protection, he said. Or maybe he just didn't trust himself to keep it—that could be."

"And it's registered in your name?"

"No," she says. "I doubt it's registered at all. Somebody gave it to Benny once after they did a private show in Las Vegas. I made him hide it in the garage."

"This person he got it from in Vegas, did he have a name? Did Benny ever tell you?"

She shrugs. "Maybe, probably. Sure. But it was a long time ago. I have no idea now. Don't ask me who he was. What I remember is, Benny said he and Al got paid really well, and it was all in cash. The gun was a little perk, like a party favor."

"Did Al get one, too?"

"That I don't know."

"Okay," I say. "So you had the gun at your apartment. Where'd you keep it?"

"In the bedroom. In my lingerie drawer." She looks at me. She's hurting, and I don't want to push her any further if I don't have to, but Alma has already changed the shape of this story in so many ways. She drove him over to Al's that night. And now the gun. "Benny was always worrying about me being alone," she continues. "Especially after we broke up. I didn't want to take it at first. I don't care about guns, I hate guns, and I really don't know how they work. But he'd done so much for me, writing checks, setting me up with this business. He gave me the gun and kept insisting I needed one now if I was going to live on my own. After a while, I just decided it was easier not to fight about it."

"And Benny knew where it was?"

"I guess so, maybe. But like I say, it was just there in the drawer. I never touched it. Never even thought about it."

Her cell phone is ringing. She looks down, sees who it is, but doesn't pick up.

"Aren't you going to get that?"

"It doesn't matter," she says. "I'll call her back. This is important." She reaches into her desk and comes up with a small vial of ibuprofen. "I do have a splitting headache, though." She unscrews the top, drops two blue tablets into her palm, and washes them down with Evian water. "It's been a helluva day."

"I think so too."

An elegant young Black woman with a pleated orange skirt and gorgeous braids pokes her head around the corner. "Hey, got a minute? I need to talk with you about scheduling next week," she says briskly. "Trisha has some kind of stomach flu and I really don't want the other girls—" She seems oblivious to the tragedy written all over Alma's face.

"Not now, Krystal. Let me finish up with this gentleman. Okay?"

Krystal points an index finger at her. "You got it." Then she's gone.

"So." She turns to me. "What comes now? A funeral? Benny never planned for anything like that. At least, not that I ever heard."

"Before there's a funeral," I say, "there'll be an inquest. The mavens down at the morgue have to make sure he did it to himself. Which, at the moment anyway, seems certain. Then, probably, yeah, it'll be time to bury him. And of course, the police are going to want to interview you about the gun."

"You're going to tell them?"

"I have to, don't I? Otherwise, I'm withholding evidence."

"But won't that get me in trouble?"

I make a face. "I don't see why. You had the gun. He knew where you hid it. He took the gun. No big deal."

"I guess you're right, Mr. Parisman." She takes another swallow from her water bottle.

"There is one other question I have," I say. "Then I'll be shoving off."

"What's that?"

"Benny made an odd comment on the phone. Something about the evidence piling up. Actually, he said that you and Margaret told him that. That you thought he might not win the case."

"Yes?"

"Well, see, that was the reason he gave for running away. Or disappearing. Apparently, you managed to convince him. So I was just wondering, you know, what that was all about—what you might have said to him."

Her eyes go wide again. "I wish I could point to something specific," she says. "We've had a bunch of conversations these last few weeks. That's all we've talked about every day—the trial, the evidence, what his chances would be."

"But you didn't know anything for sure."

"No, of course not. We were just . . . worried. There's a lot of uncertainty. It's like living with a cancer diagnosis."

"That may be," I say, "but his lawyer said the prosecution was working with a weak hand. I just spoke to her. She was sure she'd win. She's a pro. Why wouldn't Benny believe her? Why'd he hire her if he wasn't going to listen?"

She wags her head back and forth. Not a yes, not a no. "I told you before, Benny followed his own drummer. He could be brilliant in front of a camera. He could turn on the charm, light up the stage; but living with him, day after day—it wasn't much fun. I felt like I was always tiptoeing around him. He was strange, repressed, and—I have to say—a dull little man. He needed me to be there whenever he fell apart. Otherwise, I didn't exist. That's why I ended it with him. He never learned to share that other part of himself."

"And what about this Margaret? Who's she?"

"My girlfriend. Maggie. We've known each other for years. Benny was fond of her. Treated her like his kid sister. Only he never had

a sister. Or a brother, either. He was an only child, like me." She
chuckles then, to herself. "Maybe that's all we ever had in common."

*   *   *

I'm sitting by Loretta's bedside, stroking her hand, which is unusu-
ally cool today. There's a bouquet of fragrant white flowers in a glass
vase nearby; I want to say they're gardenias, but don't ask me—I'm
no good in that department. I lean over and read the little cardboard
note that's attached by a string. It's from Carmen, the wonderful
Cuban woman who cleaned our house and looked after her for so
many years when we were at Park La Brea.

I haven't seen much of her lately. I tried to keep her on when
I finally moved in with Mara, but she sold her car after she hit a
homeless person one night on the road, and the LA bus system
doesn't extend into the Hollywood Hills where we are; I would have
had to pick her up and drop her off later on Sunset for the trip back
to her home in El Sereno. It was too much.

Besides, Carmen was resourceful. She didn't need my money—
she was always going to succeed. In fact, the last time I ran into her
at Olympic Terrace, she told me she'd started her own cleaning business. I couldn't believe it. She already had six employees, she said, all
immigrants just off the boat from Belarus and Bulgaria. How they
communicated in English when none of them was fluent, I'll never
understand, but who knows? Maybe housework comes naturally to
some people. She showed them what needed to be done, divided
them into two-girl teams for safety, and set up all the appointments
by phone. She still cleans a few apartments every week, just to keep
her hand in, but now she has more time to spend at home with her
husband, who's retired from the trucking trade since he injured his
back. You're living the American dream, I want to tell her every time
I see her, but I don't.

I smell the flowers she's left for Loretta. Definitely carnations.
Well, as definite as I can be.

Loretta stirs, yawns in her bed.

"Hey, babe," I say. "Are you going to make a habit of this? Just lolling around in the sheets? You're not royalty, you know. I mean, don't get me wrong, it's nice work if you can get it." I wink, which always meant I was kidding, but I'm not sure she gets that anymore.

She rolls over in my direction, gives me a quick smile. "I was sleeping, Amos. I had a dream about Carmen."

"That was no dream," I say. I point to the flowers with my thumb. "She was here. Look what she left for you."

"Oh," she whispers, "oh, they're so beautiful. What kind are they?"

"Carnations, I think. But don't look at me. Am I a florist?"

"No," she says, clutching my hand. "You're a detective. *My* detective." She grins again, then laughs to herself.

In the olden days, before she got sick, we talked freely about what I was up to. She had opinions and a quick mind, and she'd often point out some small *nebbich* of a thing I'd overlooked. The brand of a woman's leather handbag, a Chanel, and what that said about her. The fact that someone had a huge arrest record for trespassing and disturbing the peace, but when you delve deeper, it was because he was big in the Civil Rights movement. A few times, that altered the whole picture. She would have made a damn good gumshoe herself, if she'd wanted to.

My phone rings. It's Lieutenant Malloy.

"I was just about to call it quits for today," he says, "but I thought you'd like to know that we found Benny Wolf's bags."

"Oh, yeah?"

"Turns out, he *was* planning to disappear. Well, maybe I shouldn't say that. What's true is, he had two small suitcases under a Mexican blanket in the trunk of his car. One of them was clothes and toothpaste, that kind of thing."

"And the other?"

"The other had clothes, too, on top. But below that, he had several fat envelopes full of cash."

"And where'd that come from?"

"Jason's been following the money trail. He emptied three local bank accounts last week. Also, he sold some treasury notes. We're still checking on the numbers, trying to match it all up. That could explain it. Meanwhile, it raises another question."

"Which is?"

"Well," he says, "if he really meant to run away, and if he packed a suitcase with cash, then why the hell did he change his mind? Why'd he kill himself?"

"You're suggesting he didn't?"

"Not at all. It was suicide, believe me. I don't have a final report back yet from forensics, but you don't need a medical degree to see what happened. His prints were all over the gun. The angle of the body. The path of the bullet. Okay, so he forgot to leave us a note. Big deal. Not all of them do."

I hear the sarcasm in his voice, and Malloy isn't prone to sarcasm. He's also tired and fed up and disappointed, which I understand. He thought this case was over; in his mind, he'd made his peace with it. He thought he knew how it was going to unpack itself. There would be a long, loud, sordid trial; the media would go ape and splash it all over the nightly news. Lives would be tarnished and ruined. And in the end, Wolf and Pupik would be remembered forever, but not because they made us laugh.

"I guess when a man's ready to end it all," I say, "there's no point in being polite, huh?"

"None," he says.

"You weren't able to trace the gun, were you?"

"Not yet," he says. "It's an older model. The serial number's been sanded off. We're still working on it."

I think about what I told Alma: that I had to let the cops know about where the gun came from, my duty and all, that I'd be withholding evidence if I didn't. It scared her when she heard me say that. Now I'm wondering whether her fear was justified. Alma was at the house on Beachwood the night Al died. And if she still had the gun afterward and found out about Lonny Dreyer, she had the means and the opportunity to take him out as well.

Malloy needs to hear that, I guess. I should tell him. Now's the time.

Only I don't. *She's not the killer,* I say to myself. *No way. Alma's an artist.* Alma's a hair stylist. A little too fond of chardonnay, maybe. A sad old *shicker.* But she didn't hate anyone. Why send the lieutenant down yet another rabbit hole?

I must have mumbled something incoherent then, because Malloy asks me if I've been drinking.

"No, um, no, Bill. Sorry. I guess I sorta spaced out. Senior moment. I'm just sitting here with Loretta. We're looking at flowers."

"Oh, no. Hey, I didn't mean to interrupt," he says. I suppose I've embarrassed him. He tells me to stay in touch, then he quickly hangs up.

"Who was that?" Loretta wants to know.

"My friend Bill. You remember him, don't you? Bill Malloy? Big, tall Irish cop?"

She sorta nods. Maybe yes, maybe no. Big and tall, that floats her boat, I'm sure. "Was he handsome?"

"He's okay, if you like that type. Not as cute as me, of course. I'm the one you love," I say. "I'm your cookie."

She grins at me. This is an old joke between us. One she still recalls.

CHAPTER 16

It's the weekend, the sun is just starting to burn up the pavement, and Omar is playing basketball with his brother-in-law and a bunch of the guys from work at Garfield High on Sixth Street. They're not very serious about it, I think. They're not working up much of a sweat, anyway. There are shouts of encouragement and arms in the air. Someone brought a cooler full of soda and cold beer, and the ones with their wife-beater T-shirts on seem to be scoring more than the skins, but nobody cares.

Omar sees me coming over. He sets up as if to shoot. Then he flips the ball nonchalantly to one of the other fellows leaning against the cyclone fence who is waiting his turn—a short, determined, heavy-set man with a mustache—and that guy comes in to replace him.

I point to the empty space on the bench beside me. "So, this is where you spend your Saturdays?"

"No, man, not lately. Saturday is when Lourdes and me go window-shopping. She likes to think about sheets and curtains, that kind of shit."

"So, what are you doing here?"

"Today she's going down to the Beverly Center with her cousin, Catalina. She's also pregnant, you know. They want to check out baby clothes. I can look at booties and onesies and blankets for maybe five minutes tops, then something happens inside here"—he points to his head—"in my cabeza, and I go crazy. Know what I mean?"

"So she told you to go play basketball."

"No, man. She didn't tell me. I told her."

We turn our attention to the game, which has gotten a little rowdier, but it's the same dynamic going on. The skins still can't hit the net.

"I've been thinking some more about Benny Wolf," I say.

"He's dead, right?" Omar says. "What else is there to think about?"

"That's true," I say. "Certainly as far as the police are concerned, yeah. But there are still a few loose ends, things I don't get."

"No one's paying you anymore, are they? If I were you, I'd stop worrying. Let it go."

"Actually, I just received a late-breaking check in the mail from Mr. Wolf." Omar looks at me uncomprehendingly, and I raise my hand. "Yeah, yeah, I know he's dead, but the U.S. Post Office doesn't seem to care. Anyway, I'd like to feel like I gave him his money's worth."

He sighs. "Okay, vato. So, what do you want to do?" He's been down this road with me before—many times, in fact. There's a weariness in his voice. Like Malloy, he doesn't have his heart in this case anymore; he wants to get it over with, and not just because this is his day off.

"Well," I begin, "here's what I've been thinking. Benny Wolf shot himself, right? He used a gun he gave to Alma a long time ago. He probably knew where she kept it, and he probably borrowed it the last time he saw her. Maybe she knew he took it, maybe she didn't. But the gun was hers, all along. That's the point. And that's why the cops never found it. Till now."

"Yeah, so what? I still say he's our killer."

"Because?"

"Because if he knew where it was, he could have borrowed it before. Hell, he could have borrowed it twice—first when he shot Al, then later when he did that writer friend of his. What's stopping him?"

"Nothing, I guess. Except that Alma was with Benny the night they went over there. She was standing right outside in the front yard. She never heard any shots fired. At least she never said so."

"That doesn't mean anything. Maybe she's protecting him."

"Maybe," I say. "But whoever killed Al and Lonny planned it out. It was deliberate. He or she had some beef. He or she wanted to destroy—not just Al Pupik—but his place in history. Whoever did this had *chutzpah*. You know what I mean?"

He shakes his head.

"*Chutzpah*. Nerve, cojones. And Benny was just not a take-charge kind of guy. Hell, he could barely bring himself to get on the freeway and drive into Hollywood. And then, of course, there's the suicide."

"What about it?"

"Well, it makes no sense. We're supposed to believe he put a bullet in his brain just because someone told him to. His ex-wife and her girlfriend thought his case was going badly. They talked him into it, is basically what he said."

"He wasn't depressed? I'd be pretty damn depressed if I was going to do something like that."

"Right. And he wasn't. At least when we talked on the phone. He called to say goodbye. He was going to pick up his marbles and run away. Come on, Omar. Does that sound like a stone-cold killer to you?"

"Not exactly." He looks at me. "So maybe it wasn't a suicide, then. Maybe Malloy's got it all wrong."

"There's a chance," I say. "But they'll figure it out. Those guys in the lab, they're pretty thorough. It's above my pay grade, in any case."

"So what? You think it was Alma?"

I wag my head. Omar reminds me of a feral cat at times, the way he reacts; he zigzags and pounces from one idea to the next. I can almost see his mind racing through all the possibilities. "Alma's not telling us everything she knows, that's for damn sure. She and her girlfriend Margaret talked to Benny just before he died. I don't know exactly when: they could have been the last ones to see him alive. We may never know what they said, but somehow they convinced him there was no way out."

"Didn't you tell me he was planning to disappear?"

I nod. "That's what he told me on the phone. Malloy said they found a suitcase in the trunk of his car. He had a couple of envelopes full of cash, too. I don't know how much, or how far he might have gotten, but still, that's what it looked like. Ultimately, you're always what you do, you know what I'm saying?"

Omar rubs some moisture off the side of his cheek. "How about this, then? Alma's the killer, okay. Alma's the killer, and Benny finds out. And maybe he's not as weak or as stupid as we think. Maybe he believed his lawyer, that they didn't have much of a case."

"Where are you going with this?" I ask.

"I'm just thinking out loud," Omar says. "He told you he was going to disappear. He announced it. So, what if that *was* the plan?"

"He could run, sure," I say, "but he must have known he wouldn't get far. A celebrity like that—somebody would spot him sooner or later, recognize him, turn him in."

"Exactly. And don't you think he'd figure you'd call the cops? He called you an honest man on the phone, right? A kind, honest man. Who better than you would care enough to call the cops?"

"Are you saying it was a setup?"

Omar shrugs. "I think he was torn. He could draw attention to himself if he tried to run away, and yeah, they could haul him in and he could plead guilty to everything under the sun, but that might not be good enough to save Alma."

"That's a lot to swallow," I say. "I—I don't know."

"Nobody knows," Omar says. "And we'll never get inside his head again. But think about it this way: she left him, but he didn't leave her. He's never stopped loving her, and he doesn't want her to go to prison. In the end, he finds a moment of courage and pulls the trigger. He shoots himself for her sake, to protect her. No one will ever know. Does that work? You like that any better?"

"That's a real Hollywood ending you're talking about, amigo. They don't write stuff like that anymore." My mind flips to the last scene in *A Tale of Two Cities*, the one where Sydney Carton is standing there facing the guillotine, thinking, "It is a far, far better thing that I do than I have ever done; it is a far, far better rest that I go to than I have ever known." Could Benny Wolf ever be that noble? Could anyone? I dunno.

"It's just a thought." Omar grins, seeing my dismay. "I could be wrong."

I'm about to respond when one of his comrades waves his arm and shouts at him in Spanish from center court.

"Oh, hey, I gotta get in there now, man. They need me. But give me a call this afternoon, okay? I'll be free after two."

*   *   *

I start to head home, then change my mind and wind up pulling into the lot at Canter's on Fairfax. When we lived in Park La Brea, I used to be a regular here, but now that I've moved up in the world, it's not on my radar as much. The restaurant is the same as it's always been; the bakery still has the same rugelach and apple strudel and babka stacked in trays under glass—well, not the same rugelach; it disappears pretty quickly. I see Reuben slicing salami in the deli, and across from him, people are lined up. They're coming forward in twos and threes to pay their tab to Doris and get their parking validated. Doris is eternal. I can't remember a time when she wasn't sitting on a stool behind the cash register, taking in the money and making change.

I grab a menu from the stack, and a new girl, an energetic sprite with deep blue eyes and red hair and pale skin, someone I've never seen before, someone who looks like she's destined to be in the movies someday, shows me to a booth. I'm about to ask her name, but then I check myself. *No, don't do that, Parisman; she'll take you for another dirty old man.*

I ask for a tuna melt and black coffee. I'm partial to their tuna melt because it comes on light rye, and somehow you don't see that much. What I don't care for is the dill pickle, which they always put on the plate, regardless. Nothing the matter with the pickle, mind you; pickles and delis go together. It just has nothing whatsoever to do with a tuna melt. I once had an argument—well, not an argument, more like a long talmudic discourse—with Reuben, who runs the place. Why do you throw in the pickle? I said. It's wrong. It's not wrong, he insisted. It's what we do.

I chew slowly on the tuna melt, chew it several times, in fact, because I want to savor it and because I want to fully digest it; and while I do, I mull on what Omar told me. Sure, it fits together. Alma could have gone back into Al's while Benny was slumped over in the front seat of her car. He would have let her in, they could have had words, things could have gone south, and she could have pulled out her gun and killed him. And she could have gunned down Lonny Dreyer. *Could have.* Right. Just like I could have been president of the United States if only I'd turned in my homework on time, or I could have been an astronaut and played golf on the moon. Anything's possible when you put it that way. I shake my head and take a long sip of coffee.

I'm deep in thought when the waiter comes along, holding two silver pots. "You want me to freshen that up for you?"

"Why not."

And as he's pouring, a fresh idea pops into my brain. I pull my phone out of my pocket and call Malloy downtown. Unfortunately, Remo picks it up. "He's in the ladies' room," he says, when he hears who it is. Why is it always me? I wonder. Why do I always bring out the natural snarkiness in him? "You're just gonna have to cool your heels, buddy."

"That's okay, Remo. You know what they say: 'They also serve, who only stand and wait.'"

"Oh, yeah? And what the hell's that supposed to mean?"

"Nothing. Just an expression, a line from a poem. Milton wrote it a long time ago. Before you were born."

"Milton who?"

"John Milton. You read him in high school English. You had to."

"Just because I had to, that didn't mean I always did it," he says. There's a hint of pride and defiance in his voice.

Even though it's against my better judgment, I press on. "The poem was called 'On His Blindness,'" I tell him. "See, he was blind at the end of his life, and this was his way of saying, well, that he still mattered."

"I don't know what the fuck you're talking about, Parisman. Are you always so full of shit? Anyway, here's the lieutenant."

An intelligent voice comes on the line. "What's up, Amos?"

"I'm sitting here at Canter's, Bill, and I got to wondering. You went through Benny's file cabinets upstairs, right?"

"We went through everything, sure."

"And I believe you might have found a will in one of them, didn't you?"

He pauses. "How'd you know there was a will? You go up there?"

"No," I say, "never. Cross my heart. I wouldn't do something like that."

"That's called breaking and entering, you know. So, how'd you know it was there?"

Once again we're strolling down this country road together, he and I. He keeps trying to walk a straight legal line while I keep telling him hey, it's a country road—it winds around old gnarly trees and rocks, but we still get to where we're going, don't we? "It's just a lucky guess, Bill. Stands to reason a man his age would have a will tucked away where someone would find it. Anyway, I wonder whether you looked it over."

"We did. He left everything he had to Alma. Which tells me how lonely he must have been at the end."

"How's that?"

"Well," he says, "she left him. Walked away. And still, he set her up with that hair-styling business. Truth is, he never stopped loving her."

"Funny you should put it like that, Lieutenant. That's exactly what Omar told me. *He never stopped loving her.* But that was to explain his suicide. It *was* a suicide, right?"

"I told you already."

"But I mean, that's not just your opinion. Forensics told you something more?"

"They're on board. Like I said, the final report won't be out for a few days more. But there's nothing suspicious about it." There's a pause over the phone. I wouldn't call it a pregnant pause, but Malloy is good at taking a hint. "Are you suggesting Alma might have had something to do with this?"

"I'm not suggesting anything. But it's never a bad idea to follow the money. People kill over money, last time I checked."

"That's low-minded of you, Amos. Anyway, he killed himself, and he has the right to squander his estate however he wants."

"Sure, sure. I just wanted to follow up. Thanks, Bill."

*   *   *

Mara has a swath of official papers and a yellow legal pad spread across the kitchen table the way she always does when her accountant says it's time to organize her taxes—brokerage statements, bank statements, that kind of thing—only it's the middle of summer.

"Aren't you getting ahead of yourself?" I say, leaning over and planting a kiss on the back of her neck. "Or did the market crash?"

"The market's not open on the weekend, Amos. No, with Gus gone and Violet heading off to college, I've just been thinking that . . . well, things are in flux, aren't they?"

"Things are always in flux."

"Exactly," she says. "Priorities change. And that's why now's as good a time as any to refocus my direction."

I pull up a chair across from her. "Sounds serious," I say. I frown, give her my best impression of an undertaker. "Tell me, are we breaking up? Shall I pack?"

"No, nothing like that. I plan on keeping you around. You make me laugh now and then. Besides, a girl gets lonely."

"Hey, boys too."

She squeezes my hand. "But I need to stay nimble. Make a few changes here and there."

"Like what?"

"Oh, I dunno. I'm going to sell the San Marino property for starters."

This would be a tectonic shift in her life, I think. The San Marino place covers three acres at least. And yeah, Gus bitched and moaned about the grounds crew, the pool attendant, and poor old Mrs. Loewe (the live-in housekeeper), but you couldn't possibly manage something that size without them. It's one of those smug, white, tree-lined palaces just down the street from the Huntington Library. I've only visited once; but when she lived there, Mara spent her days filling the six bedrooms they had with art and fresh flowers. She ordered around the plumbers and painters and electricians, and she put a lot of thought into the minutiae of dinner parties. She had Gus's checkbook; that helped. But still, it had to be a money pit and a lot of work. It couldn't have been all that rewarding, not for someone with her talent and intelligence. On the other hand, she'd invested years of her life there; the San Marino mansion was her magnum opus: her gift, in a way, to her husband. And now that chapter was coming to an end.

"My goodness," I say solemnly. "What's going to become of Mrs. Loewe?"

Mara shrugs. "Believe me, she'll be well taken care of. I had a long heart-to-heart with her on the phone this afternoon, and she understands. She never mentioned it, but her daughter and son-in-law have been after her to move in with them in Glendora. They have a mother-in-law unit out back, and Gracie—that's the daughter—has her old job waiting for her if she can just line up a few hours of child care. It's a perfect solution."

"And all the art? All that furniture?"

"There'll be an estate sale in a month or two. The more important pieces I'll probably donate to museums if they're interested. The truth is, I can't afford to sell them." She holds up an inch of paper. "It would just screw up my tax situation."

She doesn't ask me about my day at the office, and so I leave her alone at the table to work out the details of her new life. Sometimes I think Mara and I are like two tiny moons orbiting a giant planet. What we have in common is hard to say, but still we're here, and we're going round and round together, and it's become predictable and comforting over time. How we ever wound up as a couple at our age is beyond understanding. You could call that love if you want. I wouldn't argue.

*   *   *

Tuesday, around three o'clock, I put in a call to Omar and ask him if he wouldn't like to make some easy money.

"Doing what?" he wants to know. "Usually, when you say that it means you want me to bust into a house or beat up a total stranger."

"I pay extra for those things, you know that. No, this is simple. It might be a little time-consuming, but it's legal—and easy."

"My time is money these days," Omar says.

I know he doesn't mean that. He just wants me to acknowledge the fact that he's not quite as young and cavalier as he once was, that he's married now, on the cusp of becoming a dad, and that he's trying to juggle all those situations at once. We joke around, but we understand each other.

"I've been thinking some more about Alma Wolf," I tell him. "She's going to end up with whatever's left in Benny's estate, that's what Malloy told me. That doesn't mean she killed him, though."

"You told me he killed himself. We agreed—didn't we?—that he killed himself."

"Yeah, but with the same gun that did in Pupik and Dreyer. Which is why the cops think he killed them first. That's all very neat, and it puts this case to bed as far as they're concerned."

"So?

"So it's neat, but it's not true."

There's a pause while he takes this in. "Then we're looking at Alma."

"There's a lot we don't know about her, Omar. She put up with his shenanigans for twenty years. Somehow it didn't bother her, but then one day she walked away. I'd like to know why."

"You would, huh?"

"I think it would explain a lot. You never know what the inside of a marriage looks like, of course."

"Maybe she got bored," he says. "Maybe she got tired of being home by herself while they were always out on the road."

"That could be. And maybe she finally found someone else."

"Okay. That could happen. So, where do we go with this?"

"Alma drove Benny to the Beachwood house the night Al was killed. She's an easy drive from Lonny Dreyer's apartment. The gun that killed them was hers; she kept it in her underwear drawer. Also, she's been lying to us all along about her involvement. Now that the case is officially over, she probably thinks she's in the clear. I want you to keep an eye on her for the next four or five days."

"All day long?"

"No. Just the late afternoons, maybe till six. That should be enough. See where she goes, who she hangs out with. That kind of thing."

"I can do that," he says. "That's not hard. What are *you* gonna do?"

"I'll take the morning shift. I'll call you and let you know where she is when I break away. Also, I thought I'd go over to her place in a day or two and talk to her straight. Even if she doesn't end up admitting anything, it might shake her confidence, you know. Make her nervous. Nervous people make mistakes."

"Sounds like a plan," he says.

CHAPTER 17

I'm getting slightly long in the tooth for surveillance. On the other hand, I don't sleep that well at night as it is, so getting up at dawn to drive over to Alma Wolf's apartment is not much of a sacrifice, not in the big scheme of things. I bring along a traveling mug of black coffee, but I'm only planning to drink it if I absolutely must. And before I leave the house, I make quite sure my bladder is empty. You should pardon the expression, but that's the golden rule of stakeouts.

I had a friend once, another gumshoe, a nice guy about my age, Leo Sandoval. He was shadowing this cocaine dealer, a weasel named Arnie Bates. Bates was eating lunch at Bob's Big Boy in Pasadena; Leo could see him clearly through the window, only he had to pee in the worst way. He took a chance, he ducked into a gas station nearby, and when he came trotting back, Bates was sailing off down Colorado Boulevard. Not only that, Leo had locked himself out of his car. That was it for his career.

I pull up directly across the street from Alma's apartment. It's just past six in the morning. No traffic, not yet. LA is not like New York; it's not one of those cities that never sleeps. In fact, sleep is an important part of life here; we cherish our beauty rest. I only wish it worked for me. A pair of young female joggers in pastel shorts and tank tops goes past me at a leisurely tempo, chatting. They stop for the red light down at the corner, still jogging in place, still chatting.

I unbuckle my seat belt, drum my fingers on the steering wheel. The metal parking sign posted above my head says I'm only good for an hour, but none of the meter maids are up at this hour, so I can probably stretch it to two or three. Alma probably won't be moving around either, but you never know what'll turn up. That's another rule of surveillance. Wait. Pretend you're a spider. Sometimes good things just fall into your lap.

The sun rises, and soon after that, the summer heat shimmers across San Vicente Boulevard. I roll down my window, not to smell the jacarandas but so I don't bake. More cars start emerging from underground parking lots. They drive nicer cars in this neighborhood, I notice—new gleaming BMWs, Audis, and Saabs. Maybe that means they have money. Either that or they don't mind always being tapped out on their Visa. Hey, it's another working day in paradise.

*   *   *

Around ten-thirty she steps quietly out her front door, all dressed for business, and I track her to her hair salon on La Cienega. She drives a late-model black Nissan, which she parks around the corner in an all-day lot. I give Omar the license plate and location, and he takes over after lunch.

Upstairs at Olympic Terrace, I sit with Loretta and recite my adventures. Today of course it's all about Benny Wolf and the steep price of fame. How he seemed to have had a glorious life on stage and in front of the TV camera, loved by Ed Sullivan, loved by Johnny Carson, fawned over by millions of fans; but the truth is, he was weak. He was broken, afraid. A sad, unenviable man who had no self-esteem. A guy who walked his dog and overpaid everyone who took care of him or showed him the least bit of human kindness. I've thought about him more than I ever wanted to, I say. I tell Loretta that he was trapped, that he needed others kinda the way an old bull elephant who's spent his whole life in a zoo needs his keeper and couldn't possibly exist in the wild. Sometimes I think I bore her with my talk; she doesn't know any of the people I'm prattling on about, not in her current state, but she nods, nods and smiles at me, and every now and again she squeezes my hand, which I take as a sign of ancient affection. She hasn't forgotten everything. Finally, she closes her eyes and drifts off to sleep.

That evening after dinner, my phone rings. It's Omar.

"I followed her home," he says.

"So, just another day at the office then. No surprises?"

"Well, one surprise maybe," he says. "When she went to work, she was all alone, am I right?"

"Yeah."

"Not when she came back. She had a passenger."

"Boyfriend?"

"Girlfriend, if anything. A woman around her age. Skinny. White hair. Tight pants."

"That could be anyone, Omar. Maybe it was an employee. Maybe she was having car trouble. Maybe Alma was giving her a ride home."

"Then why'd they both go into her house? Why didn't she just drop her off where she lives?"

"Were they still there when you left?"

"What time is it now?" he asks. "I'm still here. They haven't moved a muscle."

"Seven thirty," I say. "You should go home. I'm not paying you overtime."

"I don't know why you pay me at all," he says. "Shit, all I did was sit here."

*　　*　　*

Before driving by to visit her again, I do some research. This is not my long suit. I usually just bump along with my intuition, but in this case my intuition tells me Alma Wolf is a liar; I want to know what's true and what's a lie. I call my pal Beverly, who works down in the vault at the Parker Center where the records are kept. It takes her a few minutes, but Beverly informs me that they have nothing on anyone named Alma Wolf.

"Nothing?"

"Nothing," she says. "She's clean. Not even a speeding ticket."

"You don't keep speeding tickets, do you?"

"No, but I thought I'd say that so you'd go away and leave me alone. You're a pest, you know that, Parisman?"

"How about Alma Morgenstern?" I ask. "That was her maiden name. It would be old. She came to LA thirty years ago, at least."

There's a sigh on the other end. "Morgenstern," she says. "Wait." The phone goes thunk. I can tell I'm pushing the envelope now. Beverly likes me, but she's not madly in love with me like some people. A box of See's dark chocolates at Christmas time can only buy so much gratitude. When she comes back on the line, she says that an Alma June Morgenstern was once arrested for assault and battery, plus drunk and disorderly conduct in a movie theater.

"What'd she do?"

"Looks like she was being rowdy, they asked her to leave, and she took a swing at the usher."

"That's all?"

"She broke his nose. I guess he wasn't expecting that kind of sudden response from a grown woman."

"Huh. And how was it settled?"

"The case never went to court. She spent a night in jail. Bailed out the next day. Her lawyer made some motions, and they dropped the charges when she agreed to pay the usher's medical bill. Sounds like she got off cheap."

"And does this lawyer have a name?"

"Petra Allison is what's written down at the bottom of the page. Now, anything else you need? It wasn't the crime of the century."

"No, thanks a lot, Beverly. You're a sweetie. Santa won't forget you this year."

"Fine," she says, "as long as he doesn't expect me to sit on his lap."

*　　*　　*

The next day, I phone Alma Wolf at work and ask her, would she mind if I came over to her place later on and talked. What about?

she wants to know. There's no suspicion, but mild surprise in her voice. Oh, I say, I just have a few loose ends I want to tie up. The police have quit talking to me, you know, and I'm kinda compulsive, I'd like to make a final report for my records.

She buys this and tells me I can drop by at three. Then, before she hangs up, she says she has another appointment at four thirty. Don't worry, I say, I'll make it quick and painless.

I ring her doorbell ten minutes early. She lets me in. She's all in white this afternoon. Very soigné, I think, for someone who supposedly just came from work—gold necklace, gold earrings, eye shadow, the works. She gives me her right hand. In her left is a long-stem glass of red wine. "Nice to see you, Mr. Parisman," she says laconically, leading me back to the living room, where we sit facing one another. The couch and chairs are the same as I remember, and I'm struck once again by the deliberate spareness. I glance at the paintings on the walls. If Alma did them, she's quite talented. I feel like I'm in a museum.

"I'd offer you some refreshment, but—"

"Oh, no, no," I say, "that's okay. It's way too early in the day for me, and like I told you, this shouldn't take that long."

She nods, takes a sip. "So, you said you had some questions."

"Loose ends, yeah." I pull off my spectacles, put them gently back on, find the perfect spot for them along the bridge of my nose. Then I flip open my cardboard notepad. I can already tell she's wary. "If it's all right with you, I'd like to start by throwing out a few names, people I've run across, see what they mean to you. Maybe you know them, maybe not."

"Okay."

"Marvin Rich."

"Who?"

"Sammy Abrams."

"Sorry."

"Joey Marcus."

A blank face. She shrugs.

"Charlie Teitelbaum."

"I've heard the name somewhere. I couldn't tell you what he does."

"Darius Shapiro."

"Darius—yes, of course. Darius was their manager. He quit around the same time Benny and I split up."

"Any idea why?"

"No."

"What'd you think of him? You must have met him, right? Was he decent? Was he a crook?"

"I sat across from him at a few restaurants. He liked to eat, as I remember. And he seemed perfectly fine to me, but you've gotta understand, I never tried to poke my nose in their business. I was a painter back then, they were comedians. Two entirely different worlds."

"Okay," I say. "Okay, I get it, that's reasonable. But I'm needing more. So how about this. I'm not trying to pry, but . . . how about you fill me in on your marriage."

"My marriage?" Her eyes widen, and she recoils; it's like the words leave a bad taste in her mouth. "That ended years ago."

"Understood. But you were still tight with Benny, right up to the bitter end. So, what happened? You change your mind afterwards? Are we talking buyer's remorse?"

"Benny," she concedes, "was always good to me. He helped me out, he was kind and generous, even . . . even when I walked away."

"I guess what I'm asking then is, why? Why did you walk away?"

"Why do you need to know that?"

"Because I'm still trying to make sense of what happened. Because it's not easy to shoot another person, which is what the cops think Benny did. And when someone turns a gun on himself? That's even harder to explain."

She crosses her legs, rolls her eyes desperately toward the ceiling, like she's fighting back tears, then she turns to me. "I couldn't live with him," she says at last. "That kind of love— over time—it—it smothers you. It was too close, I felt like I couldn't breathe."

She takes another gulp of wine, tilts her head to one side. This is private property I'm trespassing on; she doesn't want to talk, I can feel her shutting down.

"Why do you need to know this?" she asks. "Really, what's it got to do with your case? What's it got to do with . . . with anything?"

"Listen, Alma, Benny killed himself a few minutes after he got off the phone with me. But he didn't say he was going to do that. He told me he was going to disappear. He told me you and your friend Margaret convinced him he had no chance in court, so what was he going to do? He was going to run for it. That's not smart. That's foolish. That's crazy."

"I told you he was crazy, didn't I?"

"Yeah, you did, but he wasn't. He didn't act crazy. Not in front of me, at least."

"So, what are you saying?"

"Maybe you had good cause to leave him; you probably did. But Benny was a noble soul. He loved you to death. He'd do anything to save you. He gave you that gun, right? The one you kept in your underwear drawer to protect yourself?"

"I gave it back to him," she says defensively. Her voice is quavering. "That was the last time we saw him."

"And according to the cops, that was the same gun that killed Al Pupik and Lonny Dreyer. Now, I can't be sure about Dreyer, but you told me Benny was sitting in your car when you went back to talk to Al. So he couldn't possibly have killed him."

"No," she says, "I guess not."

"But *you* could."

"Me? Why would I do something like that?"

"Oh, I dunno. I could think of reasons. Maybe you were sticking up for Benny, for all the years of kindness he showed. Or you decided to protect him for a change. Or maybe you didn't plan it out exactly, you just wanted to humiliate old Al, give him a taste of his own medicine after all the shit he did to Benny. Is that why you told him to take off his pants?"

She puts down her glass, stands up. Her face is flushed. Now I've really crossed the line. "I don't know what the hell you're talking about, and I don't—I don't know what I ever did to deserve . . ." She bites her lip, points to the door. "I'm done with this! You hear me? Now get out of my house!"

Sometimes when things go sideways and the person you're talking to begins shouting at you, the first response is always to escalate, to raise the temperature, get in their face, shout right back. Me, I've never cared for that gambit; it's a good way to start a bar fight, but not much else. I stay put in my chair. I take a deep, neutral breath. I don't dare smile. To smile at her now would show weakness or condescension. Instead, I look her calmly, but squarely, in the eye. "I'm not accusing you, Alma."

"The hell you're not!"

"Please, please just sit down for a minute and let's think this over. You've been through an awful lot, I realize that."

Somehow, the truth, or at least the weight of this, registers. Or I dunno, it catches her off-balance. She folds herself back into the soft, welcoming couch, wipes what might have been a tear away from her face, and reaches compulsively for her glass of wine. We're silent for a moment, and it seems to be working.

"I didn't kill Al," she mumbles under her breath. "I didn't shoot anybody. I didn't. I—I couldn't."

"Why not? Because you weren't angry enough? Or because you weren't brave enough to pull the trigger?"

"I didn't kill him because I couldn't. I didn't have the gun."

"Where was it?"

"I don't know. Back in my underwear drawer, I suppose. Or Benny could have taken it. He said he had to use the bathroom before we left. My bedroom is opposite. So he could have had it hidden in his jacket. Maybe he came back to Al's later."

"Hmmm." I wag my head. "Okay. I can buy that. That's plausible. You might be right." I get slowly to my feet. She didn't really answer the question, I think, not to my satisfaction. But we're at an impasse. "Well, I guess I should be on my way. I'm sorry, Alma. I wasn't accusing you. I know to your ears it might have sounded a little harsh, what I said, but it's just my job. I try things out. I hope you understand."

The expression on her face doesn't change. It's still pinched and pained, and I can't decide whether that glare means she understands or not. Probably not. She doesn't bother to get up and show me out, either, but she's more or less back to the same temperature as before, which, if I had to, I'd call a plus.

I go across the street to my car. I can see her Nissan parked near the corner. Two cars behind that, under a lengthening shadow, I spot Omar sitting in his Camaro. He nods at me. When I get a block away, I call him up.

"She's got a hot date, vato. See where it takes you."

"Will do," he says.

*   *   *

I spend the rest of my afternoon in my office, which is also the guest bedroom, poking around on the keyboard, seeing what my computer might suss out about Alma Wolf or Alma Morgenstern. This is my second computer. It was a surprise, a birthday present from Mara; she thought it would enhance my career. At the time, I was perfectly content with the old machine, it was working just fine, and my career was practically over; but of course I didn't want to argue with her; so I kept my mouth shut, and now I'm glad I did. This machine is a whole lot faster than the first one. Not only that, I shamelessly slipped Violet a couple of twenties to add all kinds of bells and whistles that only young people know about. Now I can go to the moon with it if I want.

Alma Morgenstern's name appears in a few places. I don't know where she lived exactly, or how she paid the rent in those early days after she got off the Greyhound from Minot, but there was a singular purpose to her life. She painted. The people she hung out with were painters, poets, Bohemians. I'm guessing they weren't all that different from the ones I met in Berkeley when I came back from Vietnam. Alma fell in with them—it was as natural as rain. They were a tribe; they read the same books, sat through the same strange black-and-white Swedish movies, shared pizza and back rooms and spare couches in Silver Lake and Echo Park, passed joints around in the wee hours of the night, did whatever they had to do to get by. Alma was more motivated than most, or maybe she had more talent than the rest. She soon had art exhibits all over Los Angeles, small galleries and group shows, but she was building a portfolio, clearly on a path. She won a few grants. A critic spoke highly of her in the Arts section of the *Times*. She even taught for a semester at Cal Arts in Valencia. It was happening for her. Then, suddenly, it all stopped. Right about the time she met Benny Wolfe.

I pick up the phone, call Omar. "Okay, so where are you?"

"She's at this gallery in Westwood. I didn't catch the name when I walked in," he says. "But it's some kind of opening. Can you hear me, Amos? It's all glass and metal in here. Pretty noisy."

"I hear you. Sorta."

"I'll talk louder," he says. "They've got people walking around with champagne and shrimp on a stick. Little disgusting things with truffles, looks like shit, you know what I mean?"

"I know what you mean."

"The shrimp is okay, and the champagne is cold and fizzy, but you know me, I'd rather have beer."

"Forget the snacks, Omar. What's she doing?"

"Hell, I dunno. She's over in a corner. She just hugged some old woman with a lot of jewelry on her neck. Now she's talking to another one. Everybody's glad to see each other. There's art on the walls. Too pricey for me, but still."

"Sounds like she's having fun."

"Yeah, well, she's not a weeping widow, if that's what you're looking for."

"I'm not looking for anything in particular. Just stay with her, okay? She's lied so much about this case, there's something weird going on; I just need to iron it out."

"Right," he says. "Oh, I almost forgot. It may not mean anything, but that TV guy, the one we went to see in Laurel Canyon,
he's also here. Could be just a coincidence."

"Charlie? Has he seen Alma?"

"Don't think so. Not yet. He's down at the other end. Nice tan
suit. Him and his girlfriend are looking at a painting with another
couple."

"Alma told me she didn't know Charlie Teitelbaum. Heard the
name, is all."

"Well, maybe that's true."

"No, what's true is she's been lying."

"Listen, Amos. There's a hundred people in this place. They all
like art. Alma's one of them; Charlie could be too. You don't think
that's possible? I'm always running into movie stars in the men's
room when I go to the dry-cleaners. We all need our shirts ironed.
It happens. Accidents happen."

"Sure, they do. But not here. Just keep your eye on her, okay?
And call me back when she starts talking to Charlie Teitelbaum."

"You mean if."

"I mean when," I say. Then I hang up.

CHAPTER 18

$\mathbf{F}$ ive minutes later I'm still sitting there in front of my computer, wading through a less-than-riveting demographic description of Minot, North Dakota, when the phone rings again.

"You were right," Omar says. "They're in the middle of a deep, dark chat."

"Is Charlie's girlfriend with them?"

"No, she's off looking at a metal sculpture, I think. No, she was there. Now she's headed toward the bar. I might wanna go there myself. It's free."

"Never mind her, Omar. It's a shame we can't get closer to Charlie and Alma. I'd love to hear their conversation."

"You want me to move in closer?" he asks. "I can do that."

"Not unless you're in disguise, no. If Charlie spots you and remembers that little incident down by his pool, we're fucked."

"Sorry, old man," Omar says, "I am who I am. I didn't even bring my sunglasses from the car. That might have helped."

"Okay, then," I tell him. "So just watch what goes on."

"They're talking. I can't read lips, but Alma doesn't look so pleased to see him. Oh, now he's taking something from inside his jacket, a manila envelope. He's giving it to her."

"And is she . . . is she opening it? Reading it?"

"No, man." Omar is whispering now. "She's just staring straight at Charlie. Now she frowns. She's stuffing it into her purse, snaps it shut. She's not saying a word. She's pissed. Not Charlie, though. Charlie seems satisfied, you ask me."

"How do you figure?"

"Well, he's grinning, for one thing. Has this know-it-all kinda look. Now he's got his hand on her shoulder, he's giving her a sweet little squeeze. She doesn't like that. Nope. She shakes him off. Now she's walking away."

"Stick with her, Omar."

"What about Charlie?"

"Charlie's done whatever he came for. He'll probably be heading for the exit shortly."

"Yeah, well, first he's gotta rescue his lady friend from the bar," Omar cautions. "That might not be easy. She looks like she's settling in for the night."

He hangs up then. It's almost six o'clock, but the sun is still hanging like a fat wafer in the sky. I go out back, grab the hose, and start watering the garden Mara's been trying to put together on our hillside. She had ambitious plans, but the soil is parched and gravelly and won't allow for the practical stuff her parents had in their plot back in New Jersey. No beefsteak tomatoes or cucumbers. Now she's got a swath of ice plants in there, which looks pretty spectacular if you're into fuchsia; you can't eat them, of course, but that's life. I stand there holding the hose for ten or fifteen minutes. You can see the Capitol Records Building in the distance and hear the rush-hour thrum of the Hollywood Freeway down below. This is what it sounds like this time of day. Everyone just wants to go home.

Omar calls again to tell me Alma is now at a bar on Sunset called Pilar's. That she's been there for some time. That he thought seriously about going in, but instead parked across the street. Why? I ask. Because it seems like only lesbians are trooping in and out, is his answer, and it's a small place. "They would see me," he says. "They'd notice me, and then what?"

A little while after that, the phone in my pocket rings once more and he lets me know she's headed for her place.

"Alone? Or with a friend?"

"She's the only one in the car, if that's what you mean."

"Where is she?"

"Just turned onto San Vicente."

"Okay, Omar. That's great. You can go home now. Call it a day."

"Call it a day? You're not gonna follow up?"

"Sure I am. I'm going right down tonight to see her. That envelope in her purse is important. I'd love to get a peek at it. And Alma and I have other things to talk about. But I can handle it. You don't have to be there."

"Okay," he mumbles after a bit, "if that's what you want." I hear the doubt in his voice, and maybe more than that—anxiety. He doesn't say it, he doesn't have to, but it's clear that in the back of his mind, he's moved on from Benny; now he's convinced that Alma's the killer. I can't say I blame him. Alma's up to her neck in this mess, one way or another. "Just *cuidado*," he says, "know what I mean?"

I take a quick shower and shave, then rummage around in the bedroom for something appropriate to wear. She won't be expecting another visit from me—not so soon, anyway. I throw on my coat and tie and strap my Glock into the leather shoulder holster. It feels good sitting there—snug and secure. And best of all, loaded, though I doubt very much I'll need it. Then as I pass through the kitchen I tell Mara I've got one more meeting tonight. "What time will you be home?" she wants to know.

"Why?"

"It makes a difference what I cook for dinner, that's why. If you're back in an hour, it's shrimp salad. If you're later than that, I may do something creative with the chicken. There's a Lebanese dish I've been wanting to try."

"I see. Probably later." I tell her not to wait around for me, just make whatever pleases her and leave me a portion.

She gives me a hug and a peck on the cheek, warns me gently as I open the front door to be careful.

"You're the second person in the last twenty minutes to tell me that," I say. "You know something I don't?"

She smiles. "No, I just couldn't help but feel that bulge inside your coat. You don't normally bring a gun to a meeting, do you, Amos?"

"All depends who it's with," I say.

*   *   *

The lights are on in Alma Wolf's apartment when I ring the bell. But when the door finally opens, it's not Alma but Margaret Mooney staring at me. She's holding a half-empty glass of white wine, and she's dressed more upscale than the first time I saw her. Not much jewelry or makeup, but she's got a lovely lavender tunic on with tiny microscopic flowers and tight silver satin pants. She's barefoot, too, but I don't notice that right away.

"Hi," I say. "You remember me? I'm Amos—"

"I know who you are," she says. There's something in her voice, not anger, but despondency, a weariness with the whole world. "Come in. Alma's still in the shower. She'll be out in a minute."

I hesitate. "Sounds like I'm interrupting. I can come back another time."

Margaret shakes her head emphatically. "No, come in, sit down. You have more questions, I'm sure. That's what you're all about. So come on. Let's be done with them."

I trail in after her like a puppy dog down the hall and grab a soft spot on the far end of the couch. I pull out my cardboard pad and the stub of a No. 2 pencil I always carry around. "While we're waiting, you mind if I ask you a few things?"

"Me?" she says. "What do I have to do with this?"

"Maybe nothing," I say. "But I'll bet you can fill in some blanks. Nobody has all the answers—it's a mosaic."

"Okay, sure." She leans back, then runs her free hand through her hair to freshen it up, and squints. I've probably interviewed more skeptical people in my time, but I can't remember when. I also don't think she cares much for me. Because I'm a guy, all right, but also because I'm an incorrigible snoop. That's okay, I've been called worse.

"Why don't you start by telling me how you and Alma met?"

"Through Benny. Years ago. I don't know if she ever mentioned it, I started as a comedian. I tried out at the Comedy Store and the Ice House in Pasadena, the Laugh Factory, all those spots. I even had an agent once who thought I was hysterical. The next Joan Rivers, he called me. It never went far, of course."

"But you were a regular there?"

"For a short while." She takes a long, determined gulp of her wine, finishes it off, sets it down on the coffee table.

"So then you must have known Marvin Rich and Sammy Abrams, that whole crowd."

"Every single one," she admits. "We all fell by the wayside. It's a brutal business."

"But you're still friends with Marv and Sammy?"

"Friends might be a stretch. I see them every once in a blue moon. Not so often, though. We stick to ourselves. Besides, they bring back memories."

"Wanna tell me what happened to you?"

"Not particularly." She shrugs. "I had some success here and there. I could get people to laugh under certain circumstances. There just weren't enough of them, as it turned out."

"And how long did it take you to realize this?"

"Oh, I dunno," she says. "When my agent dropped me. When the phone stopped ringing. After six months of silence, things go sideways." She points at her head. "Your mind starts playing tricks on you. You cash in your life savings. You make believe you're on a diet, talk yourself into just two meals a day. Pretty soon, it's not enough to be thin and gorgeous, you start thinking about other career opportunities, know what I mean? Waitressing suddenly sounds exotic. Paying the rent takes on a whole new level of poignancy."

I put down my notepad. "You must have been pretty bitter."

"Is that what it sounds like? I'm not anymore. Honest."

I make a little face. "You're not very convincing, you don't mind my saying so."

"I don't mind what you say," she says coolly. "I also don't care."

"No?"

"No. That was then, this is now." There's an open pack of Benson & Hedges and a ceramic jar filled with wooden matches sitting on the coffee table. She reaches forward, taps out a cigarette, and lights up, blowing the smoke ostentatiously in the direction of the ceiling.

"Okay," I say. "So, what about now? What are you doing with yourself?"

"Right now, I'm selling dresses and jewelry in a shop on Santa Monica. I just started last week, so I'm still on probation. The owner hasn't made up her mind. Before that, I ran an art gallery in Venice. Before that, I was a dog walker. Nothing lasts forever, right? But that's okay. Kinda liberating. Tomorrow, who knows? I may run for governor."

"You're funny."

"Don't get me started," she says.

The bedroom door opens then, and Alma comes bounding out, smiling, humming to herself. Her hair is still damp from the shower. She's changed into a floppy, rust-colored sweater and jeans. Like Margaret, she's also barefoot. She stops humming the second she sees me.

"Oh, I didn't . . . I didn't know we had company," she mumbles.

"Mr. Parisman's been quizzing me about my past," Margaret says breezily. "But mostly, I think it's you he wants to talk to. Come on, join the party."

Alma finds a snug place on the couch, not too close to me but right across from where her friend is sitting. Then she notices the cigarette smoke lingering in the air. She rolls her eyes, shakes her head.

Margaret gets the message at once. "Fine," she says now, reluctantly stubbing it into an ashtray.

"I thought we'd finished our conversation, Mr. Parisman," Alma says, turning to me. "What brings you back?" She's only vaguely curious about this, I can tell. Hard to plumb another person's soul, of course, but judging by the way her arms are folded defiantly across her chest, I'm sure she'd just as soon I fell down a mine shaft.

"Oh, this and that," I say. "The thing is, at my age, I don't always sleep so great at night. I have to get up three, four times. Sometimes every hour. To pee, you understand. We men, well . . . it's exhausting. But that's not your issue, is it?"

"No, not at all. I sleep perfectly fine, thank you."

"Good, good. Because I don't, and let me tell you, I wouldn't wish that on my worst enemy. But anyway, when I can't sleep, things come to me in the middle of the night—I'm walking around in the living room, three o'clock in the morning—things don't add up and—"

"You have questions?" She glares at me. I've managed to thoroughly irritate her now; she wants this over with.

"Just a few. If you don't mind."

She nods.

"Okay," I say. "Tell you what: I'll cut right to the chase. Last time we talked, I tossed a bunch of names at you. Most of them you swore you'd never heard of, is that right?"

"I knew Darius," she says. "The rest of them, no."

"I asked you about Marvin Rich and Sammy Abrams."

"And I think I told you they didn't ring a bell."

I shoot a brief glance at Margaret; her eyes have gotten much wider, and she's leaning forward in her chair. "It's curious," I say, "because your friend here knows them well. They were all stand-up comics together back in the day, like her."

"So what? I still don't see your point."

Not everyone feels as strongly about the truth as I do. I get that. With me, though, it's always been a thing. Somebody opens his mouth and blurts out a lie, it rubs me the wrong way. Almost like a fire alarm. Or those awful jarring sounds that go off when someone tries to break into your car. Hard to ignore. For most people, though, words don't matter. It's not that they're born liars, exactly. They're just human—they just want to make more of their life. A very successful screenwriter, a guy who's won all kinds of Oscars and Emmys, once told me that the truth bored him. Truth is like a shabby suit of clothes, he said. And really, why would you want to wear shabby clothes when there are so many other wonderful things in your closet? That's something I'm still working on.

"You used to go to the Comedy Store, didn't you? And the Ice House? When you first got to town? Isn't that how you met Benny?"

She frowns. "That's where we met, yes. One of those clubs."

"So see, they would have been there, too. That's my point. They're small places. It's not Dodger Stadium. You would have met them, maybe sat down with them afterwards, had a drink, talked shop. Something like that. Especially if you were with Albert and Benny. It stands to reason."

"You're right," she says calmly. "I'm not going to say you're wrong. I might have been in the same room. But that was what—thirty years ago?"

"At least."

"And do you remember everyone you knew from thirty years ago? Everyone you had a drink with? Every two-bit comedian you saw on stage? Really?"

"Margaret here is still in touch with them."

"That's wonderful," Alma says. "I'm sure they're lovely people. But we don't share all our friends. That's not how it is."

"Okay, I'll give you that." I put down my notepad. "But you share an awful lot. And you do live together. I'm not off-base there, am I?"

Margaret beams at me, then looks over at Alma for confirmation.

"We've been a couple for a few years now," Alma says.

"More than that," Margaret adds proudly; "five years next month." She rises out of her chair and heads for the kitchen. "I'm going to start on dinner," she announces, "and maybe replenish my wine. Would anyone else care for some?" No, we would not.

There are a few awkward moments of silence between us after she leaves. Alma Wolf is a complicated person, I think. Very evolved. An artist. A fashionista. A wounded wife. A lost little maid from Minot, North Dakota.

She stretches her arms in the air, then brings them gracefully into her lap. "So, why did you bother to come here, Mr. Parisman? To see if I was a lesbian? To catch me in a lie about Maggie's old buddies? Was that so important to your case?"

"No, not so much. I really came by to talk about Charlie Teitelbaum."

"I told you before, I've heard the name, but—"

"But the two of you have never met. Yes, you told me."

"That's right."

I shake my head, raise a cautionary finger. "Well, now," I say, "that's the part I'm wrestling with."

"Oh, yeah?" she says. "And why would that be?"

"Because just a few hours ago, you were standing around chatting with Charlie down at that art gallery in Westwood. I know you were. I have a witness."

This had been a normal conversation until then, a civilized ping-pong match we were having; she was acting pleasant, self-assured, smiling, the way all women are taught from infancy to smile. Now she tenses up. "I don't believe you. I went to an art opening, okay, that's true, but I didn't speak to anyone."

"Let me help you remember," I say. "There was this slick, older, polished guy who came up to you. He had a gorgeous girl on his arm, a young thing, and you probably wondered what she saw in him. Then she took herself off to the bar, and while she was gone he slipped you a big fat envelope. You remember that? He had a tan suit on. I'm guessing it was Italian. Charlie's fond of Italian. Were you expecting him, Alma? Did he tell you he'd be there?"

"I don't—I don't know what you're talking about," she stammers.

"I'm talking about the envelope," I continue. "My witness, who'll be happy to testify in court, by the way, says you shoved it in your purse. That you didn't even open it. And then somewhere along the line Charlie put his hand on your shoulder. He was very determined, and he was leaning in and he kept going at you and going at you, and finally you'd had enough. My witness says you walked away. Shook him off. Now, are you going to tell me you don't remember any of that?"

Her eyes are fixed on the carpet, and her lower lip is starting to quiver. "He's a vicious man," she admits, "an awful, greedy, manipulative son of a bitch. I never knew—I never knew people like that existed before."

"I'll give you that," I say. "Charlie is used to being in charge. He's an executive. He doesn't like it when people get in his way."

"I was never in his way," she insists. "I didn't do anything."

"So, what did he give you? What was the problem?"

"I'll show you," she says, rising. "Wait here." She vanishes into her bedroom and a minute later reappears with a manila envelope in her hand. She lays it down on the coffee table between us. "Benny left me everything in his will. Maybe you know that. His whole estate, everything, including the winery in Sonoma. That came from Charlie. Charlie fronted him the cash for that. It wasn't a gift, he said—it was always an investment. Nothing was ever written down, but still. Now, he wanted me to sign the whole property over to him. I had to, he said, or else."

"Or else what?"

Her eyes blink, they move rapidly back and forth around the four corners of the living room. She doesn't answer me right away; and when she finally does, the tone of her voice has changed: now she is almost whispering. "Charlie . . . Charlie started talking about a Japanese friend of his. Well, maybe not a friend. Someone he knows. Akihiro, I think he called him."

"I've met the man," I say.

"And he explained that this guy, this Akihiro, was a hard worker, but he had a problem with his temper. Ever since he was a teenager, Charlie said. He was always struggling to keep it in check. One minute he'd be fine, then something would happen—a phone would ring, or a door would slam, somebody would say something rude, or look at him funny, and he'd fly off the handle. Just explode for no reason at all. Always getting into trouble. He almost killed a man once in a bar fight. Unpredictable, Charlie said. A time bomb."

"Is that all he said?"

She shakes her head, bites her lip. "No. He kept pressing me. He suggested I sign the papers right away and mail them back. He gave me a week. He's a patient man, he said, a civilized man. He didn't want me to think badly of him. This was just business. Something we can settle easily. But I need to sign. It won't go well if Akihiro gets involved. What he said. Then he put his hand on my shoulder and squeezed it. That's when I walked away."

I stare at her for a while. For a moment I consider picking up the sealed envelope in front of me. I could read it, I suppose, but it's not necessary. "So, what are you going to do?"

She frowns. "I'm an artist," she says. "I don't live in that world, and I don't like being pushed around. But it's not about me. Maybe Benny should have thought more carefully when he fell in love with a winery. He had a good heart, but he was always getting ahead of himself, tripping over his dreams. Maybe that's the big lesson."

I sense a presence behind me and tilt my head back toward the kitchen entry. Maggie has been standing there with a bottle in her hand, glaring. "Charlie's such a pig," she mutters. "Somebody should have put him out of his misery by now. Hell, I'd do it myself if I had the chance."

"I don't want to talk about this anymore," Alma says. "You hear me? You don't get to decide. As far as I'm concerned, he can keep his fucking winery."

CHAPTER 19

Bill Malloy is tucking into a cheeseburger at the Laurel Tavern on Ventura Boulevard when I arrive.

"Hey, man, I thought you gave that stuff up for Lent," I say, sliding in opposite him.

"Oh, I did, Amos. I do every year, in fact, but every once in a while, you know how it is: a man's gotta eat."

I catch the waitress's eye and order the same thing, plus an iced coffee, no cream or sugar. Bill looks more relaxed than I've seen him in a long time. He hasn't mentioned why, but word gets around, even in a buttoned-down place like the LAPD. It's because his nemesis, Captain Mason, has finally moved on. Also because the interim guy, Norm Fischer, is a pal of his. They used to play pinochle when they worked together at the Sunset Station in the olden days. Malloy is smiling. He takes another bite, wipes the juice off his chin. Norm Fischer and this burger are the two best damn things that ever happened to him, he says.

"You're probably also glad you don't have to go looking for Al Pupik's killer anymore," I say. "That must be a relief."

"You got that right." He looks at me then, lays the hamburger down on his plate. "Why are you even bringing it up, Amos? I thought we both agreed that that case was closed."

"You agreed. I'm still thinking about it."

"Meaning what?"

"Well, I agree with you that Benny killed himself. *Why* he killed himself is another question, probably one we're never going to get to the bottom of. But as far as Al and Lonny are concerned, I have no idea who did it. It wasn't Benny, though."

"Because?"

"Because, according to Alma, who drove him to Al's that night, Benny ended up in the passenger seat afterwards, and from the front yard, she could still see Al pacing around in his living room. Alma had to talk Benny into going there in the first place. She was the one who stood up for him. Also—and I just found this out—the gun Benny used on himself? He'd given it to Alma years ago to protect her. And again, according to Alma, they didn't bring the gun along. Not that night."

"Alma drove him?"

"That's what she said."

"And the gun was hers?"

"No, it belonged to Benny. He gave it to her."

"And where'd he get it from?"

"It was a gift from someone in Vegas. Someone disreputable, I suspect, Vegas being what it is."

"I see." Malloy chews slowly on his burger, gives himself ample time to swallow. Ideas are coming fast and furious now. "All right. So maybe Alma drove Benny back, retrieved her gun, then returned later on and shot him. How about that?"

"It's possible. Alma had the opportunity, and if the murder weapon was right there in her bureau, well, that sorta puts her in the hot seat, right?"

"Possibly. Maybe. I can picture it."

"Me too," I say. "But then I keep coming up short. Where's the anger? The rage? That's what I want to know. Alma may not have cared for Al—hell, he rubbed everyone the wrong way. But that doesn't translate to murder, does it?"

"Not usually. Not by itself."

"Plus, she told me she never even wanted the gun, didn't know which end was up. She just took it because Benny was so insistent.

Stuffed it in her underwear drawer, she said. Never bothered to look at it."

"And you believe her?"

"I do."

"Well, you're probably right, but we should drop over there anyway and get a statement. At this point, it'd just be a formality, of course. I mean, as far as the DA and the LAPD are concerned, this is a done deal."

We gaze out at the traffic floating along on Ventura Boulevard and make small talk. Bill carefully devours his meal. What I've just said to him is upsetting at some level; like me, he would love to drill down to what really happened, but that's above his station. I'm also guessing his recent run-in with Captain Mason has scared him more than he's willing to let on; if it didn't, at least it's made him think twice. He's very aware about which side his bread is buttered on.

It's a little before one. There's a steady cluster of leather-clad motorcyclists puttering by, heading toward an eventual rendezvous with the Pacific Coast. They don't look particularly menacing—more like a bunch of well-heeled neighbors who just forgot to shave this morning, dentists and engineers and middle managers out for a leisurely ride on their shiny black machines. Some of them are loners; a few have wives and girlfriends clinging grimly to their backs.

"I'm going to keep digging, Bill. It may not change anything, I know, but I owe it to my client. He paid me a lot more than I deserved. The way I see it, there's still time left on the clock."

Before I get up to leave, I mention that Alma Wolf's getting pressured by Charlie Teitelbaum; all of a sudden he wants her to fork over the winery to him. I guess he sorta has a point, I say.

"No, he doesn't," Bill says. "He should have thought about that a long time ago. He'd get laughed out of court."

"He's not going to court with this. That's not his style."

And then we both agree that what he's up to is not right, it's rude, also that Charlie Teitelbaum's a selfish, despicable, one-note individual. But so what? What can you do?

"Nothing," Bill concludes. "The world's a dumpster, that's all. It's made for guys like him. Unless he crosses the line somehow, we just have to sit here and wait."

"*You* have to sit here," I say. "You have a badge. I don't."

"Don't get any ideas," he warns.

As I head back up Laurel Canyon, I wonder what's gotten into me. Why the hell did I say that? I don't work for Alma Wolf. And I'm not stupid enough to try to take down people like Charlie. Not alone. Besides, Bill's right, he's not my problem. There will always be reptilian types like him out there slithering around in the dark, pretending to be saints while feasting on whoever gets in their way. That's America, isn't it? So maybe Alma's getting off easy, I think, learning this lesson now. That winery was never really hers to begin with.

I call Omar, ask him what he's been up to. "Well, I was doing what you told me to do, shadowing Ms. Wolf," he says. "But that wasn't so interesting. Hell, all she does is work and go home and drink. But then, about half an hour ago, I spotted that friend of hers."

"You mean Maggie?"

"The white-haired chick. The one you said she lives with."

"That's her."

"Yeah, well, she came out of the beauty parlor and got into Alma's car. So I decided what the hell, I'll take a chance, tail her. And guess where she ended up?"

"Surprise me," I say.

"I'm parked down the street. She just rang the doorbell at Charlie Teitelbaum's," he says. "Not only that—she has a gun."

I tell him I'm maybe five minutes or so away from where he is and to hang tight. "How do you know she's got a gun?"

There's a silence, and I can almost see the smirk on Omar's face. "How about I saw her take something out of her purse. How about she was standing there at the curb, checking to see if it was loaded. How about I know what a goddamn gun looks like, Amos."

"Hey, man, don't yell at me. I'm just asking. What's she doing now?"

"Dunno. The door opened. She was talking to someone. Now she just walked in."

"You have your weapon with you?"

"I wish. It's back at the ranch in Boyle Heights. I guess I didn't figure I'd be needing it for a stakeout. Especially, you know, for an older woman."

"Okay, okay, just stay where you are. I'm on my way." I'm over the hump at Mulholland Drive and slaloming downhill as fast as I can. There's afternoon traffic, but everyone seems to lean into these curves at a breakneck speed. I take a sharp right at Lookout Mountain, feel my holster and gun snug against my chest as the car starts to climb.

When I get to Alto Cedro, I see Omar standing around in front of Charlie's place, pacing back and forth with his hands jammed in his pockets.

"What's happening?"

"Can't tell." He shrugs. "But I just heard noises from inside. Sounded an awful lot like shots to me."

"I'm going in," I tell him.

"Not without me," he replies.

"You don't have a gun." I start to move forward, then turn back. "You stay put. Call the cops. Tell them what's happening. I don't want you getting hurt." I pull out my 9mm Glock then, release the safety, and race toward the house.

I learned long ago in the Marine Corps how to advance on an enemy. You pick it up quick when you have to. How to crawl through the tall grass on your belly with your rifle cradled lovingly in your arms. How to ignore the bugs and the heat and the fear and the pounding in your rib cage. How to filter out the screams of your buddy ten feet away. How to hold the shit in your pants and keep your eyes on the objective. This is different, though. I'm walking into an air-conditioned shooting gallery, and I've no idea whose team I'm on.

The front door is ajar. I push it open, crouch down, point my automatic east, west, straight ahead. It's dark in the foyer, but a few feet in, my foot stumbles over Wendell, the elderly butler. He's facedown on the carpet. I grab his limp wrist, check for a pulse; there isn't one. Then I slink along the side of the hall toward Charlie Teitelbaum's office. Before I can get there, I hear a soft, low moan coming from a room on the left. I poke my head in. Akihiro is down on his knees, pitched over on a white marble floor next to a toilet. He's gripping his belly with both hands, kneading it. His fingers are red and wet. He glances up at me. There's a dull, faraway look to his eyes. He's not dead yet, but the color is draining from his face. He hasn't got that long. He moves his lips, tries unsuccessfully to speak. I lower my gun and back away. I keep inching forward. Charlie's office is directly ahead. The door is shut. There's a lively but muffled conversation in progress. Behind me comes a slapping of feet, a quick scampering sound like a dog running through puddles, and I wheel around. It's Omar. He's moving fast and he's practically closed the gap between us.

"Get out," I hiss at him. "She's shooting people left and right. Get out!"

He shakes his head. "I can take care of myself," he says. "I can help."

"You wanna help?" I whisper. I wave my gun back toward the bathroom. "Go take a look at Akihiro. See what you can do."

He ducks dutifully in there, and I slide right up to the office door, press my ear against it. They're talking, both of them, and I can't quite catch the gist of it, but the tone seems mundane, almost amiable and reassuring. Like they're chatting about sports or the weather. Then there's a pause, and I hear Charlie pleading to her in a deep, terrified voice. "No, no, don't! Please! No! For God's sake!"

Two shots boom out in rapid succession. That's when I kick the door in.

* * *

It was supposed to be another working day for Charlie Teitelbaum. That's what it looks like to me when I first rush in. He's got on a fresh white linen shirt, rolled up at the sleeves, gray slacks, black Italian loafers. Half of a bacon, lettuce, and tomato sandwich left on a plate. A pitcher of iced tea at the ready. Now he's splayed out in his fancy leather desk chair. The console of his laptop is glistening with droplets of blood. One bullet is rotating around somewhere in his chest, the other has struck him directly in the left eye and passed through to the brain and out the other side. He didn't expect this. It's not pretty.

I don't see Maggie, though. She's leaning against the back wall behind the door. I've just gone right past her.

"Don't move," she says adamantly from behind me. "Put the gun down. Drop it or I'll do what I did to him."

I let my pistol plop onto the plush carpet. It barely makes a sound. And though she doesn't ask me to, I raise my hands in the air.

"Now turn around," she commands. "Turn around and face me. Nice and slow, you understand? That's right, hands up high. Now, take three steps back."

"Okay," I say. "You're the boss."

She shuts the door but doesn't bother to lock it. Then, with her gun still trained on me, she picks up my weapon and tucks it demurely into her purse.

"Just what are you doing here, Mr. Parisman?"

"You know something? I was about to ask you the same thing."

She doesn't respond right away. "I'm dishing out justice," she says then.

I nod. "So I see," I tell her. "You've done an admirable job. Charlie was a nasty SOB. I get that, yeah. And your friend Alma was never gonna stand up to him, was she."

"Alma and Benny, they're two peas in a pod. Artists, dreamers. You know what happens to artists and dreamers in this town?"

"Sure," I say. "A lot of them get ground into dust. Maybe most, in fact. But hey, that's show biz."

"It's wrong," she adds. "It's flat-out wrong, and I'm done with it. I won't let it happen to the people I love."

I can't gauge how pumped up she is, but I figure I have nothing much to lose now by keeping the talk going. She can always shoot me if she feels like it; clearly she's determined and unafraid to pull the trigger. But I'm also not an obvious enemy. I'm just a bystander, a witness to her crimes. And she knows me. That makes me a little better off than the butler I just tripped over. "Is that why you decided to kill Al Pupik? Because he was grinding Benny down?"

She winces. Her eyes race back and forth. Maybe she thought she was impervious, that she could somehow get away with it, that the cops were too stupid to follow the bread crumbs to her door. But now here's this world-weary detective accusing her. Oh, well.

"I didn't know it at the time," she says. "Not until Alma told me on the phone where she was that night. Al was being a pig again. That's what she said. And Benny couldn't speak for himself. He never could. It was going nowhere. Again. That's when I reached for the gun in Alma's dresser."

"So you went there to kill him? Or to teach him a lesson? What?"

"I was pissed. I wanted to humiliate him. Make him sweat. At least in the beginning. I remember pointing the gun at his chest, I told him to drop his pants. That got to him. He burst out laughing when I said that. Couldn't believe it. Is this some kind of joke? That's what he wanted to know. No, I told him. I'm through telling jokes. Turn around and drop your pants."

"And that's when you hit him with the wine bottle?"

"No," she says, "not then. First I told him who I was. I had to remind him because, of course, he didn't remember me from my comedy days. Why would he? It was years ago; I was nobody. He said he had sympathy for me, said he was sorry my career hadn't . . . hadn't turned out, hadn't clicked exactly the way I expected it to. It was dreadful, in his opinion. But of course he'd say that. He was standing half-naked with his back to me, a shriveled-up old man, shielding his privates, not knowing what the hell was coming next. I explained to him how he'd panned my material in front of my agent, said it was shit, and that my agent dropped me the next day. He didn't recall that episode. It was long ago and he was busy building his career, so yeah, maybe he said some things he shouldn't have, stepped on a few toes along the way. He chuckled then, as though it was funny. But it wasn't funny. It infuriated me. That's when I picked up the bottle and whacked him."

"And then what?"

"Well, he went down."

"That's right, he went down. And you didn't have to shoot him. You could have left him there on the floor. Just walked out."

She shook her head. "I couldn't do that. My blood was boiling. I thought about everything he'd ever done. It wasn't just me—it was Benny, it was all my friends. He fucked up so many lives. I stood right over him. I was shaking. The gun was in my hands. It went off again and again."

Her voice trails away, like in her mind there's still an eerie sweetness to what happened that night, or at least in the recollection. She squints then, remembers where she is, and raises the gun so that it points at my chest.

"All right," I mumble, "getting rid of Al makes perfect sense, especially when you put it like that."

"I'm so glad you agree."

"But what about Lonny Dreyer? He was another struggling writer, wasn't he? How'd you even know about him?"

"You don't understand how this business works, do you, Parisman? No, you don't have a clue. Al wasn't just a common thief, he was building himself a name for the ages. That nostalgic show they were putting together on paper? It would have aired for years. He'd have a never-ending audience. Even after he was dead and in the ground, they'd still be trotting it out on PBS, raising money for good causes. Laughing along with dear old Al. And he'd be a legend, like Elvis or Dylan or Muhammad Ali—he'd suck up all the light." From across the room she jabs at me now with her weapon, as though to make a point. "And who would remember the rest of us? Huh? The people he crushed?"

My mind is ricocheting from one crazy thought to the next. I'm guessing Omar is close by, waiting, listening, gauging the ebb and flow of our conversation, wondering what the chances are and when's the best moment to burst in from the other side of the door. I'm also

praying to God (and I don't believe in God) that he doesn't try anything stupid like that; he's fast, but still, she'd cut him down before
he could ever cross the threshold. And where the hell are the cops? If
Malloy is on the scene, which he should be, he's probably got a SWAT
team deployed around the perimeter. That's comforting, sorta.

"So you know what, Maggie? I think you can relax now. I mean,
look." I tilt my head toward the remains of Charlie Teitelbaum.
"Mission accomplished, you know what I'm saying?"

"Not quite," she says. "There's still you, isn't there? I can't have
you testifying against me."

"C'mon. Don't say that. You don't honestly imagine you'll get
away with this, do you?"

"Actually, yeah, I do."

"So the idea then is to shoot me and just go waltzing out the door?"

"Something like that."

"And you have no . . . qualms? No compunctions?"

"I've . . . done it before." She says this, but there's a wavering in her
voice, as though she's unsure and can't really think this proposition
through, more like she's just filling in a blank on a questionnaire.

"So, all right, let's back up a bit. You were dishing out justice
then. Al and Charlie and their accomplices. Giving them what-for."

"Absolutely."

"I can understand that. In fact, I might have done the exact same
thing if I were in your shoes."

"You would?"

"I might have, yeah. Somebody who treats you like shit. You
wanna strike back. It's only human."

"Right."

"But the thing is, that doesn't apply to me. It shouldn't, anyway.
I'm not the bad guy in this movie. Remember, I was trying to help.
Benny hired me."

"Benny's dead," she says. "It's too late for him now. I've gotta
think about the future. I've gotta move on."

"That's true, you do. Which would be fine, you know, except for
a couple of—oh, what shall we call them? Glitches? Speed bumps?"

She looks at me uncomprehendingly.

"Number one, there's my partner, Omar, who's lurking around here somewhere in the house. What? You didn't think I'd come alone, did you? At my age? Anyway, you don't want to meet Omar. And number two, beyond him, there's also the police."

"The police?"

"Yeah, we . . . we put in a call."

That gives her pause.

"You think I'm bluffing?" I ask. "Okay, so I get that. Take a peek outside."

She continues staring at me. Her eyes narrow. Slowly, inexorably, she inches over toward the window and parts the curtain. Then she turns back, bites her lip. Whatever she saw out there convinced her.

"I could kill myself," she whispers, weighing the possibilities. "That's what Benny did, to protect Alma. That's how much he loved her. He figured she was the one; he took the blame instead. He was wrong, of course, but his heart was in the right place."

"Gosh, I dunno, I just don't see you killing yourself," I reply, shaking my head. "And personally, from my own selfish point of view, it wouldn't do you any good to kill me. I mean, my testimony won't matter that much, one way or the other. Truth is, they've got all they need right here to send you to prison."

"Prison?"

"No question. That's where this is headed, don't you see? But it'd be a great waste to kill yourself, Maggie. You don't need to. You're not evil. You're angry, sure, but everybody's got anger. And you need that emotion, it turns out. Hell, half the time it comes with your birth certificate. And I know lawyers who make a nice living justifying things people do in the heat of the moment. I guess what I'm saying is, you don't deserve to die."

"I don't?"

"Nah, not at all," I tell her. "And you're not likely to, either. Not after it's all sorted out. There's a phrase, you know, among my people: *dayenu*. Enough. Let it be."

Her eyes are tearing up, and she swallows hard. "Let it be," she repeats. "Yeah." The tension in the air seems to dissipate. She lays the gun down on Teitelbaum's desk.

*　　*　　*

Out of an abundance of caution, when Omar and Maggie and I finally appear at the front door, we all have our hands raised high in the air, and it's a great relief to see Lieutenant Malloy standing there behind his unmarked car among the sharpshooters.

"You didn't listen to me," Malloy says. "I told you early on to stay out of this."

"You didn't say that. You said I was a civilian. Maybe you thought I'd take that as a hint."

"You should have," he says.

I smile. "I couldn't do that, Bill. Not when a man's paying me to poke around. Hell, it's what I do."

He shrugs. Sometimes I think we will probably always be at odds like this; but for now, as far as he's concerned, all is forgiven.

Two young officers, a man and a woman, approach Maggie and tell her she's under arrest for murder. As her partner turns her around and puts the cuffs on her, the female officer informs her in a very crisp and professional tone that she has the right to remain silent and that anything she says from now on can and will be used against her. Maggie nods. She looks remarkably relaxed. She glances over at me as they lead her off to the squad car, which is parked incongruously in the middle of the road. The white forensics van has pulled up in the driveway next door, and they are busy systematically unloading their gear and slipping on their paper booties. A few neighbors have come out of their homes to see what all the fuss is about and maybe to discuss, in private, what effect it might have on their property values.

Remo and Jason have taken a quick tour of Charlie's house. They're wearing plastic gloves and booties. Now they lope back to the sidewalk, shaking their heads.

"I thought you said she was a comedian," Remo says to me. "Ain't nothing funny about what she did to those people in there."

"A failed comic, is what I said. There's a big difference."

He humphs, folds his arms defensively in front of his chest. Of the two of them, Remo is the more worldly. Jason's an evangelical; he lives in a little tract home in Glendale, and the word is that his church frowns on most forms of entertainment. "Yeah, well, remind me not to buy a ticket to any future performance," Remo says. They ask Malloy if he needs them any longer, and when he shakes his head, they retreat to their vehicle.

"So now it really is over. Is that right? Amos?"

"I'd say so, Bill. It's a different story than what the *LA Times* was going to print, but now at least it's the truth. Benny Wolf died an innocent man. The only person he killed was himself, and even that was for a noble reason—to protect Alma."

"A noble but misguided reason," Bill corrects me. "She's also innocent."

"And in her own mind, even Maggie Mooney was acting out of a noble impulse. You gotta respect that. I hope the court does, anyway, at some level, when it goes to trial."

"What happens, happens," Malloy says. A member of the SWAT team comes up to him then, and Omar and I make ourselves scarce. We're strolling down the sidewalk, the sun is shining, and now we've come at last to our cars. No one wants to climb inside and turn the ignition, because they're probably baking from the heat. Still, it's time to say goodbye.

"Thanks for everything you did, Omar."

"I didn't do squat," he says. "I just got lucky when she turned up here, that's all. One thing led to another. It's not like I'm much of a detective."

"Let me tell you something, vato. One thing always leads to another. That's life. You just have to pay attention."

ACKNOWLEDGMENTS

Many people played a part in this. My writing friends who did an early read and gave me advice and criticism. Ron Raley, Cheryl Howard. Elliot Kalan. The staff at Readers' Books—especially Jude Sales, Thea Reynolds, and Rosie Lee-Parks. My family, living and dead. My beloved companion, Beth Hanson. In fact, when you think about it, there isn't that much I can take credit for, really, maybe the jokes. And they are more cute than funny. If you laugh at any of them, I'll consider that a plus.

ABOUT THE AUTHOR

ANDY WEINBERGER is the author of *An Old Man's Game*, *Reason to Kill*, and *The Kindness of Strangers*. He is a longtime bookseller and the founder/owner of Readers' Books in Sonoma, California. Born in New York, he grew up in the Los Angeles area and studied poetry and Chinese history at the University of New Mexico. He lives in Sonoma, where Readers' Books continues to thrive.